Krengel & The Krampusz

M.C. NORRIS

In Loving Memory of

J.P. "Pappy" Norris

1923 - 2014

Chapter One

"Now we are in the power of a wolf, the most rapacious perhaps that this world has ever seen. And if we do not flee, he will inevitably devour us all."

- Giovanni di Lorenzo de' Medici, in public outcry against Pope Alexander VI.

24 December, 1498

On the night before Christmas, while the midnight bells tolled, he flayed his sweet cheeks with outgrown nails. Pigeons turtled their necks and winked in the rafters. Vermin scuttled along their muddy byways, where they clashed and they tumbled, shedding thin squeals in the gloom. Droplets struck targets with mechanical precision. Dead puddles leapt briefly to life. Straws shifted. An overturned bucket plunked dully from a corner stall like the drumbeat of an imbecile herald. It was a quiet sort of night. Rain whispered secrets through the thatching. Threads of water needled downward, to bore spattering holes in the mud.

Slickened fingers rose and fell. The child toiled on. He raked his windpipe now, sucking air in apelike hoots, until at last, his legs folded when he could stand no more pain. He threw back his head and brayed at the iron ringlets that shied and returned on dangling chains to anchored ringbolts, nameless devices that drooped like a bower of adamantine vines. Someone coughed in the filthy cold air. Hanged fitments glistened, in the torchlight, with a hellish incandescence.

He knelt in the mud, grim penance complete, snowy throat red-laced as a candied confection. Eyes upturned and overflowing, the child appeared to supplicate the heavens for an appeal, for some miracle of deliverance. Blood feathered pink where his tearful streams converged. The boy listened, waited. As if prompted by an afterthought, he presented his gruesome hands, splaying his fingers to separate their sticky webbings. A ruby droplet quavered on the cusp of his chin, but did not fall.

"Please," he whispered, "is this enough?"

The child clasped his ears, as thunder trundled over the Roman countryside with godlike resonance. Hail began to clatter. Knobs of ice struck the stable's old clapboards, dry and fluted with ridges sharp enough to cut. Wood fragments flitted through the air to land soundlessly in the mud. Whole tiles shattered, tacked corners left swaying. Rain sprayed through new fissures like oceanic force upon a ruptured hull. A few orphans cried out and lilted skyward, covering their ears as if they'd just perceived the same nebulous omen, the same reckoning imparted by all those stolen before them, in a siege of phantom fists and drumming knuckles that still hated this place that took them, this makeshift dungeon, this stable that devoured children whole.

"Please. Stop."

But it would not ever. The fearsome voice inside his head matched even the elemental howling, with its oaths and obscenities, until the child pounded at his temples, curled and growling in the manure like a spine-shot dog. No refuge from it. No sanctuary. Not since the boy's earliest memory had there been much respite from the seething monologue of his Forever Friend.

He'd pushed back against the alien presence within him, hoping to will the monster into submission. He'd attempted to ignore it, to pretend for days that he'd heard nothing of its raving, to pretend he was a normal little chap unburdened by strange and unthinkable demands, which would sometimes twitch his mask of lucidity with one eyelid set a-quiver. But if there was one thing that the beast inside Klaas Krengel hated, it was being ignored.

"Grow a beard when I get older? That's all you've to say to me? Grow a beard to hide my scars?" Krengel glowered up at the sodden thatching and wiped the blood from his eyes with a knuckle. "I did what you asked. I always do. And look at me. Look at what you've made me do to my face!" Terrified pigeons flushed the rafters, wings slapping through the labyrinth of timber and chain.

"Little Klaas Krengel." Ludolf Eichmann swaggered across the stable in the direction of the wailing, imbalanced by the pendulous weight of a jug on one arm. "Imaginary mate causing problems again, aye? Say the name. Say the name of that jabbering fiend inside your head." Ludolph's demented face split in a loutish grin, perry cider oozing out the corners. "It's the Krampusz, isn't it? Little Klaas Krengel and his Krampusz."

He checked Krengel with a stiff arm that sent him porpoising through the ordure. The older boy passed the jug of cider off to another and pounced atop Krengel before he could rise. He gathered a fistful of the youngest orphan's tunic and jerked their noses together. "We all hate you, you know," Ludolph whispered into Krengel's face, nodding, "you and your Krampusz both. Not a one of us will suffer another day in your stead. No more. Today it ends. Today, the both of you shall burn together for heresy. Oh, yes. And then, forevermore, in Hell."

Had he somehow given offense? It was difficult to be certain. The Krampusz loved to invade his head during life's stressful moments, particularly conflicts, times when things were already a bit muddled, when the monster inside him would rage at the gates until he relinquished control. In an odd way, he'd come to count on these forceful interventions. Over the years, for better or for worse, the beast had become a loyal friend, of sorts. The Krampusz always stood ready to defend him, ready to suck him straight out of life's difficult moments and transplant him to a gentler place where his antagonists could not follow. And there, a boy could live vicariously through the body of his Forever Friend, stilting over the crags and crevices of Sundaloon.

Krengel's moist and blinking eyes swept the gallery of hardened faces. They all looked ready to turn him in. The other orphans had despised him from the first night he bedded amongst them, when they'd inked a smeary mustache upon his face while he slept. Friar Otto, of course, had seen nothing of their bullying, not through his dead and sightless eyes. Not when his "Little Elves" flayed the rump of Krengel's tunic, or when they packed his pointed shoes with wet manure. Plump as a cream puff and blond as a dram of wit bier, Krengel made a splendid target for anyone who might begrudge a Lambsheim brat with a hot temperament, whose pampering had failed to prepare him in the smallest way for all the world's rigors.

To think of the fuss he'd made to accompany this troupe of little barbarians along their Rhineland tour. It had been the Krampusz's idea, of course, to join their stupid choir to escape a bit of brewing trouble back home. It all seemed so silly, now. But in fairness, the notion of running away with the choir had struck him as a wonderful idea, a splendid bit of fun to brighten a summer's end. But alas, joining *Die Kleinen Elfen* had been the worst mistake of Klaas Krengel's young life.

Not a single performance. No sweets, no toys, and those nasty Little Elves had been so horrible and mean. From the Rhineland bogs to Rome, none amongst the drunken rabble had ever dealt him a moment's kindness, except for the two sisters, Mitzi, and Nele Gottlieb. And now they, like everything else he'd ever been foolish enough to love, had been taken. Apart from the murmuring Krampusz inside his skull, he'd never felt so utterly abandoned. And isolation, well that just happened to be the one torment that Klaas Krengel found most intolerable.

A growl low in Krengel's throat wound to a screeching ululation, as three months of ostracism ignited like hot phosphorus in his brain. He launched himself at Ludolf, pudgy fists balled and pinwheeling. He'd suffered quite enough of their torment. Tonight, someone else was going to cry themselves to sleep.

He supposed it annoyed them when he'd squalled loudest, while Friar Otto strangled at the garrote, and again tonight, when the Hound of God and his hooded entourage came for the Gottlieb girls. Bound and churning mud like a catch of eels, they were taken. Ropes taut and dripping dragged them into the freezing rain. The stable door trundled along its trucks to halve their parting shrieks with a thud. Slap of a latch and quick as that, Mitzi and Nele Gottlieb were gone.

Oh, they hated him completely. He could see that plainly now. The other lads had known and loved each other years longer than he, being the youngest and newest to the choir, and they begrudged his exaggerated anguish. They begrudged his looking the part of a baker's fat son, not haggard and miserable like a proper orphan, like them. He stood apart from the reeking waifs in his schooling. Just nine years of age, and already he could recite in foreign tongues. Klaas was a Krengel, after all, a polished heir to the House of Habsburg, who'd cut teeth on the finest pastries in the Burgundian Circle, and who'd obviously enjoyed many since. But would they never find it in them to overcome these small differences?

"You're all jealous," Krengel finally said, tossing his hair. A lucky blow wrought a clack of teeth, dropping Ludolf Eichmann to his rump on the stable floor. "And Ludolph, you're the most jealous one of all." The chubby tot then cocked an ear, as if to better receive some whispered bit of advisement from the thin air. "Ream out all their eyes with a pointed stick once they've fallen asleep? Don't you think that a bit harsh?"

"You're mad as a Betsy-bug, Krengel." The older boy dabbed red banners streaming from his squashed nose, and somehow found even more hate in the sight of his own blood. He spat and leapt to his feet. Others rushed in to hold Ludolph back. Oily from months without a bath, he squirted through the grips of Albert and Emil Amsel. "No one's jealous of you, you crazed little piglet." Ludolph locked an elbow around Krengel's neck, wrenching him over his hip. By a muddy fistful of Krengel's curls, he mashed the child's face into the manure, hissing into his ear through clenched teeth. "It's just that you ruined our choir."

So that was it. Krengel's blue eyes blinked. The child reared his head from the filth like a wretched golem and spat a turd.

His voice was permanently coarsened, the others loved to chide, as a result of his habitual screaming to have everything his way. He'd not a chord of musical talent, true enough, but his inability to carry a tune, that was hardly the reason that their beloved Friar Otto was strangled to death with a donkey's bridle, or that Mitzi and Nele Gottlieb were taken, or that the rest of them were spending Christmas Eve awaiting their fates inside a filthy Roman stable. No, it was the stupid wagon that was to blame for all of these foul circumstances. Or, more specifically, it was the fault of the red lion with the flicking blue tongue that had been painted on it.

It was a fine, bluebird day of particular merit that welcomed Friar Otto and his ranks of singing children into the village of Lambsheim. His rescued orphans of the Black Death, flowed bewteen Lambsheim's towers, all dressed in their emerald tunics like the callow acolytes of some nursery sect. Shepherded by their blind Franciscan monk, whose cane swept the cobblestones like a divining rod, they chanted their sacred chorals in perfect organus. The last in line were the eldest boys, who wrestled their cartload of handmade toys up toward the orphanage upon the hilltop, where it pleased God that in the spirit of Saint Nicholas, they would deliver a bit of hope to the wretched. It was perhaps by no great accident that they raised their voices clear to Heaven, as they passed the gates of the wealthiest family in all of Germania, the House of Habsburg, and humble home to Lady Adeline and Count Richwald Krengel.

Klaas Krengel dropped his ivory peg dolls to the dirt and hustled to the edge of the road. This was the travelling children's choir foretold by the Krampusz, right on the tic, and God bless his balls and breeches, once his eyes fell upon them, he decided he'd never in all his life wanted anything half so badly! He yearned, at that moment, to accompany those luckier children than he, on their merry way to travel and sing, to craft wonderful toys, to don a glossy emerald tunic! But the bloody gate, he soon found, had been locked.

The gate was never locked, and today, of all days ... as if his father had somehow intuited the choir's approach, and had barred the gates the night before to avoid paying a small tithing. Throttling the gate balusters in his fists, Krengel crooked his head and screeched his father's name far and wide, until not a bird chirped, not a horse nickered. Even the breeze through the clattering leaves seemed to swag wide berth of the Habsburg-Krengel estate, so terrible were the screams of the ignored child.

Nothing.

Wherever was that man? Rarely ever, where he ought to be. It boggled Klaas how the servant girls who moiled over him, seemed to find his father so damned alluring, swearing often to a mysterious power the Count wielded over women. How could they possibly be smitten by that aversive old glutton; that pear-bottomed, preening fat peacock, whose every inch of amplitude was accentuated with fur-lined vests saddled over a tunic, so scant it barely covered his dimpled buttocks. His pointed shoes were so long that to keep him from tripping, their curled tips needed securing to his ankles with gilded chainlets? Count Richwald Krengel wasted hours before the looking glass, brushing nits from that great flaxen waterfall of oceanic curls that fountained from his fig-shaped head. A tuberous nose beetled precariously over his small and lipless mouth, upturned at the corners in perpetual smirk.

But his eyes, Gads! They must have been his trick. For what else beyond his wife's limitless finances did the man possibly possess, but those twin orbs of unwavering blue, like swoony portals to heart of the Tropick Latitudes. Surely, those eyes were the seat of that strange and mystic prowess that somehow shattered the resolve of the chaste, for his was a confidence that commanded at any time anyone, or any thing that he desired. And he did unsparingly satiate his every craving for life's myriad pleasures, much to the chagrin of the House of Habsburg. It was blamed on the scandalous bulge that arose in Lady Adeline's midrift, which harried she and Count Richwald into an unlikely marriage.

Even in Lambsheim, an obscure little village situated in the eye of the Burgundian Circle, the newlyweds' hastily contrived nuptials were perhaps rightly scoffed. The story was told long into late evenings thereafter that even their unborn offspring had joined in their parents' mockery, by swelling stubbornly in Adeline's belly well past her ninth month. They went on to fester there another nine more, until her eighteenth month of pregnancy found her gasping in the sweltering summer heat, legs splayed, and oozing like a set of roasted hogs. And when Count Richwald slipped out for a men's holiday in Mainz, he'd scarcely passed Lambsheim's towers before Lady Adeline summoned her apothecaries to fall upon her bloated carcass like a murder of crows, and evict by blade and spatula the accursed tenants from her womb, for there were two of them.

Twisted as its parent's union, and perhaps less apt to survive, Adeline's firstborn was held aloft by its scaly limb and appraised by her chief physician, who was none but a savage witchman who loved no Christian God. He was said to have frowned in the profound silence that seemed to emanate from the thing in the manner that snowpack stifles a winter landscape. The hairy imp seemed not to mind the crude examination, or so the story was told. Without a squeak, it gawped lackadaisically back at its handler through eyes like moist chips of the summer sky.

The second infant was then uprooted with screams enough for two, already baring four teeth, fat and blushing beneath its blond tussock of tight Moorish curls. Son to an heiress in want only of a daughter, and to a Count desiring anything and everything but children, newborn Klaas Krengel was spirited away by a host of supplicants, commissioned to spoil his every whim, to drown him in delights, whilst his mother tidied up the niggling ends of her ordeal.

Secreted by the moths and moonflowers of her private garden nook, Lady Adeline's little devil departed her world wrapped in a sack of blackened leather, writhing against the Bible she bound facedown upon its breast. No prayer was offered beyond the witchman's chattering invocations. No sentiment was spoken, but the shameful stave and pitch of Lady Adeline's spade, the muffled mewling from inside the sack until her dreadful deed was done.

But that was just one version of the story.

Another version insisted that both infants had been quite perfectly human, but only one survived the rigors of childbirth, while the other was born woefully deformed. By this account, the stillborn twin owed its frightful appearance to a sort of bee that allegedly attacked Count Krengel, and stung him upon his bare buttocks whilst he and Lady Habsburg were intertwined, thus injecting a dose of evil into the transaction.

A different spin alleged that the stillborn twin was in fact, strangled in the womb by the umbilical cord of the other, so terrible was his brother's greed to share his childhood with no other. So tightly bound was the hangman's noose, some storytellers added with a whisper that the poor babe needed beheading, to relax the coils wound round its throat.

And still others swore drearily that there had never even been another child at all. Never had there been another Krengel whatsoever, but the one boy named Klaas, who soon grew fat enough for two.

Klaas looked not much like either of his parents, but it soon became evident that he would favor the Count's every defect. The little grub's meanest appetite was not at first for food or female company, but for wild adventures beyond the walls of the Habsburg estate. The boy's obsession with the treasures of wealthy kings from faraway lands, was perhaps seeded in a tease dealt him by one of the dark servants who, upon observing little Klaas leaping about in his silken braies with a slashing wooden sword, assured the portly tot he'd never survive a finger's breadth outside the borders of Christendom. Slow was the sting of a woman's insult, and how the burning did linger.

Klaas was too young for sabbatical, Friar Otto protested, when Count Richwald Krengel arrived to shove his only son through the gates unto the choir, tossing his bedroll out after. "Pish-posh!" bellowed the Count. "No need we begin behaving shabbily! It's to be no great damned odyssey, just a brief tour of the Rhine Country." He tossed a bag of clothing and threw the latch. His child should withstand the slight rigors of travel. Count Richwald nodded his head with a grunt. A dose of hardship would be just the thing for the boy.

However, little Klaas had no understanding of the ministry of Saint Nicholas, no real care for their purpose, no skill in carpentry, no formal training in song, Friar Otto retorted. He was not even an orphan. Why, if anyone happened to recognize this wayward son of the Habsburg clan on some lonely road imperiled by greedy men, he'd become not just a burden, but a terrible liability. Then, of course, there was the small matter of the child's unusual mental situation, a rather touchy subject, and known leagues beyond Lambsheim to be no small matter at all.

It was at that juncture, with Count Richwald braying through the balusters for the Friar to have more faith in God, and the Friar bartering a cask of barleywine in the unwanted child's stead that Klaas found it in him to pitch a fit of indignation, so beastly that his father was inspired to donate a new wagon and fresh horses, should Friar Ottomar for the love of God, take this boy of his away. Klaas squealed and clapped his fat hands. Friar Otto was nobody's fool, but in their weaker moments, wiser men could be had.

The new wagon was neatly covered against the elements and it smelt sharply of fresh paint. Friar Otto smiled and the children sang while they loaded. He trailed his fingertips down the buckboard, over the smooth rims of the wheels, free arm sweeping, as he groped his way blindly past the painted Habsburg coat-of-arms: a rearing red lion with a lashing blue tongue.

Northward, through the spongy fens, they forded strange peatlands that murmured and spat, where pitch-skinned mummies in fur capes were among those curiosities drawn grimacing from ancient graves in the mire. Night followed day and round again, but the friar dared not stop for an instant upon that bubbling sedge, for beneath the glade, was a mostly fluid element that sucked hungrily at a wagon's rims, and eventually drew down all things set upon it.

Led by morning's ravens that cleaved the skies like piratical skiffs, they chanced upon a band of ill-fated pilgrims, masked and mindless with exhaustion, heaving to the reigns of mounts bogged to their withers. Already, two lay dead. They warned the choir to keep back a safe distance, for they were refugees of an outbreak of the worst kind, not a league beyond the marshlands, where whole villages were being devoured.

"Bid ye turn your wagon about, good Friar. Ride hard the way ye came."

And so they did. Huddled in the wagon's paunch, Krengel clung to Mitzi Gottlieb as they raced the Black Death day and night all the way back to Lambsheim, where the child's screams reverberated the ransacked halls of the Habsburg estate when they arrived, but days too late. Leaves skittered around the corpse of Lady Adeline Habsburg-Krengel, abandoned in her throes to her plundering apothecaries, who loved neither god nor master. Her severed fingers, divorced of rings, lay scattered amidst shards of stained glass.

Southward, the wagon lilted and squealed as they climbed the craggy highlands, where frigid streams roared over shelves of polished rock. Blizzards of swallows stirred the slot of sky pinched between walls daubed with nests. Their wheels bounced over crevices where faded glyphs marked seeps tapped by gas-bottling warlocks of a forgotten age, when the science of magick was not yet forbidden. They camped in painted caves. They spread their bedrolls in natural tanks in the cavern floors, and lay their cheeks against stone blackened by ages of misuse. The children slept poorly in these places, awakened in the night by strange dreams of owl-eyed hags, who dragged children from bedrolls down into the bowels of mountains to leech marrow from snapped bones like precious lye from heartwood ash.

Beyond the upland passes and through the whispering pines, they fell upon the remote village of Ischgl, where a caravan passed them on the Feast of Saint Denis. Rumbling wagons, clopping hooves, and shuffling feet, conveyed a train of bearded Spaniards so vast as to bridge one horizon to the next. By papal invitation to *Miso del Gallo*, they in all their thousands were official Roman guests to the Midnight Mass of the Rooster. For Spanish tradition held that on the eve of Christ's birth, roosters across Spain all crowed with such extraordinary zeal that only hatchets could quiet their cawing heads. Thus, God's miracle was recognized, for never before or since, had a cock crowed so passionately at that hour.

The caravan halted, and there and then, commenced a manhunt for a defunct heretic suspected cowering in his grave. Campfires were lit. Drams of ale were poured. Knots of toiling friars gathered round great cauldrons to sparge their mash into boiling wort. Friar Otto deployed his orphans to barter casks of ale for fowl. The night never slept for all the laughter and popping fires. Having endured more than a month on desolate roads, the children were aroused by the energy of this rendezvous, which seemed to them a winter holiday. Chaperoning Franciscans from the Friary Rabida, they haunted the night with their roving torches like revenants amongst Ischgl's graves, for leading the Spaniards was none other than the Grand Inquisitor himself, the so-called Hound of God, whose camp would not break until bones had been exhumed and burned for heresy. Ischgl's sleepless peasants were flushed like chickens from their coops to collect wood for the growing pyre. So cowed were they by the foreign men in black habits that no relative of the accused dared protest.

"Look about you, now," Friar Otto said, fluttering his fingertips in the direction of the cemetery, backlit by the incandescence of a hundred fires. "Note the size of the headstone where the accused shall rest, and compare it to the more ordinary stones around it." As the blind friar foretold, the headstone that halted the diggers was a polished oolite spire that loomed over the field of common tablets. At its base, shovels stove the earth. Dark sheaves of dirt began to pitch. Krengel leaned around Friar Otto, enveloped in sweet steam roiling up from the barley, and he waved his hand before the friar's bleary eyes. "But this prophecy is no trick of the blind," Friar Otto explained, "for a Grand Inquisitor would never waste his time dragging a destitute heretic to trial, be the accused living or dead. Not when the fruits of conviction lied in the seizure of estates."

"Friar Ottomar Zimmerman, how often have you confessed as a heretic?"

Friar Otto turned his from the cauldron of boiling wort toward the rasp of the eavesdropper's voice, permitting the man in the shadows to drink deeply of his buttermilk-colored eyes. "I know better than to answer a crafted question, where any answer that I give will be wrong." Friar Otto smiled and cocked an ear toward the graveyard, where the diggers' blades struck wood. They plunged their spades beneath the coffin rim and pried until a great splintering arose. One digger covered his mouth and retched. Another clambered out of the hole and ran out into the boneyard, arms flailing. "I'm sure I've heard of you, Grand Inquisitor, Brother Ignacio de la Rabida, and the so-called Hound of God."

"As I'm sure I've heard of you, Brother Ottomar, the so-called Equalizer, minister of Saint Nicholas, shepherd of Elves, and heretical preacher of sermons against we servants of God." The stranger in their midst withdrew a sopping sponge from a leather purse situated upon his hip. Strange medicine streamed down his wrists. He pressed the sponge to his face and inhaled fiercely until the nostrum could be heard bubbling up his nostrils. Whatever his remedy against the Plague, it reeked not of pure vinegar. Something else lurked beyond the ascetic veil, darkly herbal and dizzying.

Circling the wagon slowly, methodically, eyes scanning every nuance of their cargo, the Hound of God at last paused between the wheels. A pale finger outstretched. A polished fingernail tapped against the painted image of the rearing red lion, and the hunter of heretics allowed a crooked smile.

"You ruined *Die Kleinen Elfen!*" Ludolph pumped Krengel's face in and out of the filth. "Daddy always gave you everything you ever wanted, didn't he, you greedy pig? Well, that choir was all the rest of us ever had. Only thing in the world ever made us matter!"

Krengel turtled his neck from the manure, sucking for breath. He'd already paid a hefty price for wedging his way into their choir. How could they fail to appreciate that by God's will, he'd been orphaned by the Plague, same as they. All was even.

Ludolph rolled Krengel onto his back, knelt on his arms, and began to slap his cheeks. "Go on, then. Go on, then. Have a fit, you little madling."

"Make him speak in tongues!"

"Aye, speak in tongues for us, little Krengel." Ludolph poked him in the eye. "Let your Krampusz out for tea."

"Get off me!" Krengel's eyes rolled, as the Britain struck him hard enough to release a cloud of silvery sparkles. They did not understand. No one did. People loved to provoke the beast inside him, to addle him to the point that the Krampusz would bellow up through Klaas's throat like a bullhorn.

The stable door rumbled on its tracks. They were back. Ludolph leapt off and scrambled aside. Krengel rose, smearing at his stinking mask, pinching dung from his nostrils. His robe swung heavily with nodes of muck. A hush fell over the room as they advanced, single file, beneath the swaying manacles where Friar Otto had so recently confessed. Each identical to his hooded brother, fore and aft, they invaded the makeshift dungeon in a black parade until at last, one entered distinct from all the rest in his wine-colored robe, and by the sour reek emanating from him.

One Franciscan nearest the Hound of God stepped ahead to announce his superior. "All rise for His Most Reverent Grand Friar-Inquisitor, Brother Ignacio de la Rabida."

The Inquisitor brought out the sponge. Lifting it to his face, he inhaled until a map of veins rose upon his forehead and threatened to burst. Medicine spattered against the mud at his feet. After a moment's calm, the Inquisitor returned his dank pet back to its home in the special purse. He then grasped the swaying manacles and glowered down at his captives. Craze shimmering upon eyes that burned like stars under the swathed hood, was the only sign of life in a countenance fasted to ghastly pallor. "Which of you little heretics is Krengel?" He pinched the iron ringlets between his fingers and gave them a little twist.

Krengel swallowed, shifting his feet. His eyes flicked to and fro behind the mask of mud. The last time that question was asked, and went unanswered, the Gottlieb sisters were taken. And the time before that, Friar Otto had died. The Little Elves were not apt to lose another, on his account.

The Inquisitor released the manacles. The chains swayed in the torchlight as he edged nearer the silent children. His fingers, intertwined and seething like a nest of vipers, belied any guise of lucidity. Scratching quills recorded his every movement, every word, into ledgers so thick that they seemed to account for every moment of his life, and every life that his affected. The orphans were well aware that any statement they made would be twisted into an admission of heresy, a charge so overused that it was meaningless. It was the charge to which Friar Otto had finally confessed, after being winched repeatedly to the stable roof with his elbows pinioned behind his back, ankles weighted with sacks of rye, and dropped to a jolting stop on the knotted line, again and again, until his shoulders became sickeningly limber. But it was not the "Queen of Torments" that brought about his confession. It was Mitzi's screams, muffled by the Scold's Bridle, wrought not of pain, but of sympathy for Friar Otto as she watched her beloved benefactor fell repeatedly from the rafters. But made incapable of speech by the bridle, she could not assure Friar Otto of her safety, and he confessed.

The Hound of God strode down the row of silent orphans, unblinking, one finger crooked around his chapped lips. He looked to be appraising the worth of each child, their body, and perhaps their soul. The only sounds in the stable were sucks and squelches of his shoes in the manure. He stopped before Krengel, battered and bloodied. He curled his lip at the robe of ordure draped from the child's shoulders. Drawing a dagger from its sheath, he reached out.

"Is it you?" The Inquisitor seized the boy next to Krengel, known as Rolf, and jerked him out of the row. He pressed the gleaming blade to Rolf's throat. "Are you Klaas Krengel? Son to Count Richwald Krengel? Heir to the House of Habsburg?"

"Nein!" Rolf shrieked.

"Speak the common Latin tongue, boy. You must be Klaas Krengel, so clean and kept! Are you not?"

"Nein!" For Rolf spoke none but the Germanian tongue. He hung pissing in the Inquisitor's grip, wrists drawn against his chest like a rabbit submitting to the raptor's talons. Inquisitor Ignacio spattered the children with a kicked lump of manure. A few blinked, but no one dared wipe the filth away. How the Hound's eyes burned with contempt, like something not of God's creation, radiating a contempt not just for children, but for all of mankind, living, dead, and unborn.

"One of you is Krengel, and you owe me for your benefactor's trial. And if it costs me all ten of your throats, I won't be out a ducat less." Blood welled in ashen fissures around his grimacing lips, parched from so much exposure to vinegar. "Pray you spare this fool's life, Klaas Krengel, wherever you are."

Hard palms slammed Krengel between his shoulders with such force that he had no perception of the fall. One instant he was standing in line, and in the next, he was bowing before the Inquisitor on his hands and knees.

"How saintly of you, little Santa Klaas, to turn yourself in." The Inquisitor was smirking. Blood fished between his teeth. He dropped Rolf to the dirt and squatted nose-to-nose with Krengel, where he treated himself to another go at his sponge. Crushing it against his maw, he sucked through every orifice in his face until his eyes went crossed beneath fluttering lids. Orange rivulets of bloody medicine dripped from his chin. "It may interest you to know, my little Santa," he said, without ever opening his eyes, "that we've learned the whereabouts of your father. Can you guess where we finally found him?"

"Mainz," Krengel said, wiping the back of his hand across his lips. "I suppose he went to his Krengel Bakery, in Mainz. That's where he always goes. He's got important business there."

"You speak Latin?" Inquisitor Ignacio's eyes flicked open. He hitched his eyebrows and somehow laughed without laughing at all, just a snuffling jerk that rippled his trunk. "Yes, he was found in Mainz. That much is true. But there is no Krengel Bakery there. Only a public bathhouse, where I've learned your father was found three months ago, dead--of syphilis. We burned his remains on charges of adultery."

Krengel's heart throbbed inside his ears. Why on earth he felt so compelled to defend his father was confounding. His whereabouts should have come as no surprise, not to anyone who knew Count Richwald Krengel well, notorious glutton of every pleasure.

"This is all such a shameful affair." Inquisitor Ignacio rose and cleared his throat. "But you orphans of the Friary are indebted to the Church. And to repay this debt, I've executed your sale. New benefactors will arrive to claim each of you. But first,

Baptism. And then, a final performance by *Die Kleinen Elfen* for the pleasure of our Roman hosts." He lowered his gaze. "With the exception of you, Klaas Krengel."

Krengel turned to search the hateful faces. The only expression in difference was that of Ludolph, leering behind him. He looked genuinely happy for the first time in months.

"We wouldn't have you ruining our Savior's hymns on Christmas Eve with your awful braying. Your loving new benefactor has already arrived, Cardinal Moretti of Bari, who shall keep you wonderfully close to him until an investigation can be made into charges against your heretical mother, so that your family debt to the Church may be repaid in full. These matters, I'm afraid, do take time."

Krengel breathed loudly through his nostrils, glaring back at the Inquisitor through hot and oily eyes. "My father always went to Mainz." His lower lip began to tremble. "He had important business there."

In the throes of silent laughter, Inquisitor Ignacio's trunk wagged like a boiled stalk of drawk. He sniffed a shot of air and clapped his hands. "You must despise me!" The Inquisitor groped for his beloved sponge, but he fumbled it in his mirth. He snatched it back from the manure and stamped dark blotches upon his muzzle. "Terrible, you must think me. But make no mistake, Santa Klaas, there are immeasurably worse monsters than I lurking in the unlit corners of this world." Inquisitor Ignacio licked sanguine manure from his lips. "And I pray that every one of them takes a bite of you."

Roosters of diverse kind and color ran loose about the nave. They crowed their blasphemies from the capitals and cornices, and flapped cackling over the congregation from one window pedestal to another. The fowl were wound to a terrible fuss. And as their pale droppings rained upon the richly embroidered mantles of visiting Cardinals, the question of whether including actual chickens in <u>Miso del Gallo</u> had been wise or unwise, was surely an unspoken commonality. Krengel tracked the path of a snowy rivulet down the crimson fabric of a Cardinal's tunic. He blinked his blue eyes and smiled.

"I know," he whispered to the Krampusz, who shared with him right then and there another vision of red and white. "I was thinking the same." It was a banner flapping high over a blasted ridge of cactus pads. The Habsburg Netherlands flag, of course, but displaced to a faraway realm that evidently knew nothing of flags or subjugation or geometric shapes or even the colors of red and white. "It's beautiful. Just as I imagined. If only you could take me away with you to Sundaloon, so I could see all the wonderful things you've been doing."

"Shh!"

Separated from the congregation by a partial choir screen, the clergy chanted their oaths by the flickering light of chandeliers. Their drones were vast and resonant beneath the vaulted dome. Sinuous columns soared and radiated into fans that arched over clerestory windows. Ordinarily, those windows might've filled this space with abundant natural light. But not at this strange hour, when the windows were black as blind arcades, when the church might as well have been situated on the bottom of the Adriatic Sea.

A murmur spread through the congregation. The children were coming. Paraded down the center aisle, <u>Die Kleinen Elfen</u> were dressed for what was to be their final performance in sackcloth robes slopped with red paint, with steepled <u>corozos</u> made of paper thrust down upon their heads. Still dripping from their forced baptisms in a horse trough out on the Piazza, the boys stumbled over rolled apples, recoiling from bearded Spaniards who stepped from the pews to make grabs for them as they passed. Some seized their wrists and pretended to kiss imaginary jewels on their fingers. A forceful shove toppled Benedikt Amsel. His paper *corozo* was crushed underfoot. He began to bawl. Sputum showered him. It was the darkly overwhelming presence of the Inquisition that brought out the worst in men, inspiring an exaggerated show of condemnation against the little heretics, who had been dressed for the occasion as miniature clergymen for an added bit of fun.

Pascal Schwartz helped little Benedikt to his feet, wincing, as he was struck between the shoulder blades with such force as to detonate an apple into snowy pith. This brought a low rumble of laughter, and a barrage of malicious fruit. Inquisitor Ignacio had warned the orphans that the congregation was apt to become unruly, and that some might try to tempt them to retrieve a thrown treat. But their pangs of hunger had best be ignored and every treat forsaken, for if a lad so much as looked at a thrown piece of fruit, he would experience the agonies of an expanding brass instrument called, "The Pear."

Krengel lifted his eyes to a cackling rooster flapping past successive niches of inlaid mosaics. Pixilated martyrs burned, bled, and died at the hands of men and the jaws of beasts, suffering every conceivable and terrible demise. Each scene recalled an age, not so very distant, when Christians feared only non-Christians. How times had changed. His gaze tracked the flying rooster past the choir screen to the procession of orphans, halted now by a veritable riot. Rolf was bawling so hard that his whole body appeared paralyzed. Peter Engel shouted at the crowds, twisting his paper corrozo and swatting the groping hands. Apples whizzed across the aisle and lobbed skyward toward roosting chickens on the cornices.

Fingernails raked through Krengel's hair. He flinched at the scrape of owlish claws against his scalp, and turned a questioning eye to the man behind him. Cardinal Moretti, his new benefactor, could not seem to stop touching him in some small way since Holy Mass had begun. A tumor the size of an apple bulged from his jaw, uprooting several blackened teeth from their sockets. His breath was positively noisome.

"Stop it!" Krengel hissed at the Krampusz, shaking loose the gruesome visions that had surely been belched straight up from Hell unto the backs of his eyes. He shifted the focus of his thoughts onto Mitzi and Nele Gottlieb, swallowed up by a seaport brothel. Ludolf Eichman and Pascal Schwartz were to apprentice a bloated ghoul called Bugger Snipe, who mined gold from the mouths of the dead. Peter Engel and the Amsel brothers would collect and sell manure as stewards to the City of Rome. Theodor Weissmuller, Wolfram Faust, and Rolf, would return to Spain to serve the Friary Rabida in whatever capacity they were bidden.

Whose fate amongst them looked to be the worst?

Krengel grimaced as a few hairs were plucked suddenly from his head. He turned, scowling and rubbing his scalp. Cardinal Moretti curled the stolen threads around his tongue, drawing them clumsily into his malformed mouth like angel hair pasta. He grunted and sucked, bouncing tiptoed with evident delight. On either side of him hovered his acolytes, bald and vapid. One drooled through a gap in his bottom lip, where a perfect crescent of flesh had been bitten clean away.

Krengel turned away, breathing heavily. Around the orphans, the mob surged and pulled. A torn corrozo was batted over the crowd, where flying apples and flapping chickens shared busy airspace. First one, then the whole orphan choir made an undignified retreat back toward the entry. There, a phalanx of hooded Inquisitors was positioned to receive them.

If nothing else, Krengel's fate meant travel. He'd never imagined living anywhere but Lambsheim, and now he was going to a place called Bari, where a stewardship awaited him, the Basilica of St. Nicholas. Stripped of his past, of everything he'd ever known, Krengel reckoned his own destruction. But into what would he be reformed? It was a queer feeling to stand poised at the brink of a brand new destiny, yet unknown.

"Bless you, my forever friend," Krengel whispered to the Krampusz who, for better or for worse, had never once left his side. Denizens of different worlds, never once having laid eyes upon the other, they tolerated an estranged, yet intimate familiarity, a distance bridged by shared snippets of imagery and passage from a separate reality. And as the nature of the sender was inadvertently suggested in the nature of the images sent, be it a glittering sunrise, a careful bloom amongst briars, or the bloody husk of some poor lizard bashed flaccid against the rocks, Krengel knew his Krampusz well. "Dear brother of mine, in another time."

An emerald-breasted cock burst aflutter from a clerestory niche. Feathers floated down like holy manna, as a second pinch of hair was yanked from the back of Krengel's head. This time, he dared not turn around, while his eyes welled with tears. Cardinal Moretti's tongue slapped excitedly against the walls of its hollow.

Although he couldn't be certain why, Klaas Krengel was suddenly overtaken by an urge to reach beyond himself, beyond the horror of his immediate situation. He knew enough to lower his head in perfect humility, perhaps for the first time in his young life. He then folded his hands together, closed his eyes, and he thought of delicious pastries.

Chapter Two

"I've a story to tell." The young harlot nearest the driver spun to address the jostling cartload. "It's called, 'The Three Boys and the Brine Tub.' Anyone heard it?" A crop of affrighted eyes under yellow hoods blinked in furtive glances.

"Well," the she said, clasping her hands and clearing her throat, "it was a dark and stormy night, when three orphans sought shelter at an inn. But this was no ordinary inn." Her eyes gleamed mischievously. "The orphans had not a ducat betwixt them, but the innkeeper's wife took pity and she offered a room for free. The boys thanked her, went off to bed, and soon they were fast asleep. But late that night, while the orphans slept, the innkeeper crept into their room. He pulled out a knife --" She then hooked a forearm around the driver's neck. She drew her index finger slowly beneath his chin. "And he slit all of the children's throats, right then and there."

"What did he do that for?" a small girl asked, wiping her nose on her sleeve.

"He was hungry," the driver replied, peering over his shoulder.

"Yes, the innkeeper and his wife were very poor. They badly needed the meat. So, he chopped them all up and threw their flesh into a brine tub to cure. Then, he washed up and went off to bed."

"But guess who showed up for breakfast?" The driver wagged a finger and grinned.

"St. Nicholas!" a couple of the girls shouted, in unison.

"St. Nicholas! Yes! He just happened to be traveling through that very town on that very next morning, and was hungry, so he stopped by the inn for a bit of breakfast. But soon as he stepped over the threshold, he sensed that something was wrong."

"Had second sight," the driver said, tapping his temple. "Could see a man's sins by looking him in the eye."

"The innkeeper denied killing anyone, of course."

"Course."

"But St. Nicholas made his way over to the brine tub. He stared down into the water, pointed his book of gospels at the heap of boned flesh, and he shouted--"

"Stand up!" The driver jabbed a finger at the sky. "Stand up, you three, and testify!"

"And they did." The harlot gave a wink. "Those three dead orphans rose from the tub, bloody water streaming off their skin, and they all pointed at the innkeeper. Murderer!"

The driver smiled and gave the reigns a smart shake. "You girls, you arrive in Bari on a special day. For it was on the ninth of May, five hundred years ago that our patron, Saint Nicholas, arrived here in Bari. His bones, anyway." The driver gestured to the eastern seawall, where waves spewed foamy jettisons. "The Turks were invading the city of Myra, where Saint Nicholas had been dead and buried six hundred years. But a crew of Bariot soldiers decided to rescue him before the Turks plundered his tomb. He was never happy in Myra, anyway." The driver shook his head, giving some pause to the clopping hooves of his horses. "His bones had quit seeping myrrh. And that, my friends, is how you know St. Nicholas is unhappy. His bones dry up like old sponges. Give nothing."

"What's myrrh?" asked the girl with the runny nose.

"Juice squeezed from the leaves of a certain shrub, I believe," replied the harlot. "They once used it to keep the dead from becoming all stinky."

"Not the myrrh of Saint Nicholas," said the driver, wagging his finger, "it is not from no shrub. Every drip is a teardrop from God."

"What's it look like?" another girl asked him.

"Well ... is clear, thin. No smell or taste. You see it tomorrow, every corner in Bari. Is like the lightest oil, so thin, is almost like ..."

"Water."

The driver glared at the young whore seated nearest him and cleared his throat. "As I saying, Saint Nicholas had not flowed in Myra. Not happy. Not for long time. But, when Bariot sailors arrive for him, smash open sarcophagus--"

Not yet a day in Bari, and the girls had already heard the same story retold a dozen times. A Myran monk refused to hand over the relics of St. Nicholas to the Bariot soldiers, and during the scuffle that ensued, an old flask once used to collect the saint's holy drippings had toppled from a shelf. It came to rest upon a tile, where it spun and chattered all about until the sailors took notice. They took it as a sign, pried up the tile, and below, they found the secret entrance to the saint's tomb.

"--them hammers crash down upon lid--WHACK!--and great fountain of myrrh shoot into air like blowing whale! Oh, here it come! It fill street like river of perfume, rush down to the sea. It smell so wonderful! Wind carry this wonderful smell back across the sea to Bari, where fishermen at this same harbor all begin celebrate because them know St. Nicholas is rescue! Is soon coming home to Bari. And he does, next day. And has been very happy here, ever since."

The girls' heads jogged in perfect rhythm to the knocking hooves against cobblestone. The wagon creaked. Above, a tumult of keening seabirds twirled beneath the glittering sky. Somewhere beyond the seawall, the Adriatic smashed itself into hissing foam.

"Do you really believe those stupid stories?" the harlot asked the driver.

The driver cranked around and scowled at her. "Every year on ninth of May, his bones seep myrrh. This is fact."

"Great geysers of it? Will we see great gushing fountains of perfume roaring through the streets all the way to the sea?"

The driver sighed, staring between the heads of his horses for a spell. "You know, is too bad they not tolerate you little whores in Basilica, or you go see it for yourself. Whether you love Saint Nicholas or not, he still love you. Eh? Is watching over you right now. Look and you see him, there, there, right over there, at every turn. We so love our St. Nicolas, and he so love Bari."

The former was undoubtedly true. St. Nicholas haunted every ledge, every windowsill, and every alcove in the seaport. Gesso figurines of the fourth century bishop lurked over doorways like mischievous fairies. His benevolent bearded face beamed from homemade portraits propped in windows, somehow retaining his air of humility, notwithstanding, a jewel-encrusted mitre jutting skyward like a chessboard bishop, a richly embroidered mantle upon his shoulders, glimmering heaps of medallions about his neck.

"Was he a Moor?"

"What?"

"St. Nicholas. Was he Moorish? In many paintings, his skin is dark."

The driver crooked his head around. "Girl, what is your name?"

"Mitzi. Mitzi Gottlieb."

"Mitzi Gottlieb, you do well to pray to Saint Nicholas. He had soft spot for your kind." He turned stiffly back around and gave the reigns a shake. "Always in his left hand, you will see the book of gospels, clutched to him heart." The driver raised his right hand and wiggled his speckled digits. "But in other, he hold a mysterious black bag with little treasures inside. This because the good saint once climb over darkened rooftops and drop gold down little girls' chimneys. Save them from bad world that soon will hunger for them. You pray him tonight. Maybe he bring a gift for you. But maybe not, eh? Maybe all you find in the morning is coal."

The little girl with the cold tugged at Mitzi's sleeve. "What happened to the orphans?"

"What orphans, Nele?"

"They stood up in the water and pointed at the innkeeper."

"Yes?"

"Well, did they all fall back into pieces, afterwards, or did they live?"

"I don't know, Nele." Mitzi smiled and stroked her sister's hair. "That's a very good question. You could ask the same of Lazarus of Bethany, I suppose--if they hadn't beheaded him, of course. Once a dead man has been raised by the power of God, can natural death ever trouble him again? That, I don't know. Perhaps those orphans still walk the earth today, as immortal confessors of Christ."

The driver eyed the girls over his shoulder as though he meant to interrupt, but never did.

"Why did they cut off Lazarus' head?" Nele asked. "I thought he was Jesus' friend."

"He was. But everyone else hated him. After Christ raised him from the grave, they say that poor Lazarus never smiled again, not after what he'd seen on the other side. Mobs pursued him for the rest of his days, always hunting him. They finally caught up to him where he'd been hiding--in a cave in France, I believe--and there, they butchered him, cut him all to bits."

"But why?" Nele wrinkled her nose, squinting in the sun. "He hadn't done nothing wrong, had he?"

"You don't have to do anything wrong to lose your head in this world, Nele. Lazarus was hated by everyone for what he was."

"What was he?"

Mitzi shrugged and snickered. "You tell me. But the way they hacked him all up into bits, suggests he wasn't exactly assassinated," Mitzi said, "but rather, that he was harvested!"

"For what?" Nele whispered.

Mitzi cleared her throat and looked to the sky. "There are sorts, even today, who would hunt an undead man like Lazarus of Bethany to the ends of the earth, for whatever power might be flowing through his veins." Mitzi wriggled her fingertips mysteriously.

"You mean, like warlocks and witches?" Nele's eyes lit up.

"Aye. Warlocks, witches, or just thieves and bad men, hoping to profit from the sale of a raised corpse's relics. Same as it ever was, Nele. Same as it ever was in this awful, greedy world."

"Have you seen him yet, Mitzi?"

"Who?"

"You know." Nele smiled and made a twirling gesture with her index finger about her temple. "Him!"

She hadn't thought much of Krengel, her little madling, since Christmas Eve. She and Nele's survival had been her only preoccupation. No man had yet touched them, but remaining chaste had not been a simple task. She and Nele were quite young, but it was just that youthful innocence that appealed to a most loathsome charter of men given to brutal acts of misbehavior in the bedchamber. And so it was that once the sun cooled, Mitzi was left to war through every night for their survival. And survive, they had, for she'd found a method for keeping those lecherous scads at bay.

Why on earth should a brothel not satisfy diverse hungers, she thought, after blinding a randy bishop with two handfuls of lye. Why should a man come here to slake but a single appetite, in a house where talent is limited to the bedchamber? Seemed a bit of a waste. Even a brothel shouldn't resign to the ordinary, not when a menu of fine food, drink, and fresh garden vegetables could in time propagate chatter, and make the unmentionable the talk of the town.

To confuse the appetites of men, she'd concocted a hearty pottage with pulled hinds of hare, fat chibols and white beans, sprinkled over with sage and a crushed rye tourt for a bit of crunch. But even more aromatic on a cold Roman night, her clove pullet fared well beneath a blanket of baked apple slices, nestled in a warm bed of crumbled cinnamon maslin. Germanic couplings of bacon, sugar and vinegar, paid tangy compliment to the traditionally savory Italian stews.

Like Mitzi's morbid sense of humor, there was an appealing dissonance in opposite couplings. Any cook worth her salt knew the steps of the alluring dance made by sugar and vinegar, cream and pepper upon the tongue. And in a greater sense, pairing beauty with the grotesque, naughty with nice, was just the sort of experience to draw souls to the cinnamon heat of a whorehouse kitchen. How right and how bright she'd been to intuit that Man's capital sense was seated not in his eyes at all, but in his nose, the foremost point on his stupid face. Hook the nose and their bodies did follow the decadent trails to Mitzi's kitchen, perhaps later to the bedchambers of another, if, after several helpings of pottage and perry cider, they were still able. The spice of her gingerbread medallions wafted through open windows and down dark alleys like a river of myrrh. More akin to a pub than a brothel, patrons gathered at the stoop tipping drams, while the staircase treads to Mitzi's kitchen did all the creaking.

"Klaas Krengel, you silly shit," Nele said, pinching her sister's leg, "he's here in Bari, yeah?"

"Ow! Well, yes, I suppose, if he's still alive."

"Wouldn't it be fun to visit him?"

"We hardly have time for that, Nele. They're expecting a lot from us at this seaport. We must begin cooking at once if we're to be ready for tomorrow's crowds. If we've no fine spread prepared, then it's we who'll be devoured." Mitzi smiled at Nele and swept an auburn lock behind her sister's ear.

"I wish we could find him." Nele smiled. "Remember those stained glass windows in his castle? And the butterfly gardens? And the whole cellar of beer? Imagine living there!"

"Yes, but the looters ruined the place. And besides, just look at what the good life did for him. Nasty little bugger, wasn't he? Worst little monster I've ever seen."

"But Mitzi, you took such sweet care of him."

"Hoped he might return the favor, was all. Reckoned his rich father might one day come looking for him. Maybe take us back with him to Lambsheim for caring so well for his crazy son."

"You didn't like Klaas at all, then? Not really?"

"Felt a little bad for him, I guess, with all the troubles in his head." Mitzi shrugged. "I don't know." She kneaded the hem of her tunic between her thumb and forefinger. "Thought he might just amount to something for you and me. Always got to keep thinking, Nele. Be more than just a pretty face. Stay sharp as the devil himself. Be on the lookout for opportunities." Mitzi broke her mantra with a sigh. "Thought Klaas Krengel might be one of those. Turned out, he wasn't. That's all."

The wagon squealed horribly over sheaves of red granite thrust up through the mud, and fishtailed through blue sloughs of shale that spilled from the mountain's ruptured guts like a great cache of potshards. So many fled the plagued Low Countries last fall that the roads were beaten thin to their rocky bones. But all had since settled. Here, the breeze hissed through needled boughs where solitary birds of no definite color flitted. Wolves trailed them by day and groaned all through the night, but while the sun shone, there was no quieter place than the heart of Germania.

Bugger Snipe suckled his wineskin. He belched, wiped his chin on his tattered sleeve, pursed his purple lips, and spat over the silvered wheel that was scribed by crushed rocks. The sun had not yet crested the eastern ridge, but already the wine was gushing through every whorl of Snipe's brain, dulling him to bestial complacence with regard to the world around him. It was his usual state. Since childhood, strong drink was both the medicine and the mortar with which he bricked rough memories into a life hard and fragmented as the road beneath his wheels.

Disposing of the dead was a loathsome and thankless occupation, but there was enough to be pilfered from corpses and abandoned homes to keep him in the drink. And it wasn't all rubbish. There were good moments in the company of the dead, ones that pleased him to repeat and to remember. The warm ones. The long and private interludes with those heaved aboard his reeking wagon still warm and fresh, or better yet, with a tiny spark of life yet in them. They were the lucky ones who joined their ferryman in the bulrushes for a final afternoon of intimacy before being clubbed sweetly into the hereafter.

Snipe's smile vanished when he startled at the whoosh and clatter of an arrow shaft that seemed to dart out of and into nowhere. He leaned back on the reigns, halting his beasts. "You little bastards quit wasting arrows!" He turned and glowered through the flaps. "I'll come back there and skin you both alive. You hear me?"

No answer. The still forms of his young apprentices were buried beneath heaps of sack cloth and various fitments jarred loose from the hooks. Snipe groped behind his seat. It was missing again. They'd taken his bow and quiver. Evidently, he'd not whipped them quite hard enough the last time. The older boy, Ludolph, seemed obsessed with the lethal instrument, forever stealing moments to practice with the weapon. Not even a vicious beating could deter him. Had a bit of a dark side, that one.

"Oye!" Snipe succumbed to his nagging temper, whacking viciously at the twin forms with his prod until the stick snapped in two. He threw the ruined instrument overboard. "I'm talking to you! Where's my bow and quiver?"

Snipe spun back around, pulled a quick jerk off his wineskin and grimaced. His features softened to an infantile expression as his pressurized rage seemed suddenly to effervesce. Purple wine dribbled from the corners of his mouth as his eyes turned downward, where blood streaked the wineskin pinned to his heart with an arrow, buried all the way to its fletching.

And when he spotted his boys, not asleep behind him in the wagon at all, but yonder, perched atop two ruinous watchtowers, he realized in his final moment that they'd baited him here with all their tales of an abandoned castle of stained glass, butterfly gardens, and beer. But those little bastards had meant all along to murder him here, just outside the gates of the Promised Land, for the purpose of looting the lost village of Lambsheim, themselves. Bugger Snipe's eyes fluttered closed. He slumped over in his seat. Wine gurgled from the punctured skin down the wagon's peeling sideboards, where a rearing red lion lapped its blue tongue at the streaming blood.

"A good shot? Ha! It was a brilliant shot." Ludolph nocked another arrow on the bowstring. "How far would you say it was from me to old Snipe?"

"Here to the bedchamber, at least," Pascal said, stepping over the pile of bones to point down the long hallway. "Stuck him right through the thumper."

"Reckon I could split that bedpost from here?"

"Don't waste any more arrows! We've only got a few left. Let me carry it for a while?"

"Find your own one." Ludolph bent to retrieve a shard of blue stained glass from the tiled floor. He turned it round in the moonlight, and then passed it to Pascal. "Here's a good one for your collection."

"Come on, then. Let's go check the bedchamber. Probably she's got a nice jewelry box hidden in there somewhere, maybe behind a secret wall."

"Yeah." Ludolph grinned. "Bet she does. Rich lady like her wouldn't set it out for grabs with all her servants mucking about."

Like all the rest of the rooms in the Krengel estate, the bedchamber had been plundered. No telling how many times. Every drawer was overturned. Even the mattress was slashed and stained, disemboweled, stuffing strewn by the handful. The room smelt of urine and musky rodent activity.

"Look," Ludolph whispered, bending at the waist to retrieve a scrap of linen from the floor. Embroidered upon one corner was an ornate letter "K." He pressed the handkerchief to his muzzle and closed his eyes. "Silk! Have you ever touched silk before?"

"Smells like people have been pissing in here." Pascal wrinkled his nose.

Ludolph stuffed the kerchief into his satchel and wandered over to a niche, where a stained glass window overlooked a small garden. Might have been the only window in the estate left unbroken. It was a beautiful work to behold. A circular portal was left unstained, surrounded by concentric rings of cool lavenders and blues. Outside, ghostly moths courted the spikes of moonflowers. "Look," Ludolph said, "a spot yet untouched."

Pascal pressed his nose against the glass, alongside Ludolph. "They might've gotten to it from the outside."

"How? There's no gate. Just big walls, all around."

"If I was Lady Krengel, out there's where I'd keep my treasure." Pascal groped around the window frame, feeling for a secret latch or a hinge. "It's got to open, somehow. How else would she water her flowers?"

"Maybe those kind don't need watering."

"All flowers need water, stupid."

"Maybe they get enough water when it rains. Hey, should we smash it?"

Pascal picked up an empty cabinet drawer. With one heave, the last window in the Habsburg-Krengel estate detonated in a shower of tinkling slivers. Moonlight spilled through the jagged hole, casting shadows of Herculean moths against the bedchamber wall, where they heaved their dragon wings about the domed shadow of a single headstone.

"You know what I think it is?" Ludolph said.

"What?"

"I think it's a family grave plot."

"So what? We're not going out there?"

"I never said that. I just reckoned I was done with graves after I arrowed old Snipe. Grave robbery was his bit, not mine."

"Won't bother me to rob one more." Pascal snapped off the shards of glass and threw his leg over the threshold. The drop was farther than he'd guessed. He fell to the garden in a heap. Much like the window's design, the nook's pavestones were also laid in concentric rings around a central plot of earth that was nucleated by one lonely headstone. None but a single word was inscribed upon it.

"Well, what's it say?" Ludolph shouted down from the window.

It started with a letter K, followed by an R. Pascal sniffed and rubbed his nose. He wasn't so very good at reading. "Just says 'Krengel,' I guess."

"Well, read the damned thing!"

"I am!" Pascal squinted his eyes in the moonlight. "K-R-A-M--" He stood up, put his hands on his hips, and then leaned forward again. "Krampusz?" He glanced uncertainly back at Ludolph.

"What?"

"Krampusz. That's what it says."

"Isn't that the name of the … of that thing, that monster, who used to talk to little Klaas Krengel inside his head?"

"Trying to scare me?" Pascal swatted the air. "Won't work."

Ludolph flicked a shard of glass off the windowsill. "Go poke around in the garden a bit more then, if you're up to it. See if there's anything good down there. But don't let the Krampusz get you!"

Pascal frowned, shivering in the midnight breeze. A riot of plants grabbed at his feet with their sinewy vines. A fat moth dusted his face with slapping wings. Pascal spat and swatted it away. He wiped his mouth, lurched forward, and disappeared down into the weeds.

Ludolph stared at the garden for several seconds, but his friend did not rise. "Pascal?" He leaned out the broken window. "You alright?" Tucking the bow and quiver beneath his arm, Ludolph slipped over the sill and landed with a grunt on the limestone pavers. A flurry of pale moths greeted him at the garden's edge. He could see things more clearly, now. There was more than one headstone, engraved with trumpeting cherubs and swaddled babes. He counted three, no four of them, five! Enmeshed like speckled eggs in the bracken.

"It is dark. It is deep. On the bottom, my children sleep."

Ludolph spun toward the sound of the voice, sharp and jagged as shattered glass.

"You will not disturb my children."

Ludolph staggered backward into the garden, heaving breaths of the chilly night air. His frantic eyes searched the edges of the nook where starlight dissolved into blackness. "Who is it? We weren't going to rob any graves. Honest!"

There, where a shag of lush grapevines crept up the garden wall, he could see the shine of her eyes. Or was it her teeth? Stumbling away from the face in the shadows, he barked his heel into a headstone, stumbled, cursed, and crashed into the weeds. The headstone that tripped him loomed in front of his face. The etched visage of a little girl, her young life reduced to lines, gaped back at him from a granite tablet that appeared to be smooth and newer than the rest. Inscribed like a banner over the face of the little girl was a single word: LALA.

"You will not disturb my children!"

She was coming. Ludolph could hear the slap of bare feet upon the pavers, the scratch of outgrown toenails against the limestone, the snap of branches. She was in the garden.

Pascal had been right. Partly right. It was a family grave plot, to be sure. But there wasn't a whole family buried here. This was a cemetery for children. There must have been a dozen or more headstones in the weeds. Miscarriages. Births gone wrong. Children born unfit for survival, struck down by disease, taken ahead of their time.

"Get out! Get away from my babies!"

"Pascal!" Ludolph flipped onto his belly and dragged himself forward through the underbrush. He pulled himself along by fistfuls of vegetation until his groping hands swept thin air. "Pascal!" Ludolph screamed into the abyss. But there came no reply from the gaping hole that had evidently swallowed his friend.

The Krampusz surfaced from the tide pool with a flailing grabbut in his mouth. Surging ashore, he shook a spray of dazzling droplets from his blue-black curls with a shimmy that began in his waggling nose, and rifled down through the inky carpet of fur to his dark clapping buttocks. It was going to be another perfect day. The grabbut wrenched about and bit him on his cheek, but being so terribly scarred and disfigured, the Krampusz seemed not to mind, or even notice. The destruction flowed from his crushed eye socket like solidified lava down his cheek, and up across his rumbled brow. As though suddenly self-conscious of these old injuries, the Krampusz covered his right eye with a furry palm, and gazed up to the heavens through his left. The grabbut hooked his nose with a claw and tented the black flesh of his nostril.

The Krampusz seized its tail and dashed the sea lizard's brains out upon the rocks. While the grabbut quivered, he smeared the back of his hand beneath his nose and spat. It was a big old lizard, maybe the biggest he'd ever caught. He turned it in the sunlight and smiled. He sure missed his old bix-box. Used to be, he could preserve a special moment like this one forever. His bix-box would buzz like an angry bee when he'd press that silver button, then it would flash bright as lightning and shit out a perfect painting on a little glossy card. He spent hours on the beach pointing that bix-box at himself, and making it shit paintings of his funny faces all afternoon. But there came a day when he swam with his bix-box out into the sea. The Krampusz's smile faded. How sad he'd been to learn that water killed bix-boxes, dead.

Lord swaney. He wiped his brow and smeared his face against his furry palms. Not yet noon, and already it was getting hotter than a two-dollar pistol. Dragging the dead grabbut by its spiny tail, he loped feet-over-knuckles with his heron's legs articulating between his even longer arms like a great black onion teetering atop a moving scaffold.

The beach all around was strewn with kelp. Glistening bladders and whorls of amber tubing looked like the entrails of some nameless thing disemboweled beneath the glittering sea. The Krampusz smiled at the grabbuts and isk-isks all scrambling pell-mell before him. The scads of critters he loved to eat had come to respect his voracious appetite, as he advanced upon them like an inverted pendulum with his graceful vaulting gait. The dead grabbut tilled a broken rut through the sand as he knuckled through a waldorf of belching oruks that inched and rippled toward the surf like elephantine grubs. At the feet of the beetling cliffs, the Krampusz clambered atop a rocky slab strewn with ruins of all manner of life butchered and smashed asunder, and he settled in with his picnic lunch amidst the carnage.

Isk-isks picked through the putrid puzzle all around him while he worked. Like a hatch of cherry spiders, they nipped bits of bygone creatures and ate while hitching sideways across the lava, eyestalks fixed on the Krampusz, while their delicate pincers conveyed parcels through the masticating mouthparts. They exactly matched the Krampusz's surges of motion like a living shadow thrown before him. Then, they scattered when he sat down with a fleshy smack, folded his stilted limbs in the center of the slab, and began to pick the thong of a dangling satchel at his groin.

His lithe fingers loosed the little, black bag, which was about the size of a coin purse. The Krampusz dipped into the satchel, worming his hand in to the wrist. Groping for a moment, he withdrew his hand and frowned down into the bag. He pulled it loose from his waist, placed it upon the rock and pulled with both hands in opposite directions until the bag flowered open, wider and wider, until it had stretched to a more accommodating diameter.

He doubled over, rooting around inside well past his shoulders and further still, until he lost his balance and tumbled right down into the purse. Isk-isks flattened at the cacophony of clanging instruments that crashed and bounced through untold depths that echoed the Krampusz's cursing. After a long while, there came the resonance of ascending footsteps. He emerged from his purse out of breath and muttering as though he'd just climbed up from the bowels of the earth. He held a shiny tool in his hand. It was one of his favorite little treasures, all inlaid with mother-of-pearl. One of the doodads that had once belonged to Chad.

He turned it over in his hand, pressed a silver tab with his thumb, and the Mexican switchblade sprung to life with a pleasing snap and a flash of steel. Flipping the grabbut between his legs, he jabbed the blade between its hinds and flayed the sea lizard from asshole to Adam's apple.

Weirder stuff than switchblades and bix-boxes sometimes turned up down there, lost between moments, in the Quick. Hellfire, he'd come across stuff down there that would've puzzled smarter men, things slipped through the cracks of fantastic worlds, and damned if he could figure out how to use them. Seemed like some things turned up at the bottom of the staircase just to confound him, like the mee-deep. It was like a perfect square of the smoothest coal you could ever imagine, and it just beeped and cheeped all night and day like a hungry chick fallen from its nest, and all the while, a row of mysterious numbers kept dancing past a tiny gray window on its face. Didn't take too long before he'd smashed that confounding little son-of-a-bitch to smithereens, to set those dancing numbers free, but once he'd done so, there was nothing at all behind the glass. It was all a lie.

And then, there were better days, when he found things like Chad.

The Krampusz licked grabbut blood from the switchblade and chuckled.

One morning before breakfast, he'd thrown open his purse and damned if there wasn't a strange kid stumbling around down there in the dark. Anybody's guess how he'd managed to get in there, but without the Krampusz's help, there was no getting out. This fellow wore dark spectacles, short leggings, and a billed hat. Silver rings pierced his earlobes and dark designs inked his shoulders and arms. At first, Chad hollered a lot and stunk of alcohol. He kept checking his mee-deep, but mee-deeps don't work down there in the Quick. Before long, he settled down, and the Krampusz decided to keep him. Chad was an emotional and messy creature. He cried for months about the darkness and his family and his friends, yet the Krampusz found Chad useful in his ability to explain some of the baffling items that wound up in the Quick. Over time, he taught the Krampusz a lot about his language, about the habits of his peculiar world. But much like the bix-box, there came a day came when all the fun stopped, the day that Chad was not waiting at the bottom of the staircase.

The Krampusz belched. He covered his right eye and peered skyward again. Like a hole ripped in the blue firmament, the swirling vortex in the sky rotated high above Sundaloon like a cyclone of filth, black as a warlock's root cellar and crackling with fairy lights. The Krampusz licked the other side of the switchblade, smacked his lips, and then tore out a glistening handful of the grabbut's innards. These, he slapped upon the rock.

There was a correct method to eating raw grabbut. Any part of a sea lizard could be distasteful if taken alone or in excess to any other. Maintaining a proper balance between a grabbut's intense flavors was key. The Krampusz lifted a loop of intestines from the mess and pinched a greenish extrusion of stomach contents from the flaccid tube that curled wetly upon the rock. The emptied gut he flipped to the hovering isk-isks, who seized upon the noodle and battled over the spoils like clownish knights in carnival armor. He placed a blanket of briny grabbut hide over a nugget of flavorless meat, wrapped it in a kelp leaf, and dipped it twice in the goo. That was when he heard the scream.

Clapping his hand over his missing left eye, he cranked his head skyward and watched the thing fall from the portal, arms pinwheeling, all the way down into the heart of the daisy forest. Mockingbirds flushed before a swelling cloud of dust. Not the best spot on Sundaloon to come in for a landing, but there were probably worse.

Every isk-isk rushed the carcass the instant the Krampusz leapt off the slab. They squabbled over the viscera, while Sundaloon's self-proclaimed king vaulted off over craggy fields of lava with impossible ease.

###

Every bell in Bari had a unique tone and timing. Each was synchronized to the timing of a specific, daily event. The toll of a bell would prompt a skyward glance from anyone within earshot, to make a quick check of the sun's position. The bells were so intimately linked to the passage of time that on the rare occasions when every bell in the city tolled at once, the experience rattled a Baresi to his very soul, stilled him in his tracks, for time itself unraveled and was strewn to confetti. The joyous crash of sound reverberated through the seaport's writhing arteries to flush pigeons in dappled flocks that flashed in the sky like schools of minnows.

At midday on May ninth, the first day of the annual *Festival of the Translation of the Holy Relics,* Bari came alive with clanging bells. Starlings gushed from the clerestory windows around the pealing bell tower at Basilica di San Nicola, the final resting place of Bari's patron saint. It was an imposing fortification, a somber hulk of ancient masonry that loomed darkly over the peninsula with its back to the Adriatic Sea. With its cruciform mass shouldered between Romanesque towers, it better resembled an English castle than an ordinary place of worship. And at times, it had served as such.

Across the bustling piazza from the seaward dormitories, a hooded figure emerged from the basilica's Lion's Portal. The brown fabric of his Dominican robes flapped in the briny wind, throwing back his hood as he skulked beneath the engraved names of those famous sailors who rescued Saint Nicholas from Myra, five hundred years ago. He jerked the hood back over his naked head and turned to face the wall. Head bowed as though in prayer, he reached into the sleeve of his tunic, and withdrew a steely dagger.

Cast upon the spike of shimmering steel, was a leering distortion of his broad face and blazing eyes. He lowered and tilted his chin, trailing his fingertips over his newly shaved scalp. It was another of the Krampusz's bright ideas. Krengel smiled. He looked funny bald, a bit like Friar Otto.

In five months, he'd grown in height and width. Though they might've starved a passive child with their severe Dominican diet of broth and rye, what were Krengel's lifelong failings, but symptoms of his indomitable will to have while others around him had not. Greed ran strong in both sides of his family. And it was no small irony that Krengel, now a custodian of the relics of a saint canonized for profound acts of generosity, had honed his naturally greedy edge to a perfect tool for survival. Since Christmas Eve in Rome, he'd grown meaner, stronger, and more formidable. Daily acts of theft and trickery against the hardened peasants of a foreign land had honed Krengel, right beneath the noses of his Dominican handlers, into perhaps the most dogged urchin in all of Bari.

Krengel lifted his tunic, glanced around the crowded piazza, and then sheathed the dagger back into a tight fold in his braies. He hitched up his secret contraption. The rope was itchy about his waist, and the weight of the invention had begun to chaff his flesh. The dangling wood blocks clonked between his knees. Should've wrapped them in cloth to quiet their knocking. Too late for any of that, now. This was the big day. Around front of the basilica, cartwheels rumbled against the pavers as guests and dignitaries continued to arrive.

He'd not yet spotted Cardinal Moretti, rumored still unfit to attend this evening's festivities, deathly ill as he'd been. Moretti posed him little threat in his weakened condition, but he was indeed the one person in all of Italy who could possibly spoil everything by summoning for him at the critical hour. Thus, the first phase of Krengel's plan for May ninth was simply to avoid Moretti at all costs, to meld into the visiting crowds and simply lay low until sundown.

"What in Heaven do you think you're doing, back here?"

Krengel spun to find the rector glowering out at him through the Lion's Portal. He seized Krengel by an ear and marched him along the wall toward the main entrance of the basilica. "We've been looking everywhere for you! Your benefactor has arrived!" The rector lifted him by his ear and flipped back his hood. "You've shaved your head. What is this?"

"I had lice?"

"Shush it!"

The rector harried him to the main portal, where Cardinal Moretti was being lifted from his wagon in a sort of birthing position by a host of able-bodied Dominicans. The friars set him gently upon his unstable feet. He swayed weightlessly in the bullying wind, as though might at any moment be sucked off the earth and flung through the heavens. He lolled back his head and peered at the ecclesiastical assembly from beneath his fallen eyelids. The purplish growth in his lower jaw had swelled to the size of an onion, forcing his tongue to protrude like a newly hatched chick. He attempted to speak, but his lips produced only bubbles.

Krengel's survival for five months in the favored hunting grounds of this predator was owed mostly to a bout of poor health that robbed Moretti of all but an infant's strength, slackening the musculature of his face, not a day after *Miso del Gallo*. As a result, Krengel hadn't suffered sight of the awful man since Christmas Eve, which was fortunate, but rumor held that Moretti's health was steadily improving. So said the Dominicans anyway, who'd just this morning doted over Moretti's latest accomplishment of peeling and devouring a boiled egg all by himself.

A breeze kicked up and snatched the mitre right off Moretti's head, tumbling and spinning it down the street. But the friars supporting the feeble body of their guest could only look on in despair as they goaded him forward, one cautious step at a time. A silvery thread of slobber whipped from Moretti's lip and bowed like a harp in the wind. Snowy wisps of hair all writhing on scabrous pedestals, Moretti looked for all the earth to be some deranged and ancient warlock, routed from his alpine rookery.

As the trio approached, Krengel bent his knees until he felt those wood blocks beneath his tunic touch the ground. He then stepped atop them and rose, oh so slowly, to his tiptoes, causing the special knot from which they were suspended to unwind. Through the fabric of his robe, he gathered the reigns of his makeshift stilts. Those milling around him were so transfixed by the precarious transfer of Cardinal Moretti that none seemed to notice that Klaas Krengel had suddenly sprouted a foot in height, looking quite enough like an adult friar, with his broad shoulders and shaved head, to pass before the myopic eyes of the monster.

Moretti made some unintelligible grunt as they led him past Krengel, swinging his disheveled head. Yellowed fingernails splayed as he reached for the boy, but groped naught but thin air. Those rattling claws sliced past his face without touching, only to rasp against the doorpost as they pulled Moretti inside.

Safe. Just as the Krampusz had promised.

So many friars were about for the *Festival of the Translation of the Holy Relics*, tending to all the dignitaries being housed in the monastic dormitories, that a hooded man-boy on stilts could walk freely through the piazza, disturbing only a few pigeons. The first phase of his great caper was complete. Krengel grinned at the dull impact of his clopping stilts upon the pavers. By nightfall, he'd be comfortably seated aboard a ship destined for the Habsburg Netherlands, his mother's homeland, where not even the Holy Roman Empire could touch him. But first, he needed a hostage. And not just any would do. His hostage was to be a man more celebrated in Bari than both Christ and Pope Alexander VI combined, a man with the power to lift an orphan right out of Bari.

Chapter Three

The dagger's point cleaved the last seam of mortar and the tile popped free. Krengel caught it in the folds of his tunic. He sheathed the dagger in his braies, gazed up and down the empty hall, and with a flap of dark fabric, vanished into an unlit room.

It was more like a windowless cell. A Bible, a candle, a straw mattress, and a chamber pot were the dorm's only amenities. This was the simple dwelling he'd occupied for five months. There were many others like it, mostly vacant. The rooms on either side had once been occupied by Cardinal Moretti's other two lads, but they had been empty since Krengel's arrival. Those poor gnawed waifs had never left Rome, where they'd hanged themselves rather than return here. He'd never even learned their names. Shame they'd gone under not a day before Moretti fell ill. They might've accompanied him tonight, had they lived.

Krengel knelt beside the mattress, plunged his arms into the straw, and retrieved an empty copper flask with a dangling chainlet about its neck. For weeks, he'd stashed this article for tonight's purposes. He lifted his robe and shoved the flask down the front of his braies. He gasped at its coldness against his skin. Lastly, he laid the stolen tile at the head of his mattress. The rector and the Dominicans would find it, tomorrow morning, long after he'd set sail. They would find that tile, and they would understand its meaning.

The bas relief engraved upon it was the image of Basileus, a floating boy, soaring high above the earth. Gliding beside him was

St. Nicholas with his sacred book clenched in his left hand. Flapping birds in their midst looked agog at the spectacle, while divine hands reamed the clouds to offer a blessing. This tile depicted one of St. Nicholas' miracles. When he heard the prayers of the little slave Basileus emanating from a far off land, he sent the winds of God to lift the kidnapped child up into the heavens, and safely back home again.

It was not the only instance in which St. Nicholas had appeared out of thin air in answer to prayers. The patron saint of thieves and children again proved his knack for sensing innocent lives imperiled, when he appeared aboard a sinking ship and snatched a doomed crew from death's talons. St. Nicholas said only of his phenomenal abilities that, "a life devoted to God allows a person to see others in danger, and to hear cries for help."

Krengel swooned at the thought of being whisked into the sky, where he'd hike up his tunic and piss down on Bari. He smiled, spread his arms like little Basileus and twirled through imaginary reefs of clouds, whistling through his teeth.

"Klaas Krengel?"

With a startled fart, he spun towards the familiar voice. This time, it was not the Krampusz. In the doorway stood the Dominicans, Hadrian and Giulio.

"We've found you, at last."

Krengel edged between the friars and his mattress, lest they see that vandalized tile and whip him to a hair's breadth of his life. He bowed his head respectfully. "Greetings, Brothers. How might I be of service?"

A grunt resonated through the hall.

Friars Hadrian and Giulio grinned as an oafish shadow oozed and lilted horribly across the candlelit wall, beyond them. Was this a shadow at all, or did the very blackness of Cardinal Moretti's soul precede him? The chuffing gait halted, perhaps before the vacant dorm room, next door. Brother Hadrian narrowed his eyes at the unmistakable slapping of Moretti's tongue between growth and palate. The monster was just hovering before the hanged lad's open doorway, as if fondly remembering the boy's company. The flicking tongue seemed to sample the lingering scent of the room's dead occupant.

"Your loving benefactor desires an hour alone with you," Hadrian said. "He has been ill. But by God's grace, the very thought of you he owes his rapid recovery."

"You disappointed Cardinal Moretti without a kiss." Giulio wagged his finger. "Never again disappoint him, Klaas. Children mean the world to him, by God. And none shall ever love you, quite like he."

The friars stepped aside, and a perversion of the human form filled the doorway. Wax stalactites dripped from the candle clasped in its clawed hand. It loomed darkly at the portal, motionless, but for that squirming tongue. Phlegm bubbled in its throat as it sucked air across the buds of that restless organ. Frenzied breathing, in and out, seemed to excite its senses with the muskier aspects of boys known only to monsters who love them.

"There you are. Easy, now," Friar Giulio said, ushering the palpitating monster into the room. A rope of drool fell from the bucking tongue. "Would you like us to stay here? To assist you?"

Moretti made a woofing sound and lashed out against his handlers with a strength that belied any notion of a weakened condition. Poised and powerfully indignant, the cardinal swung his hairy head to glower at the Dominicans like a great sow bear guarding its cub.

"Very well, then. We will leave you," Friar Hadrian said, backing toward the door. "It would please God if the both of you would join us later for Mass, if you're able, for the veneration of the Holy Myrrh."

They closed the door. The sound of the bolt sliding in its tracks was like an iron manacle being clapped around a wrist. In that instant, Krengel channeled the combined terror of every boy before him who'd faced this horror. Here loomed a seasoned predator of children, one whose claws twitched with every flick of Krengel's eyes. That tottering crone needing lifted from his wagon was but the ruse of a demon that stored its power for favorite moments. Its shoulders rising and falling, talons expanding and contracting, it fluttered its tongue with each gasp, and protruded it strangely with each swinish groan. There would be no plea for mercy with a thing that could not speak, and could not be easily reasoned with.

Krengel rolled as the thing lunged in a flurry of raking claws and embroidered fabric, roaring like a rutting boar. Skull struck masonry with a resonating thud. The thing reeled and toppled with a moan. Krengel flung himself at the door, throttling the handle with one foot braced against the wall. It would not budge. The monster was mewling pitifully on the mattress, cradling its head in a nest of splintered fingernails. A red flag of hide dangled from its forehead. Blood streamed over its face. Krengel hoisted up his tunic and withdrew the dagger. Its tongue churning blood and matted hair, the thing sprung to its feet and charged again with a gargling scream.

Krengel's foot snapped out to kick the candle, the only source of light in the room. The cartwheeling wick diminished in a looping tracer of light. Blackness entombed them, remembering the enraged thing where it hung, midair.

In the gloom of a lightless cell, clashing bodies rent hide by claw and steel. Ropes of fluid arched felt but unseen from new, wet niches. Cleaved bits smeared underfoot like shelled oysters. The thing howled in agony. Every plunge of the dagger drove the blade to the cushion of wet cloth against his hand, again and again, until the unseen thing ceased to come at him anymore. It was bubbling, hitching its way wetly into a corner.

There was no question whether Krengel could escape his locked cell. He'd been doing so since his first week in Bari. He slipped the tip of his dagger through the door frame and stepped up onto his blocked stilts. He rose to his tiptoes, sliding the blade up the gap until it met with the underside of the bolt. He manipulated the bolt back along its tracks with gentle pushes of the dagger. Curling his fingers around the handle, he pulled open the door.

Blood was everywhere. It streamed from the corner where the cardinal had crawled off to die. Red tracks were stamped all about the floor in chaotic patterns like instructions to an impossible dance. His hands were moist and tacky with it.

Murder, now. No worse offense in the eyes of God or man. He poked his head through the door. The hallway was clear. Slipping out the door without once looking back, Krengel pulled it closed behind him. Using his stilts once again, he slid the lock, and then jammed the point of his dagger between the bolt and the track. Once he'd lodged it tightly, he pried up with all his might and snapped off the dagger's tip.

That ought to do it. Krengel wiped a bloody hand across his nose. Moretti's body would not likely be discovered until after Mass, maybe not until the next morning. And by then, if the Krampusz kept his promise, the good Saint Nicholas would have spirited him far away.

It was sundown when the Krampusz reached the clearing. It was plain to see where something had fallen from the sky, smashed through the forest canopy and landed on the hardened lava below. Bad spot of luck, right there. He circled a strange tumulus of rocks, moving on all fours like a large and sentient spider, lowering himself to examine puddles, sallow gobbets of matter. Gnats swarmed over coagulated fluids that oozed from beneath the pile of the stones. Protruding from the rubble was a thin arm and a dead child's hand, dusty and blood-flecked.

The Krampusz stared at it for a spell. Looked to be holding a little something. He stuck out a three-toed foot and gave it a kick. A couple pieces of glass, blue and purplish in color, dropped to the lava with a musical tinkle. The Krampusz picked them up between his claws and turned them in the twilight. Kind of pretty. "Well, I'll just swaney." Loosening the thong at his waist, he dropped both shards into his purse. If they ever hit bottom, they never made a sound.

The Krampusz took the stone pipe from between his teeth and knocked the bowl against his palm. He blew the ash from the stem. Jerking a wad of dry sedge from a crack in the lava, he rolled it into a ball between his palms. It began to smolder. He tipped his palm against the pipe and coaxed the glowing wad into the bowl, puffing his cheeks until the quid glowed hotly. He winced and coughed at the bite of acrid smoke in his lungs. Wasn't nothing good to smoke on Sundaloon. He guessed he must have smoked every weed on the island twice over and hadn't found a one that didn't leave him with a splitting headache.

He turned back to the dead child's hand, like a moonflower sprouting from the rubble. Dead boys don't bury themselves. He puffed his pipe and circled the grave, then followed the single set of footprints out of the clearing.

###

Krengel sat in a polished wilderness of marble and oolite columns. In these strange woods, stags and hares avoided swooping griffins. Lions attacked goats, while serene peacocks lowered their necks to sip mead from goblets. Fantastic trials of life and death were forever intertwined in the sculpted Norman capitols. Beyond the forest of columns and flickering in candlelight, loomed the shrine of St. Nicholas.

The crypt was packed. It was hot and redolent with perfume. Russians, grizzled and ponytailed, shuffled over the marble floors in their flowing black tunics, heavy crucifixes swinging from their necks. The stairwell lines from the nave down to the crypt were moving torturously slow. Murmuring visitors inched along toward the saint's tomb where they knelt in the flickering candlelight, one at a time, and ducked their heads through a small arch beneath the altar. There, rump protruding from the mouth of that miniature arcade, a visitor gaped directly down into the blackness of a sump where the holy fragments of Saint Nicholas were supposedly weeping myrrh.

After a moment's engagement with that dark and portentous hole, each visitor backed out from beneath the altar and traipsed back upstairs to the vestibule treasury to look upon artifacts that are more tangible. There was a thorn from the Savior's crown, a hair from the Virgin, splinters from the cross and, wrapped in a purple ribbon, the very wooden planks used to transport St. Nicholas from Myra to Bari. Whenever the visitation finished, the Archbishop of Bari was set to lead a grand procession to the crypt, where the rector would crawl beneath the altar with a silver ladle and draw up the holy myrrh.

Against so many other relics, the myrrh of St. Nicholas made a strong standing. His mystical fluid was exceptional in the sense that the supply was endless. Thus, St. Nicholas bested lesser saints and their finite relics with a lucrative crop to be harvested annually, diluted and distributed worldwide. Russians were his favored customers, who couldn't seem to get enough of St. Nicholas. Their Orthodox Church had even awarded him a permanent Thursday spot in their weekly liturgical cycle.

Wood blocks clasped between his calves, Krengel stood last in line to the crypt, trying his best to remain absolutely motionless. But the urge to scratch at the dark crescents of dried blood in his cuticles was too much to resist. He folded his hands, closed his eyes and thought only of the task that the Krampusz had put before him. Tonight was five months in the making. He reflected on the hundreds of hours he'd spent training to walk naturally on stilts, his nightly escapes from the dormitory to visit the shipyards by the light of the moon.

Upstairs, the choir began to chant. The clack of shoes upon marble reverberated through the crypt as the Archbishop's altar party assembled at the top of the staircase. Krengel dared not turn around. He imagined the ranks of distinguished Friars and acolytes who were scheduled to lead the way with a crystal chalice on a golden platter. They would be followed by the rector, armed with his silver ladle. His Most Reverent Archbishop of Bari would bring up the rear, bedecked head to toe in the height of ecclesiastical finery.

The visitation line moved forward. Krengel's heart began to pound as the altar came into view. The awesome presence of Saint Nicholas seemed so close, so palpable, that the thousand-some years since his Bari ministry seemed reduced to a matter of minutes. It felt as though Saint Nicholas was everywhere, all around him.

Blood drained to Krengel's feet, leaving a lingering buzz in his lips while his heart thudded dryly against his ribs. He suddenly doubted whether he could do this. It seemed so ludicrous, now: this whole notion of teetering upon wood block-stilts up to the central apse, hoping to dip beneath the altar with his copper flask and attempt to steal the most precious relic in all of Bari, right under the nose of its most powerful bishop. In all his months of preparation, he'd neglected to consider the possibility that at the penultimate moment, he might be too awestruck in the presence of

St. Nicholas commit such an egregious sin. And he was a murderer now, with blood still on his hands. The line moved forward again. Krengel clenched his fists and tried to smooth the ragged edge that chaffed his every breath. Suppose he fainted and toppled on his stilts before the altar.

Upstairs, the choir ramped up their chanting to a staccato of glottal grunts. Russians bowed and kissed the crucifix pendants around their necks. Friars lowered their heads in veneration. As though the rector was cued by some nuance in the escalating fervor, he signaled the procession. Footsteps descended the staircase behind him, pinning him against the shrine of St. Nicholas. Why was he even doing this? The Krampusz had never fully explained.

Just two visitors left, between he and the tomb. The first crawled out from beneath the altar, stepped aside to kiss his crucifix pendant, while the second man dropped to his knees and took his place. Krengel stared at the Russian's rump poking out through the little archway.

Blood chugged through his temples and drummed inside his ears. Red spots danced through his field of vision. At last, the Russian crawled out of the tomb and stepped aside. Saint Nicholas awaited him. Krengel's knees began to wobble. It was happening. He could feel it. He was going to faint.

The Russian eyed him suspiciously as Krengel half-knelt, half-fell to his knees before the altar, dragging the wood block stilts across the marble floor behind him. It was falling apart. The plan. All of it. Mindless, numbed, he hitched into the dank aperture that only amplified his gasps. Groping through the folds of his robe, he fumbled the copper flask with an awful clatter. He retrieved it, bit the chain and yanked the stopper, then pushed the flask ahead of him down the hole. They were coming. He pretended not to hear the vessel's splash in the vat of holy myrrh, the cadence of approaching footsteps. He drew up the dripping flask, crammed the stopper into the neck, turned his head and retched dryly. This was horrible. The worst thing he'd done. Cold fluid prickled his wrists with a chill somehow more damning than even the warmth of spilt blood: the tears of a violated God.

They were right behind him now, advancing upon the altar in officious lockstep. He felt a slight pressure change as they gathered to receive him outside the tomb. "Help me, Krampusz," Krengel whispered, cringing in the crimson light that welled up from his peripheries. "Take me away from here." The red glow muted the stress of the situation, superseding the impending confrontation and consequences sure to follow, until the earth yawned wide beneath Klaas Krengel and swallowed the naughty child whole.

Chapter Four

He fell from the sky like a hawk-struck pigeon. The impact of the boy's body wrought a dull thud and a swell of dust from somewhere deep within the jungle. Every godforsaken plant wore spines, writhing up through shattered plates of slag. The ground was scored with slithering trails left by meaner forms of life that dragged through here upon their scaled bellies. The surf's distant thunder-hiss stirred the hot reek of brimstone that spewed from vents encrusted with sulfurous pustules, like gaping mouths of the dead. Such was the situation as far as the eye could see across an island so devoid of charm or amenity that it might've been a berg calved off of Hell's mainland.

Krengel rose from the shallow crater he'd smashed into the cacti, his face screwed into a knot. No part of his body had been left unharmed by the landing, though it did not appear that any bones had been broken. The bristling warren of needles into which he'd plummeted was a wicked nest befitting no earthly creature but perhaps an armored cockatrice, or even a dragon. He squinted up at the swirling hole in the sky. Though he could imagine no worse landing spot in all of creation, he knew that had he fallen anywhere else on the island, he'd have likely been dashed to a formless pulp against the jagged escarpments of hardened lava. Sundaloon was a terrible place, where a marooned monster called the Krampusz reigned king.

Krengel spat some sand and grit. He dabbed at a bloodied elbow, wincing around at all the bramble. His surroundings were not at all unfamiliar to him. Sundaloon was his secret place, a private getaway. It had always felt a little bit like a home away from home. Since his earliest nursery memories, the Krampusz had drawn him here--but only in spirit. This visit to Sundaloon was entirely different. It was real. This time, he was not living vicariously through the Krampusz, experiencing an alien landscape through the senses of another. No. This time, he was really here, physically standing on the island. And the Krampusz, he intuited, was also here. Somewhere, the monster from inside his head was waiting to meet him face-to-face for the very first time. How was that bound to go?

Krengel began picking his way through the miserable gulch like a crushed insect, hitching along toe and nail upon his belly through hot shards of black glass that slid and scraped with every thrust like blades against files. It was a painstaking process of lifting and parting cacti, worming tediously through rubble that consumed the better part of what he guessed was morning, until the sun glowered down full upon him.

Seabirds in their unseen thousands chirred like summer locusts against the rhythmic resonance of breaking waves. Krengel rolled panting onto his side and gaped up through the chaotic network of briars. In its midst, he spied the first ambient creature he'd yet encountered in this awful place. The lithe mockingbird hopped easily through the bramble, pausing frequently to cock its auger head and stab neurotically at the ground. A blinking eye of burning amber was its only drop of color, being mottled as its thicket of spine and shadow. Krengel licked his parched lips and emitted a strange wavering sound from somewhere in the bottom of his throat. The mockingbird flattened. A demure wink of its yellow eye, a burst of drab wings and it vanished as the thicket resounded with the screams of a boy buried alive.

His thirst was terrible.

He thought of the myrrh. Dare he sip from the flask of Saint Nicholas' holy drippings? If not today, would he yet? His bleeding fingertips trembled over the bulge of copper at his waistband, feeling the slosh of cool liquid inside it, until they found something else. They curled around the handle of the dagger. He worked it free of its linen trappings and brought the murder weapon before his eyes. Docked of its tip and ruddy with blood, the blade gleamed in the bleak filtered light. The sight of the instrument that killed Cardinal Moretti felt to him like a seam between worlds lost and gained, a palpable stitch in his quilt of reality.

Would the Dominicans not pursue him beneath the altar, and would they, too, not fall through the same rabbit hole as he? New fears empowered him. Plunging the dagger to its hilt in the pulverized aggregate, he dragged himself forward more determinedly than before. Stabbing the ground like a great mockingbird, he lopped cactus pads and hacked acacia, pulling his way through the bracken until by God's grace the thicket broke, at last affording him an unobstructed view of rolling cinder dunes feathered with seagrass.

Krengel crawled forth. He seized a handful of wispy sedge in his yearning to touch something soft and yielding. He ripped loose a grassy bouquet like a smitten fool and mashed the tussock to his face, inhaling the verdant familiarity of any handful of grass torn from any place in the world, and this scent somehow assured him that Sundaloon must in fact be some earthly location, and that he'd not fallen straight to Hell.

He rose in his bloodied rags and gawped about the rippling barrens, a landscape not unlike the sea itself, but frozen in a fluid moment to an ashen plain. The ocean's roar only added to the strange effect. The surge of phantom waves thundered from nowhere and everywhere at once, such that the source of the sound could not be pinpointed.

A rocky outcrop some several leagues across the swales hooked his gaze and held it fast until his feet were compelled to convey his body in that direction. Ahead, spiraling swarms of whip-tailed seabirds rode the winds and plunged in an endless promenade. Krengel staggered toward the sight of them, transfixed, for he wanted to be amongst other living things and more than anything, he yearned to look upon the ocean, to appraise the vast and unseen element that surrounded him.

Sifting dunes yielded to a range of rumbled rock pocked and riddled as meteors, shining wet, black as tar and splattered with bird droppings. Fountains of foam leapt gaily beyond the cliffs, then fell apart in dazzling displays of destruction. Something moved to his right. Krengel flinched at the explosion of scrabbling talon and slithering tail as a fragment of the rock itself seemed at once to come alive, whipping and gyrating over the knifepoints of obsidian to the precipice, where it hurled itself over with suicidal abandon.

Krengel hovered in the spot where he'd flushed the terrible thing, hand pressed to his hammering heart. He scanned the jagged formations looming all around him. Like gargoyles perched atop the blasted crags, they clung poised in their thorny crowns like regal lords of the breakers. In every aspect, they looked to be birthed of the rocks themselves, great black lizards with cracked faces and whetting stone hide, spangled with the excrement of gulls. Garish crabs crawled right over the tops of them, as if whispering secrets into their ears. Some nodded their heads in dim approval at the state of their surroundings, like satisfied wards of some ambiguous trust perceived only by them.

There was no beach at all, no transition between vastly different worlds that appeared to be hemmed only by violent collision. The cleaved edge of Sundaloon rushed straight down to the roiling sea. Gulls and gannets occupied every nook in the wall's face, however slight, indifferent to the siege that raged eternally beneath them. Nestlings perched a straw's breadth from certain doom peered lackadaisically down at the crashing tonnage of seawater. Hapless scads of marine lizards rose and fell on the frigid swells, not yet reattached to the cliffs from which they'd plummeted. Every living thing on this island appeared to be designed to endure, to suffer, to ask no more of the world than some air to breathe and a spot of rocky ground.

Krengel wrapped his arms round himself and shivered in the briny mist. He squinted his eyes against the spray and inhaled the fishy brimstone stink of what appeared to be his new home. He'd seen all of this before through the eyes of the Krampusz, but actually standing at the seaside cliffs was a bizarre transplantation. Where in the world was that chatty monster now, who'd forever teased him with snippets of this place? The Krampusz hadn't uttered a single word since his arrival. Perhaps that old means of cerebral communication was impossible now that they shared the same world. He wondered if by chance they did encounter one another, would the Krampusz even recognize him as a friend?

Krengel cupped his hands to either side of his mouth and hallooed long and hard across the wastelands, but his cries were drowned in the ocean's deafening roar. His gaze crawled eastward, long about the thorny bottoms, where lush and gradual slopes ascended to misty plateaus, where the Krampusz had once shared with him a vision of the Habsburg-Netherlands flag, flying high upon a ridge. He did not see any red and white flags. But perhaps he would find a bit of fresh water up there on the misty ridgeline. Were he to establish himself as a resident of this island, then those highlands certainly offered a more defensible situation, and probably better hospitality, than this. It could surely be no worse. Krengel bent for a round pebble. He popped it into his mouth and sucked it to relieve his thirst. Already, the sun was settling in the glittering sea. Best get moving, travel near as possible to the foothills before that infernal sun rose again.

Travelling the crest of a twilit ridge he stumbled on through the last dregs of light until the island was enveloped by the darkest night he'd ever seen. He edged down the leeward slope by feel alone until he rolled into a pocket in the cinders, a damp and pungent wallow with tracks stamped into the paunch. Krengel curled up there with his back pressed into the ash. He fell asleep imagining what sort of fantastic beast once nested here, whose prints easily swallowed the span of a boy's outstretched hand.

In the night, a rumbling from deep within the earth came like the fusillade of distant cannons. Krengel stirred wearily in his nest like a gannet chick peering from its precarious nook. He saw the northeast horizon aglow with a dull red incandescence that faded so gradually that he drifted off, wondering if it hadn't all been a mirage thrown up against the blackness by an addled and dreaming mind.

Moments or millenniums later, he was awakened again, when shifting ash spilled down the slope above him. The burning grit beneath his eyelids suggested he'd been asleep for at least a while.

Another surge came rolling down. In an instant, he was on his feet, the dagger unsheathed and trembling in his fist. He heard and felt the tread of heavy feet upon the ridge, the gaseous hiss of expelled breath. Whatever manner of creature was afoot at this hour, he could not discern, but it was big. Really big. Krengel could literally feel its mass being transferred to the sand with each ponderous footstep. And then it paused, directly above him, as if the night-walker had suddenly sensed him, too. Krengel's heart beat a catch into his every breath as he waited, knife readied, sure as sin that his every move was being studied. After a few terrible moments, those trunk-like legs resumed lumbering, pumping air sharply through the thing's throat like a giant bellows.

Once distanced by some measure from the departing monster, Krengel knuckled his way apelike down the slope of the ashen dune until he met headlong with the same spiny thicket he'd battled all day to escape. This time, the bracken could never have felt more safe and welcoming. He thrust his way cursing back into the nightmare of acacia briars until he found a small patch of ground uncovered by cacti. Krengel curled himself upon the musical shards of shattered slag. There, he blinked in the darkness and listened to the frantic movements of little things that scampered mindlessly all through the night, until piping seabirds heralded dawn's break.

The sifting ridge proved exceedingly more difficult to climb than to descend. No possible path of ascent looked to be any easier than the direct one from which he'd come, so it was the same trail he followed back up to the summit, feeling a bit like a minnow swimming upriver. When at last he cleared the summit, glassy-eyed and sucking for breath, he hunkered there regaining his wind while he studied the spore of weird craters that the night-walker's feet had pressed into the dust.

Each track was round and wide as a meat pie, lobed at the leading edge by the creature's blunt claws. Krengel had wasted years imagining what the Krampusz might look like. He supposed he'd settled upon the horned and hoofed icon popularized in prints as a result of his being told by the few, in which he'd confided that the voice inside his head could be none other than a demon--a rather foul charge to which the Krampusz was loathe to admit. The receding tracks along the ridge top were more befitting of a dwarf elephant, if such a thing existed. And that bizarre possibility shocked Krengel to keen sobriety in the sense that, with respect to the Krampusz, his preconceived image might in fact have no relation to an entity whose physical appearance was a great unknown.

###

The meadow quavered in the heat of the noonday sun. Flowers of every kind bloomed here, but all varieties conformed to an odd homogeneity in yellow color. Buzzing bees and insects rose and settled upon their petals.

Still, no water. All morning, he'd dogged the tracks of the mysterious beast along the dune's winding highway, until the cinders sloughed into a washout of shells and gravel. There, the trail veered through these fragrant midlands toward the foothills. Succulent plants with waxy lobes for leaves pulled at his sandals and crunched juicily underfoot. The creature that passed through here in the night had routed a wide and flattened trail that required no tracking skill whatsoever to follow. It appeared to have rested in places, where plants were crushed completely and the vegetation on either side had been grazed down to the aggregate. Krengel searched his imagination for a creature so lazy, so gluttonous that it preferred to feed while sprawled upon the ground.

He paused to mop his forehead with a tattered sleeve, squinting up at the brilliant sun. His robe was soaked with perspiration. The trail crushed on across the dappled flats, where no breeze stirred the meandering bees, the humidity, the tons of air so redolent with nectar, for the meadow was surrounded on all sides by ridges and grassy escarpments. Krengel stood panting at the epicenter of this sweltering field, almost concave in its design, like a vast sink or a crater, but not one drummed into the earth by any wayward object, for there were no remnants of any heavenly object to blame. He wondered if the island itself had in ancient times released a great skyward blast of pressure. Krengel swatted at an insect buzzing in his ear, and plodded onward.

From the meadows rose plateaus of pastoral expanse that finally met hard with the edge of lush jungles he'd observed from the coast. This was a forest of the strangest trees. Great heaps of cactus pads surmounted trunks as thick as Grecian pillars, which suggested that a coat of spiny armor had not sufficed to deter whatever creatures were bent on eating cacti. Riots of woody daisies clambered higher still to form canopies so dense as to block every trace of the sun. Up there, chortling frigate birds clattered their hooked beaks and billowed throat-pouches that quavered on their breasts like exposed lungs. Pelicans glowered down at Krengel over their grotesque bills as he passed beneath them, shifting their feet uneasily and averting their eyes with dull prejudice. The forest was a likable and refreshing situation, cool, quiet, and secluded. It was just the sort of place where --

Krengel froze.

There before him, glimmering coolly in the sand, was something manmade.

Chapter five

At the Devil's Hour came the most terrible scream. Not the shriek of man or beast, this was the grating agony of heavy metal against cobblestone. Like a crippled wagon being dragged on bare axles, twin streamers of sparks seared the length of moonlit alley behind Moretti Manor. When at last the hellish machine ground to a halt, Mitzi Gottlieb unplugged her fingers from her ears, and slowly rose from where she'd been cowering against a plaster wall decorated with frescoed bumblebees looping through garish flowers.

It was awfully late for visitors. Only the worst sorts came to a brothel door at this hour. She'd seen enough to know better than to answer the door at this time of night. But no one else was awake. All the other girls had retired, hours ago. Her gaze darted from one empty spit to the next. Worse yet, all the food was gone.

The great hall was richened by the smoke of roasted meat, humidified by boiling cauldrons of wash water that hung suspended over pits of coals like glowing portals straight to Hell. Greasy trenchers and blackened bones heaped long tables that had served a daylong clamor of moving dishes and drunken bodies, crashes of foreign language and laughter. Her feast had been a wild success. Even the Archbishop of Bari, who had stopped by the stews for his regular licorice bath, caught wind of her roast kid in plum sauce, her fruit and almond pottage, and he'd instead filled a trencher, hoisted a mazer of mulled ale and gave Mitzi and Nele his blessing.

It had been a fine day, but the big party was over. The throngs of Russians, Spaniards and Italians were gone. Only the swarms of fizzing gnats that rode in with the guests still mingled over wooden mugs, dried gobbets of pottage and roast kid that clung to bowls and trenchers. Rats tore from the shadows like evil fragments of the night to contest for scraps in squealing flurries. They vanished back into the walls behind the stock barrels and grain bins, or squeezed miserably beneath the door to the meat store. Leering over the carnage was the lord of the manor, a youthful Cardinal Moretti, gloating down in portrait over his ransacked hall with a queerly permissive smile, gilded fingernails interlaced upon his lap.

Padding across the earthen floor to the nearest window, Mitzi lifted a shutter on its leather hinge and peered beneath, poking her head out into the chilly blackness of the alley. The shot of cold air brightened her eyes as it displaced the meaty fumes from her lungs. She could see no trace of the phantom carriage through the gloom, but the night seemed to sharpen the resonance of grunting animals in the darkness, the clicking of strange hooves against pavers. Mitzi wrinkled her nose and scowled down the alley. The odor of the beasts was not the sweet musk of horses accustomed to a stable. Sour and gamey, the feral stench in the air belonged to something else. Something wild. The cadence of heavy footsteps rang with the jingling of little bells.

Mitzi turned away from the window, eyes darting, and lowered the shutter. Only lepers wore bells. None but a leper would comply with the ancient warning system devised to alert the blessed healthy to the approach of the Living Dead. It would not have been the first time that a leper visited a brothel. And, likely as not, if his purse was full, he would probably find a girl willing to go to task. A heavy fist thudded against the door. Mitzi left the window. Slinking past the flickering fire pits to the largest grain bin, she raised the lid and peeked inside. Nele was curled in the grain like a little mouse. She sat up at once with oats raining from her hair, rubbing her eyes in the tallow candlelight. "What's the matter?"

Mitzi grabbed her little sister by the yellow hood of their trade and pulled her close. "There's something bad outside. Did you latch the back door like I told you?"

"Latch the what?"

"The back door to the alley! Did you latch it?"

"It's probably just the Gongfermor, come to empty the latrines."

The force of the beating fist upon the door increased to the thunderous blows of a battering ram. Splintering timbers and falling mortar flushed rats from the quaking walls.

"I don't think it's the Gongfermor."

"What's happening, Mitzi?" Nele pressed her fingertips to her lip.

Mitzi flung herself over the rim and tumbled down into the oats alongside her sister. They pulled the lid down over them and huddled together like quivering vermin, peering through the crack between their musty little world and a world outside inhabited by randy monsters that smashed through doors.

"What is it?" Nele asked, squeezing her sister's forearm.

The thing was in the building. Each footfall was fringed with tinkling bells. And there was something else, another sound, one more troublesome to identify, like the hiss of driven sleet against a windowpane.

"I don't know."

"What should we do?"

"Quiet."

"Should we pray to Saint Nicholas?"

"My God, Nele! Shush it!"

Nele folded her hands, bowed her head and began to murmur. Mitzi grabbed her sister by the front of her yellow hood and forced her down into the oats. She climbed on top of her, muffling her prayers. Through the crack beneath the lid, Mitzi watched the Dark Wagoner's shadow spill across the earthen floor. Her eyes widened, for the shape of it matched no recognizable thing. Thrown upon the dirt was a seething silhouette that writhed like a nest of vipers. Pushing out across the filth in groping tendrils, the shadow hissed and whispered around the legs of chairs like dark drifts of windblown sand. One questing tentacle encountered a rat behind a trestle. The mass hesitated, gathered itself, and then struck out. The rodent squealed and thrashed about in apparent agony as its greasy fur rippled and crawled. Dozens more of the shadowy tendrils stood on end, wavering in place as though testing the air, until the whole writhing mass turned suddenly upon the grain bin.

"Oh, my God."

"What's happening, Mitzi? I can't see."

The entity slithered toward them like rivulets of ink. "Stay down, Nele. Whatever happens to me, don't come out!"

Mitzi burst from beneath the lid and somersaulted past the tide of shadows as they reached for her with a thousand yearning arms. It pursued her as a whole, hissing indignantly, as she bowled over chairs and leapt from table to table in the direction of the rows of her livestock barrels. She sprung over the drums and crouched behind them, panting against the plaster wall. On the other side of the barricade, living darkness bombarded the drums with billions of flying particles. Mitzi could feel them now. A few struck her face between the barrels, stinging her lips, and they began crawling up her ankles. They swarmed up her calves like prickly stockings.

Fleas.

Mitzi screamed and slapped at them, but there were too many, rushing up her thighs. She placed her hands against the livestock drum in front of her, and shoved with all her might, upturning an entire barrel of brackish water and live eels upon the legion of mites. The eels churned over the dining room floor in one massive wave. Those fleas already fastened upon Mitzi's body seemed at once to intuit a terrible calamity had been suffered by their brethren, and the bloodsuckers flitted from her skin in retreat.

Not about to give the bugs an opportunity to collect themselves, Mitzi dashed through the mud and writhing eels to the head of the hall, where she squatted between the fire pits. The intense heat emanating from the beds of coals and boiling cauldrons of wash-water baked the perspiration from her skin. Here, she felt safe. No flea would dare approach her.

She heard the music of jingling bells.

It stepped into the great hall, a shag of hide and muted leather, bejeweled with grinning rows of stolen teeth and bone fragments like some wandering eremite of primal wastelands, fallen haplessly through some cross-stitch in time's weave. The unshorn beard, matched in wildness by the bearskin parka and conical hat, concealed every feature of its face. Only twin pinpricks of reflected candlelight suggested that it had eyes at all.

"We're closed!" she shrieked.

The entity chuffed. As though eager for an invitation to a challenge, it swaggered right at her. Bells shivered with every step. Boots crushed squirming eels.

"I'm warning you …" Mitzi reached over the coals and seized the handle of the prong from the spit. She withdrew the bubbling shaft of greasy metal and swung its point at the dark being. As it neared her, it became apparent that much of what she'd mistaken for hides and shaggy pelage was in fact living masses of fleas. Great hanging gardens of bloodsucking parasites swung from its neck in larval clusters. As the creature neared the heat of the fire, the roiling mites parted like dark soil over a grave, to expose the cadaverous face buried beneath. Sallow eyes wept tears of pus. Slackened jaws opened and closed like the gates to a dam, its colorless lips regulating the flow of fleas that gushed steadily up from the monster's throat.

"Krengel," it whispered.

Mitzi shouldered her sizzling prong like a battle mace. Every sinew in her forearms, hardened by years of splitting wood and hauling water to the kitchen, sprung taut and readied beneath her skin.

The creature made a tentative step forward. "Make Krengel come me."

Her weapon sliced a whooping arc that clipped the forelegs of both tripods, releasing two cauldrons in a boiling tidal wave that surged over the ghoul. As it collapsed in the steam, the creature wore what was probably a rare look of surprise, as its undead mouth projected the squeals of its billion bloodsucking minions.

Mitzi stared through the humid plumes that continued to rise from the dark heap on the floor. Awful. She pinched her nose and took a couple of steps backwards, fanning the air with her hand. The body appeared to be collapsing inward, like punctured bellows sacking, deflating until its solid form had deliquesced through the cracks between flagstones. Only a pile of the sodden garments and jewelry remained.

Friar Otto was among the finest of storytellers, and his vast store of tales had no limits. All his life, he'd ministered, he'd traveled, and he'd camped along nameless dusty roads that sometimes harbored things unnatural to the world of mankind. Particularly from regions hard-struck by the plague, Friar Otto had explained, where the dead and the living were made bedfellows, came brushes with the evil incarnate. Friar Otto regaled his orphans by firelight with tales of the undead Revenant, wandering warlocks, dark forces and necromancy. Not that she'd believed a word of it, but never, not in all her nights in that old storyteller's company, had Mitzi ever heard Friar Otto describe anything resembling the sort of creature that had just dissolved at her feet.

Using her prong, Mitzi lifted a necklace of human teeth and knucklebones from the heap of wet leather. She turned its savage jewelry in the orange light of the coals. The little nuggets of ivory were interspersed with silver bells. Swinging pendulously at the centerpiece was a silver medallion. Imprinted into the metal was the image of a boy with dragon's wings. Wrinkling her nose, she cast the devilish token back to the floor with a clatter. There was something else. She pushed aside the soggy parka to see it better. There, on the floor, was a book.

She picked it up and tossed her prong upon the pile of boiled bearskins with a steely jangle. She wiped the beads of water from the book's patchwork cover, hewn entirely of cracked hide. Mitzi was hardly qualified to appraise an artifact of antiquity, but it was surely an old book, perhaps ancient. She sniffed it, wiped her nose where it touched, then opened it. Mitzi frowned as she flipped through hundreds of yellowed pages. They were left blank. All of them. Not a single spot of ink, throughout. She closed the book again and with her fingertip, traced the four letters embossed so boldly upon the leather: WURM.

What could the demon have wanted with Krengel? Had she heard it correctly? Given the meticulously detailed records kept by the Spanish Inquisition, she supposed that if someone or something had been trailing little Klaas, it could've found its way to her doorstep if it had it crossed paths with the Grand Inquisitor at some point since Christmas Eve. And with certainty, His Most Reverent Friar-Inquisitor Ignacio de la Rabida would not have suffered long with qualms about collecting payment from a bounty hunter in exchange for a tip on Krengel's whereabouts. An orphaned heir to a Habsburg fortune was a perfect pigeon, one whose wealth destroyed Friar Otto and the life of every child in his choir. The Inquisition had already carved their share of profits off the boy, but surely, there was profit yet to be pared from a pigeon plump as he.

Mitzi spun toward a dull thump near the edge of the room. There, a stream of oats spilled through a small crack in the side of the grain bin. Nele had managed to keep hidden this long, thank God. Ordinarily, fidgety as a little shrew, the girl had somehow remained absolutely still throughout the strange ordeal.

Mitzi waded through water pooled around the flagstones, pausing once to cock an ear toward the alley windows, where an animal grunted and clicked its hoof. A few blanched eels had lost their resolve to keep submerged, keeling here and there at the surface and champing their mouths. Hundreds of dead and dying fleas peppered the tops of her feet. Mitzi walked up to the grain bin and addressed her hidden sister by rapping her knuckles sharply on the lid. "You can come out now. He's all gone."

Nele's fingers curled through the crack. The lid raised, and her yellow-hooded head appeared. She peered over the rim with a single oat stuck to the end of her nose. Nele gawped down at the lake of standing water, all around her. "Making eel pies tomorrow, are we?"

"Yeah." Mitzi nodded, peering beneath a shutter into the alley, "I reckon so." She could see the beasts now, at least the forms of them. Their belled harness jingled as they bobbed and knocked their heads in the starlight. Rather small for horses. Mitzi squinted at what appeared to be branches or ornaments of some kind, affixed to their heads.

"Did he leave his team and wagon?"

Mitzi nodded, still squinting into the night. "Little low to be a wagon …"

"What?"

"Yeah-yeah. It's out there."

"Think he's coming back for it?"

Mitzi looked from the alley to her little sister, then back again. In terms of resale, the wagon, or whatever it was, held suspect value. Sounded like it might be badly damaged, missing a wheel or two, the way it had come skidding in. In that condition, they probably couldn't manage to haul it off undetected before daybreak. But the cargo and livestock … Mitzi tightened her grip on the strange book still clenched in her hand. No telling what that team of animals would bring, or what other curiosities might be out there on that cart. She cast a glance toward the steaming heap between the fire rings, stroking the unwritten Book of Wurm with the pad of her thumb. "No," Mitzi replied, "I don't guess he'll be coming back at all."

Chapter Six

Krengel squatted at the base of a cactus tree for a spell, turning the lavender shard of stained glass in his hand. He recalled a certain picture window in his mother's bedchamber that overlooked an untended garden. The window had contained pieces of the same shade of lavender. Wild possibilities with incalculable odds gallivanted through his mind. None more likely than any miracle, but the island was a queer one. It was an alien world, yet seeded with subtle figments of the familiar, as though the island itself was a sort of crucible where bits of his own memories had collected in the sand. It made no sense. What perhaps made better sense was that a bolt of lightning had fused sand to glass, and a packrat had trundled off with this shard, only to drop it here along the trail.

Sweat trickled down his brow into his eye, and it burned like a squirt of vinegar between his lashes. He pressed the balls of his thumbs against his eyes and groaned. It was so bloody hot. The humid air here never moved. The flask at his waistline sloshed torturously against his skin. If no water could be found by sunset, he'd be left with little choice than to drink it. Dying of thirst still seemed preferable. He tucked the shard of purple glass into the same fold in his braies that sheathed the blunted dagger, and he resumed tracking.

In an hour's time, he was running toward the sound of trickling water. Through an eroded gouge in an embankment, a muddy little spring dribbled from a seep in the lava shelf. Krengel pressed his cheek to the hot slag and filled his mouth with the sulfurous venom. He spat it out and hacked. But after a moment's deliberation, he was back, filling his mouth again. It was metallic and gritty with elemental fury. Though he could scarcely imagine a more hellish drink than this one in all of creation, he suckled from the devil's teat until his gut swung heavily from his ribs, and he could not possibly hold a swallow more. Satiated, he turned his back against the seep and slumped down into the mud. He closed his eyes and took fluttering breaths, as the gentle shower of mineral springs coursed over his head. Krengel felt as though he could lounge here in the cool mud forever, where even the menacing rasp of mockingbirds seemed pleasant. It was not until he'd languished in the shade for quite a spell that he realized that without even knowing it, he'd reached the trail's end.

Like a battlefield where denizens of the daisy forest had warred for year's unseen, the ground all around him was pounded to the barest mud. Deep pools of scummy water filled craters large enough to bathe many men. Brown reefs of filth and foam blanketed these stagnant wallows, where, as Krengel looked more closely, the mysterious creature he'd long been pursuing was immersed to its bubbling nostrils. Krengel rose from his ditch. There was more than one. He gasped. Dozens of them, all around him, masterfully camouflaged into their surroundings.

Like living boulders, some withdrew their blunt heads into their enormous domed carapaces, while others extended curious necks to gawp from their public baths. Those not immersed rested on the banks, or shambled lethargically about on trunk-like legs barely able to support the tanks of jigsaw armor bore upon them.

Krengel gazed back into the weeping Mongoloid eyes of the giant tortoise. He detected no malice in the creature that passed so near him in the night. None at all. And it was not frightened of him. To his human presence, the beast appeared utterly indifferent. Krengel strode the scalloped banks through the middle of the herd, awing over their matrix of contrasting textures, the mystic designs of ancient provenance etched into the plates of their shells. The giants blinked their sleepy eyes, inset like black buttons on those hammered knobs for heads. And on the end of that weathered proboscis, was a set of chipped sheers that looked capable of delivering a mighty pinch, but a moment's observation of these beasts' stiffly lethargic mannerisms was sufficed to intuit their benignity.

Krengel circled one, standing dumbly in the center of a trampled path. It looked as though the beast had completely forgotten where it had been headed and was left utterly paralyzed by indecision. Krengel whispered softly to it, trailing his fingertips over its shell. He threw a leg over the top of its back and mounted it like a fat pony. Krengel smiled when the tortoise groaned, teetered a little, and expelled the air in its lungs with a sickly hiss. Krengel shouted and clunked its shell with his heels, but the tortoise did not respond. Front side first, it surrendered itself to the ground. Faced with even the most incompetent of predators, an animal unfit as this would be positively doomed. The implications were clear enough: there were no predators, and probably no people at all on Sundaloon. He was marooned on an island unknown to Mankind. And worse, what if there were no Krampusz at all. What if the raving counterpart forever lodged inside his head was none other than a shadow of himself, a lost part of his own soul, howling premonitions through a tear in the fabric of space and time in an effort to warn himself away from an inescapable trap. Krengel's head felt suddenly light.

"I've been following a turtle," he whispered.

His pumping heart drew all the moisture from his mouth. He slid off the tortoise's back and staggered away from the reptilian cesspool. He clambered up the embankment and thrashed through brambles. Krengel's sandal pulled loose as he splashed through a stream, but he did not stop to retrieve it. He followed the creek, trickling coolly through mats of verdant moss and legumes from a source uphill. Groaning pelicans rose and beat their wings as he burst upon a glade. They sidled drunkenly away with wings spread, mouths ajar, wagging the translucent sacking beneath their chins. Krengel whined with every exhale. He lurched through the marsh with his ragged arms outstretched and flailing like some enraptured hermit who believed himself lord of the pelicans.

From the bluffs, he overlooked more of the same patchy landscape, to the north and to the south, corrugated with cinder dunes that rippled darkly toward more ridges crowned with more of the same daisy forests. To the west, grassy escarpments, thicketed lowlands and lava flats. Eastward, a craggy swale rumbled down to a beach of the blackest sand, where an orgy of sea lions reveled in the torrid sun. Beyond, and in all directions, seen or unseen, the glittering sea spanned to limits of the imagination.

Krengel fell to his knees atop that bleak ridge. Tears tilled clean streaks through the grime that coated his cheeks as his sobs resounded over Sundaloon. But his lifelong habit of screaming to have everything his way was a useless trick on an island apart from anyone who might hasten to his cries. Ancient tortoises with drooling mouthfuls of cacti craned their necks, but no beast amongst Sundaloon's inbred menagerie could possibly appreciate the poetic justice of a boy who despised isolation above all other torments, being marooned for his sins of desire to a place devoid of anything desirable.

***

One lackluster day faded into the next until Krengel's shaved head had again become covered by curls. And over the months he'd trekked Sundaloon's dunes and ridges, he'd come to accept the fog of sleep deprivation as being just another miserable condition, to which, he was as powerless as he was against the heat, the humidity, or to the infernal taste of the water. The comforts of home that he came to miss by each long day's end were no longer the distant luxuries of a civilized world. Those had been replaced by simpler comforts, like a bath in the cold springs, a crackling fire he'd learned to start by focusing the sun's rays through his shard of stained glass, a hot meal cooked on a plate of slag, a soft bed of sea grass. The days were hot and exhausting. The nights were restless. So many things moving. And the tremors were more noticeable after dark, when the ground muttered with titanic resonance as massive cogs at the earth's center seemed to turn.

Curled in a wreath of sea grass, Krengel sometimes felt like a flea on the back of an angry dog. If he managed to fall asleep, he was usually awoken within an hour or two by chuffing gasps, the dull impact of blunt feet, grating shells against slag. Tortoises were always on the move, lumbering myopically through the darkened wastelands like the members of some ill-fated search party. Roughly the same numbers of the creatures seemed to be active after dark as during daylight hours, as though they made little distinction or preference between night and day. And why should they, when no particular time of day imposed any real advantages or disadvantages upon their slothful lifestyles. They moved when they felt like it. Otherwise, they rested. A tortoise would often wallow in the same spot for weeks without food or water, and seemed not the least bit uncomfortable.

They were part of the landscape on Sundaloon. Krengel had not yet brought himself to kill one of them, though it would have presented no great challenge to do so. A fellow could stroll right into the middle of a whole herd of them, if it pleased him, and slaughter the lot of them by casually knocking them over the head, one at a time. But killing turtles for survival was not yet necessary. The island harbored plenty of other options for food that were more sizably portioned than those great boulders of flesh. There were eggs, chicks and seafowl aplenty. Fish and shellfish abounded in the shallow tidepools. Sea lions lounged on every beach. Light-footed crabs by the hundreds could be herded down the beaches and into simple corrals of sticks jammed into the sand. Island living was relatively easy. Krengel had learned to hunt and gather, to scout fresh water by scanning the mountain ridges for verdant belts of daisy forest. Wherever the giant daisies grew, pools of fresh water were usually nearby.

Krengel stirred as the ground reverberated with a groan so cetaceous that it was felt more so than heard, like the lowing of some behemoth chained to the earth's core. Krengel rolled onto his side and pulled an armload of grass over his head. Through his closed lids, he perceived the flash and glow of a neighboring island across the sea that was a favorite battlefield of the elements. Hellfire and explosions lit up the night sky. He'd named the island Ursa after the constellation just above it, the night he'd watched the battle rage until sunrise. Might be, Sundaloon was just one island amongst a chain. He'd never been from one end of the island to the other. It was a substantial chunk of land. But it was possible that even bigger islands were just a day or two away.

He'd considered building a raft, but thus far, there had been no reason to leave Sundaloon with its utter lack of dangers and abundant resources. And the idea of pushing out to sea terrified him. The currents that swept in all around Sundaloon were cold as rivers in snowmelt and terribly powerful, as if they'd flowed downhill all the way to the ends of the earth. Might be. But Krengel had come to accept Sundaloon as his new home. He had no justification to risk his life in order to escape. Every day, he scanned the horizon for a ship, but as each day closed and he did not see one, he came closer to accepting the possibility that Sundaloon might just be the trap where he'd grow old pacing and eventually die. Alone.

Krengel's eyes flicked open. He stared into the bed of dying coals.

By day, the boy was generally preoccupied with the routine his life had assumed, much as life assumes anywhere, dictated by a need to acquire basic resources. His began whenever he awoke, and it ended at sundown. It entailed the acquisition of wood, water and food. And then, wood, water and food a second time. But after dark, when his mind was not occupied by the sights in front of his eyes, when his thoughts were allowed to wander far and wide, that's when the trouble began. Most often, his thoughts would drift back to Lambsheim.

Strangely enough, whenever he revisited his birthplace, it came as a bit of a surprise that the situation of Lambsheim was one markedly less attractive to him now, than ever before. But what had changed? Especially in the company of Friar Otto and the Little Elves, in contrast to the long and dusty roads they'd traveled forever sparkled a smitten memory of a child's paradise of lurid colors and sweet delights. But on Sundaloon, it was the road with Friar Otto and the orphans that did glamour against the shallow farce that Lambsheim had probably always been, so misleadingly temporary. It now struck him that it had never been his mother and father he missed, whenever he'd missed Lambsheim, for they'd been missing from the very start. No, it was the spoils he missed, the toys and flowing sweets. He missed the security of knowing, each night when he went off to bed, that the river of treats would still be there when he awoke. Never had he considered the possibility that he might one day awaken curled in the dirt with every comfort known to him, gone. But his parents? Ye gods, they were no further from him here at the end of the earth than they'd been when they'd lived beneath the same roof. Not really. And this was a horrible revelation! Where had they been all of his life? Had anyone ever really shown him love? The servants? Anyone? Or had he actually been loathed by every goddamned person to have ever suffered the displeasure of his company, since the day he was shat upon the world? And the more he brooded over his sad legacy, further dissecting a phony childhood, the more those memories of a privileged upbringing festered hotly.

His father, flighty but forever forgiven by flowing gifts, had all but abandoned him at birth. Krengel saw that now. When the man would return from his frequent holidays in Mainz, Krengel would run to him, arms pinwheeling, all the way down the lane to embrace Count Richwald's fat thigh as he stepped through the gates, but he was hardly so excited to see his father as he was mad to seize upon whatever surprises his father had brought him. Treats were a very significant part of his everyday life, and his expectations were doubled on those days his father returned from holiday. What fits he'd pitched whenever his father neglected to bring him a gift! But all those gifts, they'd been but distractions from the absence of a father's love. He saw that now. Love was not there. And it never had been. Count Richwald cared for no one but himself, right up until the very end when he'd abandoned his ailing wife to flee their infirmed estate for the pleasures of a brothel.

His mother, on the other hand, had never bought him a gift. Not once. Cold, statuesque and forever distracted, her proximal unavailability somehow made her so much more intriguing and alluring than his father, who was nothing but a stupid aristocratic clown who bribed his child's affection. Gifts were never satisfactory. They did not satiate Krengel's yearning, his constant craving for something, anything, to the fill the emptiness inside himself. The joy of gifts was a fleeting thrill that lasted but a few minutes after receiving it. And then, the gift would lose its initial allure and his insides would darken. His mind would become anxious, aggravated, needy, as the cravings began squirming in his brain, once more. And it was in that state-of-mind he'd done some very naughty things. But no one would dare tattle on the heir to House of Habsburg. Heads turned. Servants scuttled the evidence. And Krengel was left to the sordid afterglow of unpunished sins like a pissing troglodyte squatted in the wellspring. No one cared enough to stop him. No one prayed he repent. Truly, there was no more miserable creature than a spoiled child.

The fire burned low. Krengel broke his trance from the pulsating bed of coals and sat up, scratching his head. He began to rummage through his small cache of driftwood, twigs and sedge that he'd piled at the foot of his bed. Driftwood was best for keeping a fire going at this time of night, but it had to be dried out completely, or it would smolder with awful clouds of fishy smoke. He picked up a log and gripped it to determine its moisture content. Felt pretty dry. He shoved one and then another into the fire. The first popped.

A blast of fiery agony and bewilderment spun the jungle all around him with an arching spasm of pain. Like a partial spectator, he regarded the sound of his own gargling screams with a dull bemusement, as though he'd been jarred clean loose of himself by the piercing impact against his hindquarters. He hooted mournfully, lolling on his side in a pile of sea grass wet with blood. Krengel felt its warm slickness, the smooth and slender certainty of an arrow shaft protruding from his rump. And he was off, crashing horribly through the starlit bracken like some wounded ape fallen from the canopy.

So much blood. Spurting through his fingers. All the energy of the arrow's flight had been piped right down the rigid shaft to the very marrow of the leg-bone that halted its point. He hadn't felt its puncture or the plunge through the meat of his thigh. He felt only the crash of channeled momentum from his ankle to the base of his spine, as a howling ache that numbed his toes and filled his head with a sickly lightness that made him want to vomit.

He dragged his ruined leg through the underbrush, pawing at the bracken and the night as he stifled a mighty urge to fall snarling to the ground, to roll about, screaming, cursing, and crying. It was his natural reaction to point a finger at the culprit, be it a faun or a naughty forest puck, and scream out against the cruel joke played upon him. For whom alive would actually mean to shoot him with an arrow? What wrong had he done? What goods had he to steal? What had he to offer a stranger but companionship here, in this desolate place with food and water aplenty? The attack made no sense.

But some instinctual part of Krengel knew that the shooting was no accident, no joke, and that for whatever reason, there was someone out there in the surrounding wastelands who meant to kill him. And they were probably pursuing him. Wherever he stopped running, that would be the place where he would die.

He grunted now, with every leaden footfall, heaving the dead leg along beside him. Krengel lost his footing and crashed downhill through alternating bands of sedge and daisy bramble. Up again, splashing through septic wallows where unseen tortoises gasped and bubbled in pools of sewage. His hands swept their great domed backs. How he wished he'd a shell of his own. An arrow flitted right past his ear and clattered off through the forest. The shooter was right behind him.

Krengel knew the terrain well. There was a bluff, just ahead. Beyond it rolled cinder dunes for a hundred leagues to the lowland thickets. Those briars would provide him with excellent cover, but in the open ground between here and there; he'd be cut down with another arrow or two, then clubbed or hacked to death out on the ashen plain. Couldn't risk it.

Without further deliberation, he abandoned that doomed course and plunged instead off the tortoise trail down into a nearby pool. Surging through the water, he elbowed his way out amidst the languid herd of reptiles that wallowed there, and he hunkered down between their shells. He was trapped. If his attacker didn't fall for the misdirection and pass harmlessly by, he'd be in for a siege. But at least this living fortification might buy him time to craft a plan, or even to negotiate.

Pinkish strobes rumbled at the sky's restless edge. Backlit by the distant volcano, an onion bulb-shaped silhouette bobbed through the daisy forest, bow in hand. Krengel's eyes widened between tortoise shells. In the darkness, it was impossible to see anything clearly through Sundaloon's weird mishmash of woody vines. It was vaguely humanoid in form, but not by any stretch of the imagination could the assassin be mistaken for a human being. It was something else. Krengel's nails gripped the textured shell of the huge tortoise as his eyes narrowed upon his enemy, his inhuman stalker, bobbing through the flashing pink until its form melded with the night and the forest. It was gone.

Krengel clenched his teeth. He reached back and curled his fingers around the shaft that twitched with every throb of his swelling thigh. It occurred to him that the proper way to remove an arrow was to push it clean through and snap off the barbed point, but the arrowhead was set dead against the bone of his thigh. He pulled gingerly. Firmly rooted in his flesh. But it would have to come out. The island's jungles would be impassable with that crazy thing sticking out and flopping around. It would prevent him from ever entering the briar thicket, the safest place of refuge on the island. No arrows could strike him in there. The sheer density of the undergrowth would level the battlefield and bring the combat hand-to-hand. If the archer tracked him across the dunes into that nest of acacia, Krengel could double-back along the trail, ambush him, and stick a knife into his liver. Krengel slipped his hand through the tattered folds of his robe and withdrew the rusty weapon that had already taken the life of the last one who'd threatened him. In his hand, the blade felt eager to take another. But the arrow, it would first have to come out.

He reached around and took hold of the shaft. He closed his eyes, already moistening at the prospect of what agonies were to come. His lungs pumped measured breaths through gritted teeth until his will felt properly inflated. He pulled and the arrow tore loose, not quickly, but gradually, with a terrible effort that dragged a rope of meat out through the hole in his tented skin. He had to pinch off the connective tissue between his outgrown nails. Only then was he free to collapse. Cold sweat streamed from his face over the shell of the tortoise on which he sprawled.

A twig snapped, just behind him.

"Well, I'll just swaney."

Krengel raised his head and turned toward the sound of the voice. Not just any voice. It was <u>the</u> voice. The voice to which he'd always been so intimately connected that it might as well have been the narrator of his life's story. He could see it. Something. Rising and falling at the lagoon's edge.

"Ain't seen ye in a month of Sundays, fat brother and forever friend." The creature sidled closer. "Got daddy's eyes, blue as blazes, and every one of his curls. Mama's nose and sweet mouth. You're the pickings of the patch."

Krengel slid off the tortoise and took a step backwards. The bulbous entity took a step forward. It slung the bow over its shoulder, and then slowly advanced out into the water, reaching out with its long spidery arms. Krengel flashed his dagger and stabbed the air. It hesitated.

"Come on now. Put that pig-sticker away. You're all hat and no cattle."

The softly drawling accent harkened to a land unbeknown to him. But the voice, and more impossibly, the distorted form of the creature itself, favored best the same attributes of his father. Perhaps redrawn, redesigned into a form more befitting his flawed existence, even glorifying his defects in a perfect living caricature. There before him stood Count Richwald, or something wrought of the essence of the man, hovering on the nighted shore like a dark drop of dew, dipping restlessly on legs like straws of sea grass.

"Are you a demon?" Krengel whispered, making the sign of the cross.

"A demon?" The creature cocked its malformed head, a glimmering rack of teeth in the starlight. "Can't be no more nor less a demon than you, fat brother, seeing's how we quit the same womb." The Krampusz outstretched its arms. "It's me. And it's you alone I've done favored, Fat Brother. And that's how's come I got to punish you for all you done."

Chapter Seven

"What are they, Mitzi?" Nele curled her fingers through the bend in her older sister's arm and sidled close to her in the blackness. The alley sounded cavernous in the fog, resonating with every scratch and click of hooves upon the pavers. Whatever the animals were, the girls had crept almost close enough to touch them. One of the beasts let out a long and menacing grunt that halted both girls in their tracks, hearts thumping in tandem. Nele clenched her sharp nails into Mitzi's skin. "I'm scared."

Mitzi was frightened, but she was propelled by some sort of morbid fascination paired with a sisterly duty to explore and exploit every potential resource made available to them. She squinted her eyes and bobbed her head up and down like a lizard in the starlight in her effort to identify the sort of livestock stood before. They smelled of the boreal hinterlands, wolfish musk and pine sap, and the pungent undertones of excrement. It was a stench that confused the senses with jumbled images of wild things from remote places.

Mitzi's eyes brightened when one of the beasts grumbled and clattered the ornaments atop its head against those of its neighbor. "Why, they're deer!"

"What?"

"They're stags, Nele. Stags, like Papa used to hunt down along the river. With the great big antlers, don't you remember?"

Nele was silent. She did not remember the stags. There were times when Mitzi suspected her little sister might even begrudge her for being able to recall so much more about their childhoods, their parents and older brothers, before the Black Death turned their village to dust. Nele only remembered strange things, like the eyes of a favorite doll, the shiny pebbles in the mortar around the fireplace, the time she was stung by a bee that she tried to put in her pocket. She was too young when it all happened, for better or for worse. She could not remember the faces of their family, or much of anything about them.

"Want me to lift you up?"

Nele nodded.

Mitzi set the *Book of Wurm* down on the pavestones, grabbed her sister around the midsection, and hefted her up. She was getting too big to carry. Mitzi took a few tentative steps toward the team of animals until she could see their paddled antlers, their great rolling eyes.

Nele gasped. "They're white ponies!"

"Deer." Mitzi corrected her. And then, she corrected herself, as a long-forgotten word tore through the scar tissue of her mind. "Reindeer."

"Do they like the rain, then?"

Mitzi laughed. Because long ago she'd maybe wondered the same thing. But her eyes moistened as she collided with flitting memories from bygone days and better times, when Papa once lifted her into his strong arms, pointed his finger at herd of animals, and whispered: "reindeer."

Flitting grains stung her eyes, her cheeks ... something crawling across her lips ...

"Nele!" She dropped her sister as a dark sandstorm came blowing through the fog. Fleas again. Rushing upon them from both ends the alley. Gushing down the outer walls. Flooding in upon them from every direction. The layer of mist began to spin like a vortex as fleas fell from the sky in dark torrents, hissing against the pavestones in spattering gobs. The girls pulled their hoods tightly over their heads, swatted at their legs and screamed, but they were drenched in a bloodsucking tempest. A billion creeping particles.

The reindeer stamped and snorted, as roiling masses streamed over the ground like spilt blood to converge at the alley's center in a pool so black that it denied even the starlight to reflect upon its surface. A dark column then rose from the middle of the pool until it reached a man's height, casting a villous shadow over the *Book of Wurm*. The mass seethed and shifted until a black skeleton leered down at the girls through empty sockets of bottomless hatred. Wreathes of fleas unfurled over the living framework, assuming organic shapes and working groups of muscles, until the same dreaded form had been fully resurrected. Fleas parted to reveal that floating cadaverous face. Lashless lids fluttered open, and the bleary eyes of a clubbed carp locked upon Mitzi Gottlieb as she was lifted off the ground by a squeezing tentacle of fleas.

"Where is Krengel?"

Mitzi gagged in the freshly manifested face of the demon that reeked sweetly of rancid meat. Squirming veins pulsed rivers of fleas beneath its membranous skin. They spilled from its gasping mouth, springing from its colorless lips.

"The book will not show him."

A trunk of fleas formed, and began to sprout from the alley. Rising between she and the demon, it bore the opened *Book of Wurm* upon its canopy. Writhing branches of bloodsuckers leafed through the blank pages.

"I don't know," Mitzi said, "I haven't seen him since Christmas Eve."

The dreadful hissing intensified, and the living tentacle that held her began to thicken, drawing in billions of stinging mites from every rat in Bari. They surged up her body in a prickly sleeve, engulfing her, inch by hitching inch, as a serpent might swallow an egg. She screamed as the slurping hulk rippled over her neck until her face floated in a living frame that threatened to cinch closed over her face. Fleas began pouring into the corners of her mouth, down her throat.

"Tell."

She retched against the invasion, struggling to free her arms, but the sleeve only constricted, replacing air squeezed from her throat with a ramrod of fleas. Mitzi gagged on the living proboscis of mites until her eyes fluttered back into her head.

"The Basilica!" Nele shouted. "Krengel went to the Basilica of Saint Nicholas," Nele said. "I swear it! Let Mitzi go."

As though scrutinizing the air for any trace of insincerity, the monster hesitated, eyes listing in their sockets. Tendrils writhed about its base like the gnarled roots of an ancient tree. It seemed to believe Nele, though it was noticeably stricken with a sort of confusion that was evidently confounding to demons not accustomed to uncertainty.

"Why the book can't show this?"

At last, it released Mitzi Gottlieb. Nele fell to her knees as she received her sister's limp body. They collapsed together in an alleyway puddle. Nele wept, pawing frantically at the black hundreds of mites still coating her sister's tongue, impacted between her teeth. At last, Mitzi's eyes blinked open. She began to cough and spit.

"Go." A forked tentacle seized Nele by the jaw. "Fetch clothing. We go north of Novgorod, where all is ice. All is cold."

"What are you?" Nele stared into sallow eyes of the living cadaver before her, whose irises swirled yeastily like coagulated globules of chilled wort.

The creature parted its lips. Translucent hooks dropped from the roof of its mouth on membranous hinges. Milky droplets exuded from the fangs' needle points. "Black Pete."

"Once knowed an ol' lady, done swallered a spider. Wriggled and wriggled and tickled inside 'er. She swallered that spider to catch the fly. I don't know why she swallered that fly. I reckon she'll die."

Krengel thrashed in the webbing of another nightmare until at last he'd torn free. He groaned and blinked his eyes in the impenetrable blackness. Rolling onto his belly, he hitched his way through the nest of garbage like a sightless chick, arms sweeping, until he'd found the one and only thing in the world that he trusted, anymore.

He rested his cheek against the staircase's cool limestone landing until his night terrors subsided. Or perhaps it was daytime. No way of telling. Not without sun or moon or stars. But whenever he awoke and could not immediately find that reassurance of solid stone, an icy geyser of terror would spout up through his core. One false move in the wrong direction and his bearings could be irreversibly thrown askew, separating him from his single landmark in a lightless world, though perhaps not a stone's throw away. The very thought of that situation terrified him so much that he refused to move from within arm's reach of the staircase landing.

"Please let me out." Krengel peered skyward, desperate for just a pinhole of light. "If you let me out, I can help you. I can catch fish, crabs, and lizards. I'll do anything you want. I can start fires. I can be useful."

"You're useful as goose shit on a pump handle." The voice of the Krampusz was no longer a private monolog, ranting inside his skull. The beast within him had become a very real external threat, his words vast and resonant, emanating with grandfatherly surliness from somewhere outside the void, beyond the trappings of the sack.

"Please. All I want is to see the sun."

"I doubt that. You was miserable when you had every danged thing, and you was miserable once you was quit of it. Truth is, you just want whatever it is you ain't got, and once you got it, you don't tend it no more. Nine years, you been living the good life while folks all about ain't had a pot to piss in. I ain't got no sympathy for you, Fat Brother. Well's run dry as a popcorn fart."

"No one but Mother ever knew the truth about whatever happened to you. I had nothing to do with it, if that's what you're upset about."

"I don't blame ye for how they done me. Never once did. Nor how good ye had it while I was down there, suffering all alone. But Fat Brother, if I done learned one truth thus far, it's that folks is happiest when they got to struggle some. That's a fact. And it's one I aim to teach ye. I aim to make you struggle like I done. Make ye love to suffer and endure."

"But I've been suffering ever since I left home with that stupid choir!" Krengel said, gawping up through lightless abysms. He sifted through the trash to clamber blindly upon the reassuring solidity of the staircase landing. "And it's all mostly because of you. For doing every stupid thing, you've ever asked of me. Look at where it's all gotten me! What I need is--"

"You don't need nothing, no more. Your life has stopped, Fat Brother. Dead in its tracks. You done ceased."

Krengel slid his palm from one side of his chest to the other. There was no heartbeat. This had to be a dream. It was impossible. This place was impossible. There didn't seem to be any passage of time. It was just a boundless trap filled with unrelated junk that precipitated from one end of infinity to the other, piled-up like a layer of trub at the bottom of an ale cask. But no, he couldn't be dead. Krengel pressed gingerly at the damp spot on his rump where the arrow had struck him. Dead boys wouldn't be able to feel pain.

"You ain't dead, Fat Brother. Just ceased."

"Why did you shoot me?"

"How else you reckon I was supposed to catch ye? Didn't shoot ye nowheres fatal. Didn't aim to ruin ye for all my purposes, and I don't reckon you're ruined, yet."

The wound from the arrow had not even begun to heal. He kept it packed with garbage wadding to slow the loss of blood, or he feared he'd bleed out. It was as though his body's natural processes had just stopped. His urges to feed and to relieve himself were absent. He slept, for lack of anything else to do. He drifted in and out. But distinguishing between the periods of wakefulness and nightmarish sleep was becoming increasingly difficult. Besides the patches of luminescent mold, no natural light permeated the blackness of the Krampusz's sack. There were no familiar sounds. No points of reference except for a monolithic staircase that pierced the terrible void to heights unseen, an invisible marvel thrust upon a boundless nightscape. Twinkling fairy lights betrayed the distant peaks and yawning canyons that resounded with the groans of things lost and lugubrious that haunted those blackened grottos. He was not alone. Just as life has always managed to find a foothold in the bleakest deserts, the same warring castes of parasites and peons and fearsome agents of balance, probably perpetuated a blind circle of life throughout the cavern's whorls. He sometimes heard them, scuttling through their warrens and bellowing challenges from the crags.

No telling how long he'd been in there, with no means of measuring the passage of time. Wounded as he'd been, he'd not fought back against the Krampusz's spindly embrace, as he was lifted from the wallow and lowered into the sack upon a stone landing. The Krampusz stepped back, and dark folds of leather began to rush upward all around him, like endless bolts unraveling from spools and racing toward the starlit firmament. Titanic sacking rumbled and vacillated, as the cavern expanded while Krengel clung by his nails to the stones beneath him, lest he plummet to his death, not downward, but inward, as he hurtled toward infinite smallness. The sack cinched tightly around a moon eclipsed, and the nothingness of the sack enveloped him.

"I sometimes hear things down here." From those distant mountain slopes that blinked to life in waves of sequenced incandescence, there often came the squalls of wayward babes, fallen between moments and forgotten in the depths of vast hollows where they developed without aging, maybe scrambling on all fours over lightless ridges, wizened but forever neonate.

"Surely, you do hears things. You ain't alone. For I heared them too in all my years spent trapped down yonder. Mostly memories of things I done, I reckon, but some of what's down there ain't on my account, already down there when the Sack of Shadows falled into my keep. Further you depart them stairs, lessed is apt to be my doing. They's been owners afore me and owners afore them, and things alive down there ought not be, but are, things I ain't had nothing to do with and don't never intend to. Because the Quick ain't begun when that sack of boiled manhide got hewn and cursed, and it ain't bound to end the day that sack gets burned asunder, as one day it surely will."

Krengel closed his eyes and whimpered. If this were all but a bad dream, then when did the dream begin? Had those who'd labeled him a madling all his life been right all along? Real as it all seemed, could it be he was not imprisoned in a monster's magic sack at all, but back in Bari, rotting in a dungeon cell for the crime of stealing myrrh, or back in Lambsheim, hidden away in a secret room in the bowels of the Krengel estate, drifting forever through the gulfs of insanity? It was so difficult to be certain at what point in his life the real had become surreal.

"See, better folks has got lost down there afore you, Fat Brother. Like ol' Chad, huh. Just showed up down there like sometimes they do.   Lest I took him in drunk and ain't remembered doing it, but I don't reckon that's the truth.   Chad, I think, was one showed up on his own down there, like sometimes they do.   And they's others was my doing.   Like my Ala-bama critter.   My little Sugar Beet.   Thought to have me a sort of family, that way.   Leastways, a friend.   But I ain't never had none of neither for long.   She gone.   And they's been others, all taked. Reckon them dead as down yonder allows.   But it's you going to find out, Fat Brother, soon as you let go of them stairs."

"Why are you doing this to me?"

"'Cause I love you, Fat Brother, like I love all my best things. Don't ye see?   All things is down yonder for good reason.   Maybe I might could use something for later, if not straight away, or maybe I done kept it 'cause it recalls some special place or another, reminds me of someone, or maybe it's got some kinder value … but they's a reason it's down there, if it is, and it's 'cause I love it somehow.   Just like you.   Things will keep just fine at the bottom of them stairs, but people don't.   Ain't nobody lasts for long who clings to that landing.   And you won't neither, if you don't quit your bellyaching and take to your chore."

"What chore?   What can I possibly do down here that you can't do better yourself!"

"Now, there's aptly a reason I'd have bagged you, ain't they? You bet ye.   Ideas don't just spring up in a feller's brain for no reason at all.   They's a reason you down there.   You bet ye."

"But I don't know what to do."

"Nor did I.   Took me ten lifetimes, I'd reckon, but I done found me my whole purpose for living.   This time it's your go-around.   Bag's hewn up with threads of space and time, with time's a-running one way and space a-running another.   You got to learns to foller them threads kinder like an ol' map to get around down theres.   That's the best hint I'll give ye for taking to your chore."

"What bloody chore!"

"Find 'em.   Find all them ones has got taked.   Find me my Chad, my little Sugar Beet and all the rest.   Find 'em and lead 'em out.   That there's your how's-come and what-for."

"If I had a candle --"

"Nope. You'd just set things afire. Draw all kinder evil upon ye. Best ye go without light."

"But I'm your friend. I'm your Forever Friend. Don't you remember? How it's always been, you and I, together forever?"

"Darned right. You bet ye. We always going to be together, you and me, but you going to spend the best part of forever down there on them stairs lest you done that chore I said, 'cause you ain't coming out a click sooner."

"I've got your flask," Krengel said, desperation cracking his voice.

"What's that ye say?"

"Your flask of myrrh, the one you asked me to steal from the tomb of Saint Nicholas. I have it."

"Wouldn't be where you're at if ye ain't stole it first, like I said."

"Well, I've got it right here, if you want it. But you'll have to agree to let me out before I give it to you."

"Thank ye awful kindly, but I ain't got no use for such poison. But you will, Fat Brother. I guaran-damn-tee you surely will."

"Why?" The Quick all around seemed to await a reply. Only a slight breeze and a rumpling of leather sacking like a calving glacier. Krengel's eyes searched the blackness. "What will I need the holy myrrh for?"

"Can't say no more about such things, lest she hears and comes for ye too soon."

"Who? Who will come for me? Who are you talking about?"

"Shush now. Best ye go. Go straight away."

"But why are you doing this to me?"

"Because it's you alone I done favored, Fat Brother. And that's how's come you getting punished for all you done."

Chapter Eight

"Put it back, little Klaas, straight away." Friar Otto crumbled a fistful of dried yarrow. He let it rain through his fingers into the cauldron of boiling wort, and then he clapped the chaff from the palms of his hands. The flower's sharp bitters effervesced at once, somehow brightening the cave with a meadow's essence. "Thievery will play no part in my ministry. You know well that it's greed, Klaas, above all other sins that I find most intolerable."

The orphans on either side of him were still sound asleep, but somehow, the good Friar had managed to hear his groping fingers through the dried crusts of bread. Krengel sheepishly withdrew his hand from the Friar's stores. He rolled over and pulled his bedroll to his nose, scowling hotly at the ceiling, where stickmen lobbed spears at a fantastic herd of spotted horses thundering over the cave's painted whorls. This was supposed to be the ministry of Saint Nicholas; he was the patron saint of thieves, after all …

"A wiser man than I once said that the true measure of a man is what they'll do when they think no one is watching," Friar Otto said, scattering more flower petals into the boil.

Their usual slice of bread and cheese twice a day had slimmed to a cup of muddled flour and barley. Two quarts of ale were now but a weak quart of tea that tasted as though it had been brewed from dirt and iron filings, and filtered through a dungeon mattress. And that was probably not far from the truth. Highway vendors rangy enough to stalk the Germanian hinterlands to make customers of refugees didn't abide by any standard of decency, let alone purity. The circumstances seemed to bring the worst out of the woodpile. It had been a hard trip, even for the toughest children amongst them.

"If you're having trouble sleeping, then come and brew with me a spell. You need a skill in this world, Klaas, a secret to guard. Learn one, and it's you who will become valuable, regardless of where in the world the winding road takes you. And besides," Friar Otto lifted a steaming sack of sparged barley from a smaller kettle and dropped it wetly to the cave floor, "you may be useful tonight in helping me dispose of spent grains."

Krengel was upright in a shake. Wrapping his bedroll around his shoulders, he goose-stepped through the enmeshed blankets and bodies all around him, padding up to the Friar's frothing brew kettle. He sat down cross-legged on the cold cave floor, shivering in the terrible drafts whistling up from the earth's frigid bowels, and shrugged his bedroll up over his head.

"The bread you were about to steal from my stores is for brewing, and brewing alone," Friar Otto said. "All the magic of transformation of stagnant water to purified ale lies within those crusts. Unless, you'd rather eat them, and take your chances lapping water from the seeps of foreign lands."

"No." Klaas shook his head.

"Why aren't you asleep like the other children?"

"I can't sleep in this bloody cave." Krengel shivered and rubbed his arms. "I have bad dreams in these sorts of places."

"What's wrong with a good cave?" Friar Otto dabbed his trembling fingertips along a natural shelf on the cave wall, until they met with a little leather pouch amongst several other purses and corked vessels that he'd evidently arranged there. "You don't like the dark?"

"No. I don't suppose that I do care much for the dark, or for dank spidery holes beneath the earth that could collapse at any moment and seal you in forever."

"But there's something else," Friar Otto smiled, "isn't there?"

Krengel licked his lips and shifted his feet. He stammered over a reply.

"You've lived all your life in Germania, where accused witches are burned a hundred at a time. Killing them takes on the air of a festival, doesn't it? And it should. It's as much a jolly part of our Hun culture as brewing the finest beer. Fearing witches is what we do."

"My nannies all told me --" Krengel froze after blurting the first of his thought.

"Don't be embarrassed," Friar Otto said, "I will not judge you."

"They told me that if I was naughty, a witch would come for me in the night."

"Yes. She'd drag you right out of bed by your ankles and throw you into her big, black sack, and then off you'd go to her horrible cave, where she'd roast you alive and eat you. And the hag's name was Berchta!"

"Yes!" Krengel gasped. It felt as if Friar Otto had reached into his head and plucked the witch's name right off a dusty shelf. "Old Berchta!"

"Those stories have been around as long as children have been around. The good children are always rewarded by some sort of gift-bearing fairy, and the naughty ones are taken in the night and eaten by some awful thing that has a taste for unloved children. You cannot hide from her. Wherever there is darkness, there is always Old Berchta, always lurking in the gloom just an arm's length away. This, they told to a blind child." Friar Otto blinked his marbled eyes. "I too was threatened more than once with a visit from Berchta."

"You?"

"Aye."

"You were a naughty child?" Krengel appeared delighted by the revelation.

"I was orphaned, same as you. My father's murderers took me deep enough into the woods that only God would hear my screams, and for a week in Hell, that's all I did, until they put out my eyes and they left me. I survived. I groped my way out of those woods to become a pickpocket and a beggar, a blind boy who'd fight anyone for a ducat. I had a lot of anger inside me, back in those days. A lot of rage against a world that seemed only to despise me. It took time to find my path through the darkness." Friar Otto gestured to a reed mat with a flap of his hand. "Strain off the foam, if you would, before we boil over."

Krengel did as instructed, screeding the toasty froth off the dancing wort. He closed his eyes and inhaled the cloying vapors of steam. The bittersweet yarrow mingling with the bucolic caramel aroma of malted barley smelled amazing. There was no other smell like it in all the world.

"This batch will be mulled to a Christmas ale, to welcome the season of Advent."

Krengel peered down into the bag of spent grains and licked his lips. The stuff inside looked like chickenfeed. "Will we not grind any of the leftover into flour?"

"No."

"We're out of bread."

"Have faith. In two days, we will arrive at a village called Ischgl." The Friar dipped into a pouch and retrieved a pinch of Irish moss. He passed his hand over the boiling cauldron, sprinkling the seaweed hash in a slow and deliberate circle.

"Oh," Krengel replied, after a moment of peculiar silence. He supposed the Friar meant that it would be a waste of time to spend all day bothering with drying grain and grinding flour and baking bread, when they could produce several casks of fermenting ale in half a night, with which, they could barter for just about anything. To that end, a friar's brew was a perfect form of travelling currency, forever in demand. He bent and scooped his fingers down into the wonderfully warm texture of cracked and boiled grain. He shoveled a steaming heap of the malted barley into his mouth and closed his eyes. Sweet as candy. He could not remember the last time he'd eaten something half so delicious.

"You keep straining."

"Sorry."

"Brewing amounts to a one-hour boil, once you've steeped your malted grains into a nice tea, added your yarrow, and finally your honey and rinds and spices. Any three-toed fool can do it, but we fools have learned to closely guard our secrets."

"Why do you brew beer? Friars, I mean."

"It's a shepherd's call to his flock. Beer brings many parishioners to worship."

"Is that all?"

"Mmm." Friar Otto cocked his jaw. "Well, to a man who lives by his vows, brewing beer is not a duty entirely devoid of pleasure."

Krengel smiled up at the Friar. For the life of him, he could not remember ever having experienced the pleasant company of cooking alongside someone. It felt good and satisfying on a level that merely eating food with another did not. Something deeper and more meaningful there. His parents, of course, never cooked. Even at the Krengel bakery in Lambsheim, it was his father's servants' doing. They did the toiling while Count Richwald sponged all the credit. Even the children of the servants were employed as delivery boys and girls, toting baskets of pastries all over Lambsheim and to the villages beyond. His father, in all likelihood, was no cook at all. Klaas had once been rather naïve to that fact, assuming his father to be a marvel in the kitchen, whose many flaws were balanced and perhaps tolerated on account of his culinary genius. But alas, it was simply not so.

On the odious occasion he'd secretly followed his father to the bakery, hoping to steal into the kitchen and spy on him baking bread, he'd peered in to find the man all covered in sweat and flour. But so were two of the baker girls, sprawled before him upon the counter, their better parts stamped all in white from his father's groping hands. When the nearest girl turned and shrieked to find Klaas standing there, Count Richwald's powdered face sprung wide with theatrical surprise, and then split in great floured chuffs of laughter. Both girls contracted his fit of the sillies, and all three cackled crazily in the fog of dust. Klaas spun round to quit that weird kitchen, but he slipped in a dollop of slopped butter at the final turn, and upset a great tower of clattering trenchers. He could still hear their laughter.

"Klaas?"

"Aye?"

"Sometimes you seem distant to me. Though you're standing here, right beside me, it feels as though you're a thousand leagues away. Keep straining the wort."

"Sorry."

"The bread crusts will be added once the wort has been cooled and transferred over to the fermenting casks. That's when all the magic of the transformation begins."

"You keep saying 'magic.'"

"So?"

"That makes me a bit uncomfortable."

"Transforming a boiling cauldron of undrinkable solution into a pure and wonderful beverage?" Friar Otto smiled. "What else could it be? I've known brewers to turn buckets of castle sewage, snails and all, into drams of the finest nut-brown."

"It's just the word, 'magic,' that feels wrong to me."

"It's a dangerous word. Very dangerous, indeed. They'll burn a friend of anyone accused of practicing the least of it. But here I ask you, what words did our Lord and Savior utter at the very moment he raised Lazarus of Bethany from the dead?"

Krengel shrugged.

"Tabitha cum."

"What-what?"

"Tabitha cum. It's Aramaic. An ancient incantation designed to summon the walking dead. Magic words, Klaas. Old ones."

"Are you saying that Jesus used black magic?"

"Absolutely not! The holy Gospel merely states that he uttered the words of a necromancer's spell. Rest assured there are those who'd burn me alive for pointing out that fact, but check your scripture and you'll see that it is so. Tabitha cum."

Krengel glanced up at the blind Friar, who rarely turned his head to address the person with whom he was speaking. If he ever turned, it was for dramatic purposes. Krengel cast a glance over his shoulder. The other orphans were still asleep.

Friar Otto uncorked a flask and shook a few curiosities into the palm of his hand. They looked like dried baby ears. He brought them to his nose, inhaled, and then cast them into the boil. The little flaps unfurled in the scalding water, revealing veined and translucent segments. The aroma billowing out of the cauldron now pinched to a sharply citrus tone that burned with an oily astringency inside his sinuses, moistening his eyes. Surface tension relaxed and the layer of foam dissipated. Krengel gaped down into the wort and blinked. Through his tears, there appeared a roiling distortion of his own fat face, staring back at him.

After Krengel fled his father's bakery, he'd crashed off into the glen to be alone. Birdsong drew him deeper to a rotted bridge and a burbling brook that he hoped might bring some solace. He'd heard of the bridge, but never seen it. There was a troll with an appetite for naughty children rumored to lurk beneath its wormwood pilings. Krengel leaned over the mossy railing and stared down into the water. The only troll he saw was himself, staring back. He spat down into the face of his own reflection, eager to disrupt so many traits that he recognized as being inherited from his father. Chilly breezes bullied the trees. A crispy leaf tagged his shoulder as it pirouetted down over verdant reefs of moss where fish popped and minnows shattered like mirrored glass.

He closed his eyes, but he found no peace within. His fingers tightened upon the handrail as the chugging cadence of its words seeped up through a fissure in the cellar of his mind, and it grew louder, more insistent that he do something outward, something bad, like inflicting pain upon himself or another creature as a means of dumping some of the imbalanced bilge sloshing heavily in his mind, things lewdly intertwined, powdered in flour and cackling like gorgons. He groaned and rocked back and forth against the railing. When his eyes flicked open, a new face leered up at him from the water.

He pushed back from the railing, trying to divorce his mind from the image of a demonic Count Richwald Krengel, with skin black as tar and eyes chipped from glacial ice. He growled and pressed his fingernails into his cheekbones, yearning to drag them all the way down his throat. But it would only want more and more. How it nagged, darkening his emotions as it raged, throwing itself madly against the asylum walls of his mind. Krengel bit down on the insides of his cheeks until he tasted a little blood. Only pain satisfied the Krampusz, but he worried that if he started it would be too hard to stop.

He quit the bridge, kicked off his shoes, and dropped to the stream bank, where he squatted with splayed toes in the greasy mud and peered beneath the bridge for trolls. He didn't see any. There were signs of habitation, scattered potshards. A fire pit festered like a cancer on the earth. Nearby, a couple of wadded rags, the remnants of a ratty blanket, but no trolls. He stooped under the trusses and duck-walked over to the fire pit where he knelt and plowed through the moist ashes with his fingers. His face again, pale and bloated, glowered pugnaciously up from the water like a drowned boy's ghost. He wanted to hurt himself, to rake at his face until ribbons of flesh curled beneath his nails. He brushed back a lock of hair and left a blackened streak of ash like an extra eyebrow. It surprised him. Gawping down at his reflection, he turned his head back and forth, examining the loud black streak from every angle. His eyes brightened when he felt the Krampusz gurgle in approval.

The demon cooed as he dipped his fingers back down into the ash and brought them up to his face. He closed his eyes and smeared char from bridge of his nose to the lobes of his ears, and then opened them again. The paint really accentuated their burning blue. War paint that is. And it felt so right that he didn't even want to harm himself much anymore. It was as if he'd found a brand new way to placate the monster within. It liked to see him in war paint. With his index fingers, he blackened his lips, and then dragged streaks from the corners of his mouth down either side of his chin. He smiled, opening and closing his mouth. He looked like the most demented sort of puppet. Gads, if only he'd looked this way when he'd entered his father's bakery. It would have changed everything. And it was at that moment that his ears pricked to the crunch of footsteps in the forest litter.

He had a good mind to keep still and not reveal himself, lest they snoop where they ought not beneath the Troll's Bridge for today they'd find a nasty troll indeed. Her singsong disposition did beg for a bit of trouble, but Krengel wasn't sure what exactly to do. He just idled between the pilings, hunched with his arms dangling oddly at his sides. Filth rained between the planks as her wooden shoes clopped over the wormwood ties. She hesitated, just above him. He cranked his neck for an angle to see up her tunic, but a shower of dust neatly blinded him. Fucking hell. She spat over the railing as he rubbed the grit from his eyes. Concentric rings expanded from her foamy coin of spittle to the water's edge. A couple of crumbs fell.

Krengel's eyes snapped back upward. A minnow ascended from its green abysms to pop a crumb from the surface of the water. Krengel hitched his chin and sniffed at the buttermilk sweetness in the air. He recognized that smell as surely as a calf knows its mother's teat. They were pastries. And not just any pastries. Krengel pastries. The best in the Burghundian Circle.

Krengel freed the blanket remnant from the mud and pulled it over his head like a miserable shawl. He slipped carefully out the backside of the bridge, and then stole up the bank behind her. He peeked over the knoll. The girl, about his age, rose to her tiptoes and leaned out over the rail. The wind billowed her rose-red tunic and flapped the long white ribbons in her hair. She wore the red and white colors of a true daughter of the Habsburg-Netherlands, but she was certainly not. She was their property. He recognized her as a girl named Lala, a courier from the Krengel bakery and the only daughter of Miss Luludja, one of the very bakery girls that Krengel had so recently encountered, bare breasts powdered in flour.

"What you got in your basket?" Krengel rose from the grass and stepped dryly onto the road. He felt bolder than usual with a painted face and hood, meaner, as if anything he said or did could never be directly connected to the boy beneath the disguise.

The girl caught her breath at the terrible sight of him, but somehow, she did not scream. Instead, she gathered herself, frowning at him as she adjusted the basket crooked over one arm, smoothing the napkin that covered her precious wares. She cleared her throat and excused herself, attempting to push past him, but he countered with a bold sidestep that brought them nose-to-nose at the end of the bridge. Her breath smelled like buttermilk and nutmeg.

"You've been pilfering from your master," Krengel said, trying to speak without affect to heighten his puppet-like appearance.

"I have not."

"Pay the toll," Krengel said, unfurling a filthy hand, "your whole basket of pastries, or I might decide to eat you, instead."

The girl rolled her eyes. "They're not mine to give away. Now, if you'll excuse me, I've a delivery to make."

Krengel watched her anxious chest rise and fall, noticing the subtle throb of her heartbeat within her throat. She was dark skinned, like her mother, like so many of the servant girls that his father seemed to prefer. He supposed she was pretty, for a gypsy.

"I know who you are," she said at last. And at some cue, some evident change in his expression that belied a bit of uncertainty, she shoved hard past him and marched off down the woodland path.

Her shriek pealed the twilit glen. Blackbirds spilled from the trees like pieces of the night racing into place. She was shoved to the ground. Her basket of pastries was ripped from her arm and hurled into the woods, releasing a herd of bouncing tumbling buns and stripy confections. He grabbed her by the ribbons in her hair and they struggled in the dank forest leaves that smelled of mushrooms, until he clambered with reptilian purpose upon her, clenching her ribbons in his fist. Bent on reenacting some rendition of what he'd seen earlier in the bakery, he pinned her slim wrists to the ground and stared meanly into her eyes. But in a switch, one wrist popped free, and she found a stone the size and shape of a baked potato, bringing it broadside to Krengel's head with a blinding crack that resounded all the way into his chest.

He awoke with sticky leaves matted into his hair. It was dark. Something was wrong with one of his eyes. A tooth clear in the back of his mouth throbbed like a hornet sting. He reached up to feel the swollen side of his face, and found her white ribbons still entangled in his fingers.

There would be no repercussions for him. What he suffered instead of worry was burning humiliation. Once he'd managed to recollect the better part of his senses, he took the basket and hurled it angrily into the stream. He tried to throw the wadded napkin in after, but it settled in the weeds of the lower bank. He kicked at a pastry and then hovered for a while in the moonlight, just breathing, and a trickle of blood leaking warmly from one of his ears.

No father to greet him at the gates. No mother to ask worriedly where he'd been. Krengel slogged across the darkened estate to the servants' quarters, around back of the house, where lithe silhouettes loitered in doorways. The second doorway to the end belonged to Luludja and Lala. A crimson tunic draped from a clothesline. Krengel peered deeper into the gypsy women's dwelling until he caught sight of Lala. Just her head poked over the rusted rim of the washtub. Lantern light exposed the innumerable pinholes, some so low there couldn't have been more than a few inches of water in the tub. Her mother sat behind her on an oil cask. She was brushing leaves out of her daughter's raven-silk hair.

Krengel had meant to terrify the girl this afternoon, but she and her mother appeared not the least bent out of shape. Despite the trials they'd both endured at the hands of their masters, the girls appeared quite happy, without fear over what the next day might deliver. They had each other for the time being, and that appeared to be enough.

Lala suddenly turned her head toward the night and stared in his direction, narrowing her eyes. Her mother stopped brushing. After a moment, Luludja rose and closed the door.

The house servants stood ready to receive him. They asked no questions. They'd kept the coals warm beneath his nightly licorice bath, gently stirring the water with a silver paddle shaped like a willow leaf to keep the bottom of the basin from getting too hot. One bather knelt beside the stepping stool with a towel draped over one arm. He presented the usual woven basket filled with soaps and oils. Another held a pitcher of milk painted with the images of fanciful peacocks and a gilded platter of cakes. Krengel eyed them all hotly as he undressed, feeling a bit like a pale queen termite amongst his trimmer and darker-skinned supplicants.

He settled down into his bath, immersing himself like a frog in the snowy layer of bubbles all the way to his eyeballs. His eyes flicked from the face of one servant to the next, as they gathered woodenly round to tend to him. Something was different, tonight. Their brushes were rougher than usual, their attention lackluster. He let out an indignant honk when one of their combs grated over the injured side of his head. Sputtering up from the basin's paunch, he clutched the knot upside his head and grimaced down at the bloody tint upon the bubbles. Out of the corner of his eye, he caught a smirk.

They knew.

Krengel smacked his palms against the water. Somehow, the realization that the servants all spread gossip behind their masters' backs, was even more infuriating than the possibility that they disliked him. He imagined them howling and reeling in the servants' quarters as the story was told and retold of the gypsy girl knocking him out cold, and leaving him in the woods. They reveled in his misfortune.

Krengel snatched the towel from its bearer and stepped out of the tub, pushing past the usual offerings to squish barefoot from the bathroom, down the main hall, all the way to his mother's bedchamber. He stood half-naked and dripping before the crimson upholstered door, afraid to knock. The memory of the gypsy girl's mother lovingly brushing her daughter's hair, invoked a queer feeling of desperation in him, as if perhaps there were some confounding moments in life when more than anything else, you just needed a mother's embrace to make things right. He stood tiptoed to reach the enormous golden knocker, and gave his mother's bedchamber door a few sound whelps.

Almost immediately, his stomach wound into knots. How would he ever explain that he simply needed to be with her? That's just not the way they were, or ever had been. He rarely ever saw his mother, except on the occasions that she made scheduled public appearances. She was cold, hard, and beautiful, like a porcelain doll.

The sound of hastening footsteps down the hall turned his head toward the encroaching phalanx of bathers. They were upon him, taking him gently but firmly by the arms and ushering him away from the crimson door. "No one must disturb her for any reason when her bedchamber door is closed."

"But I'm her child."

"No one."

"But her door is always closed! Always!"

The door opened. Standing there was a shirtless, glittered man in a golden robe. His head was shaved clean, and his face was made-up like a woman's. He smiled quizzically down at Krengel.

"Forgive us," said one of the bathers, "we beg the Lady's pardon."

"No!" Krengel wrenched in the grips of his handlers. "I want to see my mother!"

The man in the doorway placed a manicured fingernail against his bottom lip. He turned and glanced over his shoulder in the direction of a murmur that issued from somewhere in the bedchamber behind him. He turned back to the boy, smiled down at him, and then gestured to his entourage that they wait for just a moment. The crimson door closed to a sliver of light. Krengel and his bathers straightened up and composed themselves, releasing grips of one another and adjusting their garments.

After a few moments, the crimson door reopened and the glimmering man was standing there. But this time, he was not smiling. He avoided eye contact with Krengel and addressed only his handlers. "No," he said.

Krengel's jaw dropped. "What do you mean?"

"No is her answer. She kindly asks that you all go away."

"Did you tell her that her son is with them? Her child?"

"She asks that you go away."

Foam boiled over the cauldron rim in a great slopping wave. The coals below spat and hissed like scalded cats, as the cave grew darker. Friar Otto shook his head.

"I'm sorry. I'm so sorry."

"Klaas, what have you learned if anything, in the weeks you've spent with me?"

"Well … that it's important to give … to others."

"Selflessness? Generosity?"

"Mmm." Krengel horse-lipped a grain of barley stuck to the inside edge of his hand.

"Greed. It's the dark side of our most powerful instinct, that of self-perpetuation. It's fuel for our survival, both individually, and as a whole."

Krengel nodded. A dollop of masticated barley fell from the side of his mouth. He retrieved the glop from the cave floor and sucked it from his fingertips.

"A loaf of bread will always contain some measure of sawdust and bone meal. Gin will always be cut with turpentine. Soured ale will likely always be mulled with ginger or licorice, and sold for an even higher price. Greed drives our civilization forward. It has always been around, and always will be. But never before this age has greed worn a face so terrible."

Friar Otto sighed, dipped into his pouch and cast another quid of Irish moss into the cauldron. He gritted his teeth and turned then to Klass, and penetrated his soul with those vapid, colorless eyes. "I believe it is no accident that delivered you unto me, Klaas, to my ministry of Saint Nicholas. Just as I believe that Saint Nicholas was predestined to enter the world at the precise time when he arrived, I believe that every orphan in my choir was delivered unto me for a grand and specific purpose. Our world has a way of maintaining balance. Have you noticed this? And when there's an imbalance of greed, God always sends a Christkindel."

"A what?"

"A Christkindel is a Gift-Bearer, an equalizer, a little saint delivered unto the world to teach us selflessness and generosity by his example. Saint Nicholas was the first Christkindel."

"But people call you 'The Equalizer.' I've heard them!"

"Then they've heard my sermons."

"Are you a Christkindel?"

"History will be the judge of our deeds in life, Klaas. And history is always watching. I'm just doing my part to balance the injustices of an imbalanced world. As we speak, a thousand Jews are burning throughout the Low Countries, blamed for the outbreak of Plague. They're accused so the Great Wolf will have something new to destroy, some new estates to devour. The Wolf devoured the Cathars, the Conversos, the Muslims and the Rosicrucians, and now; even the wealthy Christian dignitaries are unsafe. The weight of the Wolf creates imbalance, as he slides over the land devouring all wealth in his path like a great rippling slug, appointing rich Romans as Cardinals only to slay them and consume their estates. It is the Wolf who slavers at the paddock gates for all the lambs of a New World, overseas, for every slave of dark hide. Yes, and the Wolf's fleet grows rapidly. If you hear not a word of my preaching, little Klaas, hear instead the knocking of all the hammers in the shipyards, for every driven nail will equal ten-thousand lives smashed asunder. I promise you this. You must rise. You, Klaas. Pledge to take a stand against the Wolf. Become an agent of balance in an imbalanced world. Stand and fight the Wolf wherever you encounter it. Never show your underbelly. Save the children, Klaas. Especially the children. Deliver them all from evil. You are so important, Klaas. Know this! You--have--purpose."

Klaas nodded agreeably. "I think so, too." He lifted the bag of grain, tilted back his head, and funneled barley into his mouth. "Maybe my whole purpose is helping you brew beer, Friar Otto."

Chapter Nine

And they ran. Dropping through a slot beneath a pried wagon plank, each hit the road rolling through a vast machine of spinning axles, grinding wheels and hooves. Cloaked in predawn gloom, they scuttled unseen through the roadside graves of last autumn's pilgrims, and over the shoulder where they slid, tumbled, and bruised hide to the marrow against jutting rocks the color of dogs' teeth. A peaceful tribe of boulders offered them sanctuary. Huddled for hours, the three boys listened intently to the caravan's distant clamor, while hawks patrolled the shoaling skies in their endless hunt for a sort of vermin that stood and chirped, before plunging down through cracks into a labyrinth of tunnels.

By noon, an ominous stillness pervaded the countryside. The air hung heavily from dark and ponderous clouds that crowded like a herd of brooding beasts. At thunder's first mumble, the boys' spirits lifted, as they were certain the Spaniards would drive their caravan harder and without rest until they'd reached the relative safety of the cliffs at the valley's head. Still, the boys remained hidden until the rains came at nightfall, cold, hard, and relentless, and they peered from their warren like marmots toward the valley head where a string of torch lights twinkled.

Senses drowned by the tempest, they embarked on a slow and treacherous descent. Glimpses of hazards leapt brightly into existence by the wild play of lightning. Clattering rocks loosed by their stumbling feet were muted by an almost continuous, titanic rumbling from the heavens. Unable to navigate any path other than directly down, they slid blindly over crumbling shelves, slick boulders, and through gushing fissures. Torrents of rainwater sluiced through slippery channels between stones and stands of brush, and around the first trunks of trees that gratefully deflected some measure of the frigid downpour that plastered rags to their emaciated bodies, ghosting through the forest like revenants in burial shrouds.

Phantom wolves found them in the woods and set upon them, testing them, circling, panting, and jagging so close that the boys could smell the reek of their hides and sanguine breath, and they felt in their bones the impact of galloping paws until little Rolf mouthed his fingertips and began to cry. But, still they ran. Downward and deeper into the valley where undergrowth choked their path with bramble and briar, the wolves abandoned their game before blood was spilled, when the distant roar of a new force demanded reckoning above all other threats, man or beast, as this one would subjugate them all.

Drenched and gawping before a thunderous channel of elemental fury, they saw whole trees rafted by like spat toothpicks upon lightning-white foam. Beyond, the opposite slope ascended tantalizingly toward their broken road to freedom, leagues ahead of the stalled Spanish caravan.

For an hour, they picked their way downriver, until Theodore Weissmuller found a birch lilting precariously out over the churning chaos to a point near enough the opposite shore that it was worth a chance. He straddled the trunk and shimmied up, followed closely by Wolfram Faust, and reluctantly by little Rolf, who loitered uneasily on the bank until the older boys reached the canopy. Made more anxious by separation than threat of drowning, the little one finally hugged the trunk with both arms and legs, and began to inch like a wet caterpillar after them.

The roar of the floodwaters blasting beneath was both disorienting and deafening. Teetering from vertigo, Wolfram lost a shoe. It fell and was instantly erased from tangibility, converted wholly to the river's wild religion.

Enmeshed and dangling in the birch's sparse canopy, Theodore found good footings in the crooks of lower branches and readied himself for the big leap. He clung to branches on either side while pumping his legs, causing the tree to rise and fall like a sort of springboard beneath him. When he felt the moment was right, he sprung forth like a treefrog, but to his horror, the tree absorbed all the thrust of his legs and he gained no forward momentum. He dropped wild-eyed and grimacing down into the roiling element.

The boy was tumbled in the icy amalgam of whipped air and water, until miraculously, his raking claws found purchase in some overhanging tussock that kept rooted, as the floodwaters tried to strip the hide off his bones. He drew himself up over the edge, gasped for breath, and then hauled himself quivering and depleted from the torrent.

Slogging back upstream to the sagging tree where his companions remained roosted, Theodore extended a long cane-like branch across the water to Wolfram. He shook the branch in Wolfram's face until the boy understood, and took it first with one hand and then the other. He closed his eyes and dropped with nothing more than faith into the river, which seized hungrily upon him and rushed for deeper and wilder places like a hooked pike with a mouthful of live bait, but Theodore dug in his heels and pulled back with all his might, until Wolfram was swept ninety degrees to the water's edge. He clambered out, retching up brown lungfuls of water.

Both freed boys shouted insistently, angrily shaking the branch of deliverance in Rolf's crumpled face, but he clung bawling to the birch, and he would not let go. It was a mistake to have allowed him last place in this deadly relay. Yelling was no use. The floodwaters emitted an impenetrable sonic barrier that dissolved and absorbed all lesser sounds. Rolf shook his tearful head back and forth at the wagging branch. They prodded him with its crooked tip, jabbing the limb at his chest, until to their astonishment, Rolf suddenly reached out and took it. He wiped his tears against his shoulders, sniffed, furrowed his brow, and finally nodded his head. The boys on the shore shrieked unheard encouragement, howling and beckoning crazily with scooping arms.

Rolf hung crucified over the river, clinging to the branch with one hand and the leafy boughs with the other, still unable to commit fully to the new way. On the bank, the faces of the others contorted in every flash of lighting. Birch leaves were slipping through his fingers, snapping. He was bound by circumstance to make the terrible plunge when he at last fell, and the released tree snapped upward. But before he hit the water, something rose from the depths like a mighty Kraken.

The boys on the bank looked on in horror. A gnarled form breeched the foam to impact the child, midair. Theodore's staff snapped in two. Rolf had time enough to turn his head with a parting visage of submission, as the thing that snatched him from the air sounded back into the depths with Rolf ensnarled in its roots like a pale shrimp caught in a whale's baleen. It vanished into the froth, a forty-foot column of solid lumber armored in bark that glistened like crocodilian hide.

For a timeless spell, the remaining two paced the riverbank, shaking in the wet and cold and shouting the name of their lost one into the night. But in their hearts, they feared every shout more in vain than the last, until eventually, they turned and quit the floodwaters to begin their slow ascent, allowing every so often a hopeful backwards glance, until like flowers upon a grave, they cast their last petals of hope down into the cold valley that had swallowed their friend.

When at last they reached the mountain road, they thought it best to walk its rocky shoulder and leave no tracks in the mud for those Spaniards, who, if it pleased God, were impossibly bogged to their axles in the sloppy ruts, a whole day's travel behind them. It was a race against the Inquisition back to the village of Ischgl, where the road would split in the very location where the Hound of God had first sought to ruin their lives. There, the boys would cut back over the highland pass toward the Low Countries of Germania. The caravan would waste little time pursuing runaway orphans much past their own southwest fork toward the Friary Rabida in Spain. They would be homesick after six months on the road, and eager to return. The mountain pass represented their gateway to freedom.

The night drizzled on and the boys didn't care to speak much to one another. They picked their way miserably along the shoulder's jungled rocks for long hours, until their feet hurt so badly that they quit the careful way, and instead took their chances and walked the road. It was not half as muddy as they'd thought, for better or for worse, but as the night lagged on, they worried less about the dangers behind them and just kept on. The caravan was slow to get started, even on the best of mornings. And on such a narrow mountain road where none could pass any other, all it would take was one troubled wagon, one balking team, to stall the whole train.

By dawn's break, it was apparent by the stillness in the puddles that the rains had so gradually ceased that the boys hadn't noticed. The winds hadn't yet begun to blow, and the sun hadn't burned through the mist, if the sun was even up there at all. Nothing lived up here. They still did not speak, trudging woodenly along, half-frozen in their sodden rags, staring down at the mud, rocks, and the puddles. And then, they heard it.

The boys stopped in their tracks and turned toward one another. It was impossible to tell from which direction the disturbance was coming, the rhythmic pummeling that resounded dully at first throughout the valley and grew louder, reverberating off the canyon's walls with something of the cadence of theater kettle drums. Horsemen of the Inquisition. And there was nowhere to hide. Frozen like rabbits in the rush of a raptor's wings, they were pinched between a stone wall and the leanest of a chasm that dropped straight down into Hell.

Theodore shouted at Wolfram to run, and they ran. Down the road's center now, theirs was a mad sprint ahead to any route of escape, no matter how foolish or imperiled, because no outcome was more terrifying in all the world, than that of being recaptured by the Spanish Inquisition. Wolfram slipped and fell. Theodore stopped and helped him up. They ran again. Covered with mud and limping, but still running, grimacing like apes in the thin morning light, they slid round a bend in the road where Theodore grabbed Wolfram tight to him and drew him to a halt, where a washout of stones had tumbled down onto the road. He crooked his neck and gazed up the wall and his eyes brightened.

They were soon perched two fathoms above the road, braced between the canyon wall and the backside of a precariously balanced boulder, large as two oxen. Its situation was just so, and the ground beneath so saturated that two young boys just might be able to topple the behemoth, if they pushed with all their might. They waited in fits, eyes walling, chests heaving in terror, while the hooves of Spanish mounts drummed harder, sharper, less resonant, and more immediate, until at last, four billowing wraiths came flapping round the bend like the four horsemen of the apocalypse, doubled over their beasts' pumping necks and tilling limbs.

"Push! God, push, Wolfram!"

When its footings crumbled, the massive slab was quick to pitch. Wolfram seized Theodore by the arm, lest he follow the boulder to his death. It toppled, trundling down the mountain to a ledge where it vaulted outward, cart-wheeling soundlessly through the air like a titanic chunk of space debris. Four riders stalled in the dusk of its shadow, heaved to the reigns of screaming animals. One beast reared to perform a crazed sort of dance, before tipping off into the chasm. The other animals rolled their eyes, collided with one another, and fell, as crushing tonnage was delivered inexorably upon them, cleaving off an entire section of the road in one massive wallop of sodden soil, scraped so sheer from the wall that it looked to have been chiseled right off the mountain's face by a giant stonemason. The entire mess boiled downhill in a rumbling deluge of mud, blood, and twisted man and horse hides that gathered mass, all enmeshed, to make the throat of the canyon tremble.

The two boys gripped each other's thin arms and grinned maniacally at one another through taut and filthy masks. The road to Ischgl was theirs, and theirs alone.

Hewn of boiled manhide and cursed. The Sack of Shadows. A finite trap of infinite contradictions, blind and boundless to fuel the madness of things ceased, yet ongoing, the walking dead, forever imprisoned between moments in a realm called the Quick.

He would find a corner. He would find a hem in the fabric of time and space and follow it to a corner where all threads meet. There, he'd gnaw through the fabric. But it was hardly so simple. There was something else here. Something that watched and waited. Something that took.

Klaas Krengel held in one hand, a torch of phosphorescent mold that cast about him a blue halo of ethereal light. In the other, he gripped his knife. Even after all this time, the handle was somehow still tacky with the blood of a murdered Cardinal. Paranoid, conspicuous, he was a beacon of flickering light set upon a blackened desert, a reeking target that oozed blood from a wound that would not heal, a wound that slowed him. He could not have been more perfect prey.

The Krampusz hadn't spoken to him in the longest time. The utter isolation of the Quick was agonizing. Krengel talked to himself for want of a human voice, but cringed in terror every time he heard the sounds of another. They howled sometimes, the lost ones. Their cries suggested that at one time, they might've been human, but the Quick was entropic in nature. It disorganized and devolved. The prospect alone of spending eternity in a lightless wasteland of garbage, was quite enough to attract the attention of madness.

Krengel froze.

There was movement ahead. He could hear something. Something rustling softly in the garbage. He stared into the gloom. Glowing spores drifted from the head of his torch like motes of neon ash. It was impossible to gauge distance. The source of a sound like that could be as near as twenty feet, or far as twenty fathoms. He began to walk again, but more carefully, staring out beyond the ring of torchlight into a world of utter blackness. Things could adapt to this place, he supposed, as things adapted everywhere. Fishermen sometimes captured strange things when their nets dragged too deeply, things luminescent with agape and needled mouths, gargantuan eyes seared white by the light of the sun. Things always adapted. Things trapped here in the abyss had an eternity to adapt, because death was never an option. Robbed of eyesight, the other senses were honed. He could make it. He had faith. Friar Otto had made it out of the forest, where his kidnappers had blinded him. He'd adapted. He'd found his path through a new world of darkness.

The rustling sounds were growing sharper now, nearer. Krengel squinted and adjusted the focus of his eyes near and far in the blue torchlight, until he was standing over the precise spot where his ears told him the source should be. He hunkered down, lowering the torch near the ground, where a few waste papers shifted. Something was here, buried alive. Setting the torch aside, Krengel knelt and pushed aside rubbish with both arms, until he'd excavated quite a hollow. At last, he picked away a few crumpled wrappings and there beneath, was a patch of soft fur.

"Hello down there. And what are you?" Krengel smiled and stroked the thing with one fingertip. "You wouldn't bite me, would you?" Working his hands ever so gently around the creature's round sides, he lifted it like a melon from the garbage and turned it over.

The realization that he was holding a severed human head came as a horrible jolt. Brown eyes rolled upward and blinked soullessly from their sockets, mouth chewing mechanically, but no sound coming out. Silver hoops pierced the earlobes. Black ink designed its glistening stump of a neck.

"Chad?"

The mouth stopped working. The eyes fixated and sharpened, as if to indicate some semblance of understanding, some distant recognition.

"Who did this to you?"

The lips parted, and a spit bubble bulged, but did not break. Krengel laid the head back into its grave, but facing upward this time, so that it might better see its surroundings. The head's eyes tracked his every move, as a newborn infant studies its parent. Saliva trickled from the corner of the mouth. Krengel took a piece of paper and wiped it away. Then he took up his torch and rose. There was nothing more that he could do for a creature so pathetic as this one, fit only for death, but deprived of it. The mouth champed away in silent protest, as Krengel walked off toward the electric-blue slopes, the only visible landmark in this realm. To that end, those mountains were probably the destination of everyone who'd ever found themselves lost here. It was the only point of bearing, the only direction in which the Krampusz would have traveled when he escaped, and the last place that Chad was likely headed.

###

Shrouds of mist veiled what remained of the village of Ischgl. The few miserable cottages not burned to their footings, were but blackened remnants, charred to their heartwood and scalped of their thatching. Mass graves left uncovered and powered thinly with lime, moaned at the leaden skies where an unseen raven croaked. A thin dog appeared and trotted mindlessly through the ruins, circumventing the burial pits with a glance of the guiltiest regard.

"There's no one left." Wolfram sniffed, shifting bare feet in the ash. "All dead and gone."

The Black Death had followed them to Rome. It had seemed as though the plague were no plague at all, but rather, a sentient entity bent on destroying them. Devastation had for months, dogged their heels, appearing at times to have anticipated their next moves, making shortcuts ahead of them to meet them at their destinations, as if in ambush. Particularly at Lambsheim, while they backtracked the boggy fens, the plague had swung wide around the swamps to meet them at the gates of the Habsburg-Krengel estate. It was most uncanny, too unsettling to consider much past the daylight hours. Hundreds of Spanish pilgrims at the trailing end of their caravan were swallowed by the pestilence on their way to Rome. It was winter's purifying chill that finally halted the Black Death's advance, or it might likely have sacked the holy city in its weird vendetta against Friar Otto and his Little Elves.

"I feel sorry for them," Theodor said. "They were just living here ..." He shrugged. "They hadn't done nothing wrong."

"Nor have we," Wolfram said. "What wrong did Friar Otto ever do to deserve what he got in the end? Or us? Or little Rolf? None of us have deserved any of this."

"You know when it all went sour."

"Aye," Wolfram spat into the ash, "the very day we took him in."

"The very hour."

"Remember what a fine day it was when we arrived in Lambsheim? Remember the blue skies and fair weather? It was a beautiful day."

"An unusually beautiful day." Theodor nodded gravely.

"Aye. The perfect day."

"And then it all changed, the very instant we met him."

"All the screaming."

"We'd never seen Friar Otto in dispute."

"Never."

"He knew." Theodor cast a solemn glance at Wolfram. "Friar Otto had a way of knowing things. He knew it would be a mistake to bring him into our fold."

"He didn't want him."

"No, and had you ever seen him turn down a child before?"

"Never."

"His arms were always open, but not for Klaas. He didn't want him."

"He knew." Wolfram spat.

"He sensed evil in that boy."

"An evil clear as day. The townspeople warned us about that family."

"And it was plenty clear why."

"Why'd he go and take him in then, you reckon?"

"For the wagon. The wagon and fresh horses."

"He made a terrible mistake. Cost him his life, it did."

"Got him caught up in the wrath of God. All of us did."

"He was bedeviled, that boy. Had the devil in him."

"The way he would talk to it," Theodor shook his head, "like it was his friend."

"The way he'd claw at his own face! Remember that? All the blood!"

"We're damned for ever knowing him, you know that, Mate? Every one of us. Damned on Klaas Krengel's account."

"He's cursed us, that one. Cursed us for the rest of our days. But you and I, you think we've outrun it? The evil? You think now that we've left it all behind us that his curse, it'll leave us alone?"

"I think," Theodor said, suddenly clutching Wolfram by the arm, "that we'd better leave here. Straight away."

"What's the --"

Theodor pointed at the ruins of a nearby cottage.

Wolfram squinted his eyes. He stared through the darkened doorway of the structure, through a haze of mist and shadow. His eyes gradually adjusted. And then he saw them.

Inverted, they hung from the charred rafters like a clutch of blanched cocoons, human in size and size alone, suspended by knuckled feet. Molten eyes burned secretively through folds of slackened hide that bulged and stretched in response to their larval twitching with a sickening elasticity. Dimly aware, softly stirring, their activity seemed to be mounting at the same rate as the sun was slipping down over the horizon.

"Let's go, Wolfram."

"Aye." Wolfram's eyes widened. "This Ischgl is an accursed place."

And again, they ran.

Northbound, through the woods and twilit glen where scads of bats chipped and fluttered through the shag canopy of pines. A sliver of a moon peered eerily through the shelved clouds like the watchful eye of something bent on perverse malediction, tracking their flight up through the crags of the highland pass. Things moved through the forest around them, things that shied the light of day. They dared not stop to rest. Not until they'd reached the Low Countries, would their stiff penance ever feel complete for accompanying that accursed little child who'd somehow invoked a terrible wrath designed to punish not only him, but every fool unlucky enough to encounter him along his errant path estranged from God, divorced from grace, and direct to Hell.

Wolfram seized Theodor's shoulder, reined him to a halt, and pulled him suddenly to the ground at the mouth of a confluence of paths that funneled through the pass. Not far from the painted cave where they'd once camped with Friar Otto and the others, they lay panting in a weed-choked saddle between peaks that afforded a sweeping view of the leeward pass.

"What is it?" Theodor whispered.

"God in Heaven!" Wolfram clutched a fistful of Theodor's rags and pulled him tight, his strangled whisper ascending to a whine. "I think they've seen us."

"Who?" Theodor's heaving breaths caught with every hammer of his heart. "Who saw us, Wolfram? Spaniards?"

"No." Wolfram extended a quavering finger toward the pocked and cavernous walls, where the moonlight played coolly upon the jungle of slabs and crevices. "Them."

Chapter Ten

Like a lost Atlantean traversing the ridges and lightless trenches of his wayward kingdom, Krengel knelt before a patch of bioluminescent mold amidst the Mountains of Light. He dipped his torch into the cytoplasmic gel and rolled it gently to and fro. Krengel rose. He blew a glittering cloud of fairy dust from his torch. The strange life on the end of his stick resembled a wad of viscous electricity, pulsing frantically, communicating some message back to the pool from which it had been stolen in a weird language of light. The pool pulsed back some reply of reassurance that seemed to settle things between them, a bit.

At the crush of Krengel's footsteps through swells of garbage, clutches of polyps glowing from nests of neural masses winked out, one after another. He bent and touched a darkened one. It felt slick and yielding to the touch as he might've anticipated, but as Krengel pulled his hand away, his fingertips were left feeling oddly numbed, weighted. After some time of rubbing his fingers together, shaking his wrist, he found that the buzzing sensation in his right hand had not abated in the least. He stopped and held his fingers to the torchlight for a quick examination, and there he found, to his horror, that his fingers appeared flaccid and drooping in the sapphire light. He clenched a fist and for an instant, they became normal and firm, a familiar skeletal structure supported by muscle, sinew and skin, but when he relaxed, they melted again right before his eyes. The effect lasted for a length of time he would have guessed to be an hour, before his hand felt wholly normal and appeared as such. But when it subsided, he could never decide whether it was the polyp that had infected him with a mind-bending toxin, or if it was the Quick itself that gave precedence to consciousness over existence, interpretation over reality. Either way, it appeared that nothing could be trusted in this place.

After a long and lackluster ascent, Krengel clambered upon a ledge near the summit to find that it was already occupied. Krengel froze before it and stared. The thing stared back at him through its one great eye. Therein, was something of the wisdom of a mountaintop oracle. It was not alive. It was a square machine of some kind, with a perfectly round, glass porthole recessed into its front panel. Once Krengel was reasonably certain that the thing presented him no harm, he cautiously approached. He knelt before it, and peered in through the circular window. There was something moving, inside. He pressed his nose against the glass. He could see the poor thing dragging itself eternally forward upon the machine's perforated inner drum, which just rolled squeakily round like a wheel on an axle. The trapped creature inside was quite certainly a severed human hand.

Someone must have been here before him. Dismembered hands do not imprison themselves. Krengel pulled at a handle on the porthole's silver rim. When the metal hasp at last gave with a resounding pop and the porthole opened, a pod of opalescent creatures flushed the garbage all around him, rising weightlessly into the air like gas-filled bags. Whipping electric fringes against the blackness with glittering puffs, they ascended, until they became a constellation of living stars.

Krengel removed the hand from inside the machine and closed the porthole. He sat cross-legged on the ledge and placed the hand in his lap, stroking it between its knuckles. It seemed to like that, fanning its fingers. He sat there stroking the thing and wondering if it had once been Chad's, while he awed over the twinkling nightscape that swept down from the jagged peaks to those littered and featureless plains from which he'd climbed. The Sack of Shadows was a hauntingly beautiful place, where little rebellions of organization still survived under the rule of chaos, its king.

Strangely, Krengel felt not the least bit exhausted from his ascent. He felt fresh enough to climb mountains week in and week out without ever tiring. In the Quick, it seemed as though the body was impervious to natural wear, yet it could be affected by other bodies that it encountered. You could numb your fingertips, and evidently, you could lose your head and hands, but in all cases, the body carried on, impervious to ruination. Each fraction of the body, once a body had been hacked all to bits, seemed forever to retain a proportionate amount of that animation that had once propelled its whole.

The realization that was removed from death's reach was a difficult precept to digest. And it wasn't settling so well. It was commonly understood and generally accepted that the promise of eternal life at salvation was a blessing, perhaps the greatest gift of all. Krengel poked at the wriggling wad of fingers that tried to clamber out of his lap. It seemed now to him that he could imagine no state of being so perfect, so sublime that he would care for its everlasting continuation. Let alone a state of being so limited as Chad's, hacked to bits upon a lightless wasteland and left to ponder his miserable condition for all eternity.

Friar Otto had once described eternity to the orphans as a mountain of solid diamond, where once every billion years, a sparrow would come flitting along and it would fly all the way up to its peak. There, at the tippy-top, that silly bird would deliver but one little peck to that mountain of the hardest substance on earth, and then it would fly away. After another billion years had elapsed, the bird would return to peck the mountaintop again, just once, and so on, and forevermore. The time it would take for that sparrow to pulverize that entire mountain of diamond into dust, Friar Otto had concluded, was naught, but the very doorway to eternity.

As Krengel gazed down over the surreal countryside, he was struck suddenly with the most intense feeling of dizziness. He closed his eyes against the vertigo and hitched back away from the edge of the precipice, crabbing his way over to the relative safety of the wall. He smeared his face and groaned, sucking deep breaths to dispel the nausea. The dismembered hand became suddenly anxious, wriggling sickeningly in his lap in an effort trying to scramble over his thighs. He seized the pitiful thing by a finger, and flung it hard out over the ledge without ever opening his eyes, breathing deeply, fighting against the bout of sudden illness that had so suddenly overtaken him. Quickly as it had begun, his nausea lifted.

Krengel rose. He rubbed his scalp and the back of his neck, exhaling loudly through pursed lips. The feeling had completely passed. Eager to find some surer ground in case the vertigo returned, he dragged himself up to the rim of a sprawling plateau. There at last, he found the summit.

"Halo?" Krengel screamed up at the starless sky, where that aversive Krampusz was somewhere roosted. "I found Chad!" Krengel breathed heavily, on the verge of tears, marching aimless circles upon the flattened expanse of garbage. "I found Chad and he's dead! Dead! Do you hear me? There's no people left alive down here! They've all been hacked to bloody bits by some damned thing, for God's sake; will you open this bloody bag and let me out of here? I've done all you ever asked of me!"

As suddenly and violently as the first time, Krengel was struck to the ground by a dizziness so intense that he could hear the blow resonate through his body. Sprawled and rocking on the lightless plateau, he caught a glimpse askance of some flicker in the sky, not unlike the dance of lightning through gathering thunderheads.

The blow came again, closer, more focused this time, spinning all of creation before his rattled eyes, like a crazy top. It was moving in, pulsating with mysterious light. But Krengel could now discern that what approached him was no thunderhead. It was something else. Something bigger.

Palpitating in the tremendous front of air pressure, Krengel threw away his torch, swapping it for the bloodstained dagger in his braies. His ears popped. A great weight fell upon his chest and crushed him flat. He found the strength to raise the blade against the unseen force, poised, and ready to sting like a scorpion in the shadow of a falling shoe.

The fourth blow stunned him so terribly that it seemed to dissociate his mind and body. He perceived his form bouncing up from the garbage, and he even heard the impact when his carcass landed, though did not feel any sensation. The terror he experienced was more objective than any drive for self-preservation, in a normal sense, such that he sympathized mightily for the crippled child in the garbage, as he watched a hovering leviathan descend hungrily down upon him.

Its many rows of sequential lights streaming excitedly, the ballooned monster eclipsed the bare blackness of the firmament with its vast and weightless dimensions, veils of silvery filaments dragging the plateau like fishing nets, parting gently as a pair of curtains to reveal an abysmal hole, a fringed and vacillating mouth. The sky-devil boomed impossibly harder and faster, as it targeted the lifeless form of the boy, its festooned curtains drawing in while the filaments still engaged every living thing in their path, plucking polyps and all manner of gentle and blinking creatures from their nests, and drawing them skyward into that galactic maw.

And when Krengel was certain he was about to witness his own destruction from his displaced position, there came a volley of whistling projectiles that spat sizzling trails of sparks. They arched high over the plateau to bombard the monster with white flashes of light and sharp reports. And with each strobe, truer aspects of the thing were revealed, its ballooned segments all striated with veins, collars of fur around its many blood-red eyes, as it retracted its deadly filaments and fled for the heavens like the ghost of an enormous grubworm, called back into the arms of its bent creator.

Barely conscious, Krengel was on some level able to perceive that his rescuers were approaching. Lanterns swung pendulously from pikes. They rode atop the black carapaces of their otherworldly mounts that tossed their shoveled heads and rattled menacingly. Massive, segmented legs articulated through garbage, as the riders prodded their beasts into a half-circle formation. A few of them dismounted. They walked upright, humanoid in stature, but with the perilous gait of uncoordinated children. Their teeth were set aglow in the most brilliant moon-blue beneath their lavender headlamps. Bejeweled with luminous pendants, glowing streaks of face-paint, flickering strings of tiny lights, a tribe of natives to this world of eternal darkness formed a twinkling circle around Klaas Krengel, and loitered as sensation gradually returned to his body.

"He's not Pancha," someone whispered, "it's a boy. You think it's him?"

"Look at all the blood on him."

Krengel cracked a bleary eye and saw that every trace of blood on his tunic, on the blade of his knife, were all set incriminatingly aglow by the weird light of their headlamps, every droplet and spatter. Whether the blood was mostly his own, from the arrow wound, or that of Cardinal Moretti, he appeared saturated with death's drippings. Krengel sat upright suddenly, and the tribe of glowing children leapt back. He rose, turning slowly in a circle, still terribly discombobulated, knife clenched in his luminescent hand.

"Saved your ass from that damned Mauna Goba. Ain't you least going to say thank ye?"

A few headlamps bobbed.

"You ought not go pointing that pig-sticker at none of us. You'd be dead six ways from Sunday if ain't for us."

"'Sides, might just kill ye yet."

"Dang straight we might."

Krengel continued rotating mechanically upon one heel, directing the knifepoint round at each of them like a clockwork assassin. He felt that he had to keep moving in some way, or else he'd fall over. And if that happened, he mightn't be able to get back up again.

"Who are you, boy? Speak up!" One stepped forward to jab him in the chest with a long tube. "You down with the Pancha? Yibrasaw? Uano bembe Santa Klaas?"

"What's that?" Krengel froze, cocking his head to one side. "What's that you just said?"

"We're out a-looking for a feller named Klaas. You him?"

"I'm Klaas Krengel, heir to the House of Habsburg."

Headlamps swerved in the direction of their spokesperson, whose voice had sounded crudely feminine. The tribe murmured and hissed, shuffling restlessly about.

"What are y'all waiting for? It's him. Let's round up the numbaecs. We're going home."

Two tribesmen broke away, spearing polyps dropped by the sky-devil and shaking the glowing remnants into satchels at their hips. Shortly, the rest of the tribe quit the weird standoff in one movement, heading back to their mounts without a word. All but one. She flashed a neon smile and stepped fearlessly forward, extending her open hand.

"I'm Hiley, and you'll be coming with us, Mr. Krengel."

Krengel retracted his dagger and clutched the blade protectively against his chest, out of reach of her eager hand. He waited until she'd lowered her arm before he relaxed again.

"Where you from?"

"Lambsheim of the Low Countries," Krengel replied.

"Ain't heard of it."

"It's set right in the heart of the Burghundian Circle, just a few leagues west of the Fens ... how do you know me?"

Hiley shook her headlamp slowly side-to-side. "Don't know ye from Adam, Mr. Krengel. But there's a feller called the Ike Man, sure does. Been talking for weeks about you, Santy Klaas. Seems he'd somehow knowed you was coming. Ain't that something?"

Her drawling accent and unique vernacular struck Krengel with such niggling familiarity. He and Hiley had never met, not in this lifetime, nor any other. Of this much, he was certain. Yet, there was something unmistakably familiar about her voice.

"Ye ready?"

"Well, yes, I ..."

"Good." Hiley turned and whistled. One of the numbaecs tossed its massive head.

"Are you ... from here?"

"Well, no," Hiley replied. "We all come from somewhere's else, originally. Just like you."

"Where are you from, then? Originally?"

"Alabama."

"Alabama?" Wheels of recognition whirred inside his head. Where had he heard that word before?

"Heard of it?"

Krengel slowly raised a hand and pointed a finger at the girl. "You're his little Sugar Beet! Aren't you?"

"What?" Hiley's neon smile faded. She cocked her headlamp and took a step closer, placing her hands on her hips. "What the heck you just call me?"

"I've found you! His little Sugar Beet. That's what he called you."

"How do you know him?" Hiley whispered, her breath catching in her throat. "How the heck you know about me and my Forever Friend?"

Chapter Eleven

Somehow, it knew that it had once been a priest. How it knew such a thing with such certainty was a strange thing, yet it did. A priest no more. Perhaps as far-flung from God as an earthly creature could be divorced, its reason for being was yet essentially unchanged. It remained a fisher-of-men. A crier whose tireless purpose was to spread a particular message to mankind, far and wide, to every corner of the earth. In that sense, its life had not much been altered by the great transformation, five hundred years ago. Critical parts of the old were absent or missing from the new, like a network of family, friends, and acquaintances. Those things were gone, grown old, and to dust. It sometimes missed them, in a way. But what it missed perhaps most of all, was its name.

It once had a name, a name that meant something, a name that evoked intense emotions in those whose lips dared utter it, in those whose ears received it, and that name was Father Pabichka Napien. Or, as he'd otherwise been known by the remote tribes of reindeer herdsmen he'd come to know so intimately: Black Pete.

Black Pete's head forever swam in slushy memories from earlier times, from a past life as devoted missionary of the Russian Church, a former war criminal and defector from the army raised by Yaroslav the Wise, who'd pledged annihilation against Svyatopolk the Accursed. Names and bygone places, little details loaded with nostalgic portents, like a strange excitement that he remembered over the smell of braided leather, the thrill of driving hard into the white and bracing winds. Each league of rushing wasteland erased another layer of an unbefitting social system, away from the confounding habits of people who felt so entitled to a basic level of respect they'd never earned, slashing his whip against the scouring grit of snow, away, further and further into the wild.

Trust was one of those habits of people he'd never fully understood. It was a strange thing, trust. It was nonsensical behavior, in which a poor fool would for no good reason at all, fancy rolling clean over to show another his underbelly, begging to be used and subsequently destroyed. Black Pete had never failed to oblige the trusting, in that respect. His beloved church had once trusted him, much to the same degree as he'd once been trusted by the commanding officers of Yaroslav the Wise, and ultimately, by the various tribes of nomadic herdsmen and hunters he'd been sent to convert to the Russian brand of Christianity. He'd betrayed them all, of course, once the walrus hunters had left him in the company of their women and set out on upon the pack ice, where a great storm fastened itself upon them.

Imbibed on distilled spirits in the sweet smoke of manure fires, he'd hunkered with his new harem in a ring of firelight like faceless, flickering gnomes, while somewhere up above, a blizzard moaned its spells of corruption over the long and lightless months. Buried alive in their rank and intimate burrow where children wailed in want of their fathers, the lost walrus hunters, they all boned meat until none cried but little strewn bones that clattered, suckled of their marrow by mindless forsaken mothers and savage brides of the dwarf king, deep and dark in their cavern beneath the snow. But those days ended when the walrus hunters returned. They dragged him like a seal out into the brilliant white, naked, and glistening with the rendered fat of their children and there, they reamed his innards with harpoons and clubbed his brains steaming upon the ice.

Now, he felt no joy in the rush of elements, the mission or the message, having no connection to the church or to the lives he touched, with no faculties available through which to derive the least pleasure from driving a thundering team across the frozen wastelands north of Novgorod. Now, he only obeyed, like a Russian thistle bobbing its empty head in affirmation with the breeze. For he had no more control over his existence or the direction in which he was headed, than either of the two girls bound and gagged in the front of his sleigh; girls whose soul purpose had just been reduced, in much the same capacity as his own, to finding and destroying a little boy called Klaas Krengel.

Cheeks blistered from the cold, the girls squinted through rows of bobbing antlers, as the sleigh rails screamed over leagues of blinding snowpack. Black Pete leered down at his captives. He studied their reactions as he whipped his team of reindeer up the crest of the final rise. It always intrigued him to watch the birth of emotional nuances upon the faces of others, however fleeting or cruelly inspired, in those moments when he showed them the unimaginable. He watched the girls closely, anticipating the lift of their visages from one of hopeless misery, to gawping awe as they rafted to the edge of a sudden precipice, and skidded to a halt in full view of his fortress, far below, a frozen citadel situated in the heart of a glacier valley where the rays of a peripheral sun could never shine, a hidden marvel of clustered towers and brilliantly painted onion domes, striped and checkered in a dazzling contrast to the bleak ice walls of the fissure in which it was nested like some fantasy plundered from the mind of a dreaming child.

Somehow, Black Pete remembered that it was not a league's distance from here, where once he lay naked and bleeding upon a field of barren ice, that he first encountered his new employers, legless and unfettered by any natural force to solid ground, mammoth horns arching from their cowls like crooks upon the arctic sun.

The Fates had plainly told him that he was going to die that day, but that afterward, death would never bother him again. And the Fates had not lied. For it was upon this bleak ice field, five hundred years ago that Black Pete's life ended, and his indentured servitude to the Guild of Wurm had begun.

Chapter Twelve

She'd been down in the bog seining mudbugs the day her devil come falling from the sky. Pap had just passed. Been weeks without eating. Been days without a sip of water beyond what he could draw from chewing a damp sponge. And, well, Mama reckoned it was time to go ahead and call in the family.

She went into town with a purse full of dimes, and from the grocer's pay phone, she called up all the aunts, uncles, and cousins from both sides. Told them Doc Quin ain't allowed her man but three days to live, and they'd better come a-running if they cared to say him, goodbye.

Not every death allowed such forewarning. So, everyone came. And when they arrived, Pap looked the part of a dying fellow. Folks cried, they turned and walked just looking on the wan and wasted shed of someone who'd always reeked of hard work and sunshine. Just wasn't believable, how a tan and sinewy master of his land, lord of everything that grew or swam or crawled upon it, could be so utterly consumed. Everyone reckoned Pap might not last through the night, with his family gathered round. A prayer circle formed. Around Pap's bed, folks chanted down the night. Dawn broke with bee martins gaily a-twitter.

Two weeks passed, and Pap was yet alive. The prayer circles abated. Folks sipped things, rocked the porch, and visited late into the evenings. The crowd began to thin. Folks who'd come so long a ways to be a part of Pap's final experience had to leave again.

Regretfully. Had jobs to get back to. World don't wait. They packed up, shook hands, hugged, and left. Locals it seemed, stepped in to take their place in the vigil. Time passed slowly. There followed a seemingly unending benediction of whispered stories of who'd died how, and when, and who was getting bad, and who was fixing to go, and who'd just went and why, while the midnight coffee pot percolated.

Thirty seconds between breaths.

Pap's eyes changed color from hazel to gray. His feet went black to the ankles. His knees mottled. The preacher looked in daily, and prayed over him. Again and again, last words were whispered into Pap's ears, by the same people. Folks bent to hug him, again, to kiss his forehead, to hold his hand. But even with all that attention and all the say-so of gods and doctors, Pap didn't aim to die until he'd convinced every last one of them that he wouldn't ever die at all. And if that was the old trickster's last wish, then by god, he got it, because it wasn't until every last guest had cleared out of the house and Mama left into town that Pap decided it was time. His time. A minute passed between breaths. Two minutes. He awoke, blinking up at Hiley through unseeing shale eyes, and that last breath? It never came. Locusts chirred in the elms outside his bedroom window.

It had taken too long. Hiley grabbed her cane pole, her throw net, and her tarred bucket, all she'd ever needed in the whole danged world to make for a perfect day, and she ran without stopping, all the way to the bog without ever looking back once at that old house with the dead man in it.

"Spent most of the whole day crying. Just by myself. And I s'pose it was nigh sundown when I heard it. Kinder like a coon squalling, but from somewheres high above. I looked to the first stars to try and find it, squinting you know, and there's when I first seen him. Black as a raincloud falling out the sky, he come screeching and bitching straight down from Heaven, skinny arms and legs all just a-paddling the air until, ker-whoomp! Down he come, right-smack into the middle of a paw-paw patch.

"Fall didn't hurt him none, far as I could tell. Just got him a little perturbed and cussing, in his way. Me, I didn't worry for him or myself, neither one, and I can't rightly say why. It all just tickled me so. I crept right on up through the sawgrass to have me a look at him. And my land, when I parted that grass and his eyes met mine, I swore I was looking straight back at my ol' Pap. Not all drawn and haggard like Pap had been afore the consumption ate him up, but kinder young and handsome-looking, way he'd use to been. Black-skinned, though, and rightly out of proportion ... but, it looked enough like Pap, that thing in the bog, that I suppose I was apt to trust it further than I ought of. Stayed there with him, I did, through the night and into the next day. Can't rightly say why, but I didn't once think to leave. Just stayed with him down there nigh to the next evening afore I heard folks a-hollering for me, and then's the first time I remembered where I really belonged. But I couldn't bring myself to call back.

"Something about that ol' devil, see, called so awful deeply to me, like to somewhere way deep inside my mind into a set of ears I never knew I had. Guess it probably sounds crazy, but I felt like I had to keep quiet and keep right near him until they passed. Wasn't no two ways about it, so I let them. Never called back. And that made him awful proud of me. 'Cause he knew he was all alone in the world without me, and he needed me bad. Him and I both knew we was bound to be Forever Friends.

"Weeks went by and I kinder made myself a mama to him. I teached him how to seine mudbugs and how to fish and how to catch frogs and tadpoles, and even how to snare rabbits and opossums the way Pap taught me, though we never caught none, and roundabout I even teached his ass how to talk. Yes sir. That was me done teached him. And didn't take long as you'd reckon, as he was real quick at learning. Couldn't tell you how long I spent in the bog with him, because time with him all kinder runs together, like you get attached so hard to one another that you don't even stop to think about nothing else.

"Then one morning, Lord knows how long later, they done found me. My family did. They caught up to us and when they at last seen what had hold of me, Uncle Luke aimed to blow his head off and there come an awful fight. I wouldn't have it, and Mama wouldn't let him do it as she rightly feared he'd hit me by mistake. Mama grabbed my arm and fought that devil tooth and nail 'til he'd decided he'd had enough. He pulled out his ol' black sack, opened her up and drug me down in there after him.

"Now, I could tell he hated to be in that dark place, as if he'd been there before and didn't aim to never go back again, but that devil knowed his way around down here like an ol' barn rat knows its hayloft. He can drop in here from any-ol'-wheres and pull his sack right on through behind him. That's how he does it. See? Slips from one world to another through holes in this here sack, then pulls the sack on through after him and kinder vanishes clean from one place to the next with all of us prisoners in tow. Leaves big ol' holes in the ground of the place he leaves behind, whenever he does it, and rips big ol' new holes in the sky of the next. Course, no one can see them holes but him."

"How can you possibly know all of that, from in here?"

"Cause, Silly, how you think most all the folks trapped here wound up down here in the first place? Half a dozen's from right back home. I knew these kids. Course, most were babies when I left, but I knew their folks and families. These was kids who'd heard the story of the way the Bog Devil come and took me, and kids being kids, some had to go sneak off and dare each other to visit the place where it happened. If ever they found that accursed spot, they fell on through. Ain't no creature but a devil can see things like rabbit holes. I s'pose they last forever, wherever he leaves them, because every day new things fall through, things from way back and way on forward that ain't even happened yet, like time don't mean much of nothing."

The realization then struck Krengel that the Krampusz had been in the tomb of Saint Nicholas before him. He'd crawled purposefully beneath the altar and slipped into his sack, creating a rabbit hole to Sundaloon when he pulled the sack through behind him. It was intentional. It had all been a trap. But the Krampusz could have trapped him that way any time, in any location. Why there, beneath the altar of Saint Nicholas, unless the flask of holy myrrh was something he'd needed, but he didn't even seem to want it. The demon had gone through a great deal of trouble to get him and the flask of myrrh here. And why? Why myrrh and why him? Why goad a particular child all the way to Bari from heart of the Low Countries, directly through the path of the Black Death and through the clutches of the Spanish Inquisition. It made no sense to go through so much trouble, unless there was something more, something special about him in particular.

"Your Bog Devil, your Forever Friend?"

"Yeah?"

"I believe that he cast us down here for a very important reason."

"And what reason might that be?"

"Well," Krengel said, clearing his throat, then taking a deep breath and straightening his shoulders. "First off, I believe that he sent me down here to rescue you."

Hiley snorted, furrowing her brow. "I believe you're windier than a bag of assholes, Klaas Krengel." She turned, kicked a polyp, and edged off toward her waiting numbaec. The great beast wagged the tips of its horns in the garbage. Krengel skipped after her.

"He told me I needed to find my own way, a new direction in life, and since I've been down here, I believe I'm beginning to understand what that new direction should be."

"How long you been down here? Few days? Maybe a week? And when's the last time you heard from him, your so-called Forever Friend?"

Krengel shrugged.

"Not since the first day he dropped you down here. I'd bet my life on it. And that's because he's moved on. He's already got him a new 'forever friend.' You and I? Huh, we ain't nothing to him but a distant memory. Now, before you start to argue with me, keep in mind that I been down here a whole lot longer than you, with lots more time than you've had to think this through."

"Whatever his reasoning, I don't believe he cast either one of us down here out of malice."

"What's it matter? Why he don't never talk to us no more? Why he ain't never come to get us out?"

"He threw you down here because he loves you, Hiley. Strange as it may seem, he loves us both, and this is how he shows it. He holds onto things that he loves the very most because he doesn't ever want to let us go. Down here, we'll keep forever. Down here, we're safe from harm."

"That's what you think, Mr. Smartypants." Hiley removed a clear tube of phosphorescent light from her belt and held the glow-stick between their faces. "But it's pretty clear to me no one's told you a dadgummed thing about what's really going on down here, have they?"

"I don't suppose … what exactly do you mean?"

"You don't know nothing at all about the witch."

"Witch? What witch?"

Chapter Thirteen

At the darkest hours, when he could not bring himself to sleep, it was Krengel's nightly habit to slip down to the kitchen stores. The spiraling staircase he knew so very well, dank and close, each step readied to receive him like a flattened old friend, walls encroaching so near that two people could scarcely pass, glazed and greasy from exposure to roasting meat. They buckled inward at the second turn, swooning over treads concaved from generations of tramping feet. The ceiling sagged so low, an adult was made to stoop with hitched eyebrows, wondering with every step if the shaft had been excavated by some ancient race of dwarves. It was, after all, the oldest passage in the Habsburg-Krengel estate, corkscrewing down into a dynamic grotto that had been retuned over the centuries to meet the specific needs of its stewards.

Through the dark ages, the Habsburg's bustling kitchen had long served as an impenetrable keep, a treasury, a dungeon, and a torture chamber. Three of the six ventilation shafts now employed as chimneys over cooking fires, were found by Lord Friedrich Habsburg to be choked with two cartloads of mixed human and animal bones back in 1455, evidencing deplorable stewardship for untold years, while the estate was something of a remote fortress in the lawless heart of Germania. While the towers, halls, and great rooms above had been sacked and leveled asunder, burned, ruined, and refurbished, exterminated of all occupants and eventually repopulated, annihilated, and raised again, the cyclical clash of iron and spattering blood, clambering barbarians and infernal consumption, the bowels of the fortress had remained absolutely unscathed. Not a single tile had ever been chipped.

From ceiling ringbolts where bygone enemies once hung flayed and screaming oaths to unspeakable ends, now draped a meaty arbor of smoked sausage. Inverted hogs, bilaterally-transected, pirouetted on halved snouts amongst a dangling rookery of denuded ducks over brimmed barrels of cloudy oil, Roman olives, pickled herring, live mussels, and whelks in brine. Drowned flies speckled the surface of every open drum, every cloying pool of leakage that oozed from kegs of spiced hippocras and metheglin.

As Krengel rounded the final turn of the staircase, vermin scrambled in terror from his ring of candlelight, plunging through gnawed holes in sacks of oatcakes and ginger wafers, squeezing beneath bins of malted grains, through great barricades of kegged ale like little sinners fleeing the wrath of their rodent god. In their haste, they upended stacks of trenchers and goblets from the counters that clattered crazily about the floor.

Unaffected by the usual din of rodents, Krengel paused before a sconce and lifted his candle to light a torch. Grotesque walls flickered dimly into view. He crossed the room and lit another. Windowless, the room had not since the days of its construction been illuminated by any other source of light but fire. Rats' eyes burned from every recess where the torchlight could not reach.

The countertops were cluttered with supper's spoils. Krengel edged up to the nearest surface and by the light of his candle, surveyed all that was available. He leaned through heaps of trenchers to push his fingers through the crust of a minnow pie. He scooped up a warm handful of the silvery filling and shoveled it into his mouth. Sidestepping while masticating the squishy mouthful, he seized a drumstick of broken crane and tore loose a long ribbon of pinkish flesh. Dropping the bitten leg to the floor, he moved on, draining a goblet of metheglin in six gulps, inhaling a handful of lark pottage, munching ginger wafers gnawed by rats.

A baked crust collapsed hollowly beneath the pressure of his fingers like a cruel joke, but he recognized the ruse as the unused cover to one of his father's live blackbird pies. Between courses, Count Richwald delighted in carving a pie at intermission that would set his dining hall gaily aflutter with piping birds, while musicians played and servant girls performed their scandalous dances. Krengel wondered how many of the servants' children were his own half-brothers and half-sisters.

Suddenly disgusted, he winged the gutless tin across the hall like a discus shedding spokes of crust, until it struck the far wall with a terrible clatter. He sent a heap of trenchers over the counter's edge with a wild sweep of his arm, wincing at the horrendous noise. Krengel cared not. He clambered right atop the table and strutted right down the center of the mess with pottage squishing warmly between his toes. This was his court, and he was its king. He quaffed a second goblet of metheglin, threw the vessel against the wall, hiked up his tunic, and began to piss all over the food, the floor and the counter, filling goblets with foam. Yes, it was a fine life indeed for a king left alone to do whatever he wished, whenever it pleased him. Spattering urine upon rounds of boiled venison made him grin. And it further pleased him to imagine the servants at daybreak eating these scraps, no doubt, while sopping up his leavings.

He resented the help. Although many of them had a hand in raising him, he still resented his surrogate parents for being commanded to love him when they clearly loved their own so much more than he. The memory of Luludja brushing out her daughter's hair stoked the darkest chambers of a furnace in his heart. It was the way she'd spotted him standing there in the gloom, and had not so much as acknowledged him. She'd simply stood up and closed her door -- just as Mother had always done.

No one had ever really loved him. No one wanted to be near him. The ones who were supposed to love him didn't. The ones who were forced to love him couldn't. They all acted so put-out, so extraordinarily burdened by him. They hated him. And perhaps that was all just as well, because deep down, Krengel hated them right back. But he'd tried to bury it. Out of pure human decency, he'd shelved his lifelong resent and he'd tried his best to make a go of it with these people, who merely tolerated him, all stuck with him by circumstance.

He's not forgotten the way that Luludja had always rushed his bedtime stories. She'd skipped whole verses and sometimes whole pages in her haste to complete what was evidently a loathsome task, so that she might rid herself more quickly of him and return to the servants' quarters, where she probably spent long hours brushing nits from her beloved Lala's hair.

Rip it out. Catch her alone in the woods and rip it all out.

"Shush, my Forever Friend."

But as time went on, Krengel learned to read quite well and the first night, he decided to follow closely along with Luludja while she read his bedtime story, he was shocked to discover how often and how badly he was being shortchanged. He began to interrupt her, pointing out the skipped verses, halting her attempts at more than a page in a single turn.

She closed the book.

"I no read no more," she said. "I tell you a story, instead."

Luludja blew out the candle. They sat together in the darkness for a spell, just letting their eyes adjust, before she cleared her throat and commenced to tell her tale. "Wherever there is darkness, there is always Old Berchta. Always watching you. Always waiting."

"Who is Old Berchta?"

"A witch," Luludja said. "A witch of the old world, when things were not so gentle as they are today. An age when children kept still and huddled close to their mothers in fear of what the darkness might bring. Is why all children still fear dark places to this day, but cannot explain why. It is in your blood to fear the darkness. Because there was an age when children disappeared from their beds, when things came for them in the night." Luludja splayed and popped her fingers. "Old Berchta was an eater of children."

"Why?" Krengel asked, after a long moment of silence. "Weren't there better things to eat?"

"No, Klaas. There were not. You are probably too young and stupid to understand why there is no better dish on earth than a naughty child, slow-roasted on a spit, whose sins render sweet as cinnamon butter." After a moment, Luludja relaxed back into her chair. "But, be this as it may, Old Berchta ate children for altogether different reason. It was all owed to a fear from which she'd long suffered her terror of growing old and dying. Because it was in some tattered old book of witchcraft that the flesh and blood of children held the cure against aging. She was convinced that it was so. The idea was a wicked one that festered in her mind until she could think of little else, as it came to possess her wholly, as wicked ideas often do. And once her hunt for children had commenced, there seemed no turning back for her.

"She trapped them in the forest with the use of pits and snares, baited with fruits and toys and sweets. She tricked them by disguising herself as a frail old woman in need of help, or as a kindly merchant lady offering free kittens. She became a prolific and expert killer with children practically clambering onto her cutting block, but no amount of spilt blood ever seemed quite enough. Another was always needed to slake her appetite, until she grew quite bold, stealing into the homes of sleeping children and butchering them right in their beds. But no matter how many she destroyed, each evening when she knelt before her cauldron and peered down at her wretched reflection, she saw the lines in her face growing ever deeper.

"Well, there came a winter's day while she was out checking her snares, when she heard a small voice trickling down through the forest. Dragging herself on her belly through the snow, she crawled toward the singing until she caught sight of a little boy pulling his sled of firewood down the woodcutter's trail. She slipped ahead of him, hunkered like a cat in a copse of pines until he came singing around the bend. As always, she timed her attack precisely to be certain that she would kill him before he could cry out."

"Did she get him?"

"Of course she did. But this time it was a bloody mess!" Luludja shook her head and hissed. "Despite all her efforts to cheat death, Old Berchta was growing old! She was not as strong or quick as she'd once been. This boy, he turned out to be a real feisty one, a little warrior, and he just gave Berchta fits with all his screaming, kicking, and biting. At last, she finally silenced him, as she always did, but it was a drawn-out, messy affair, with so much noise and blood all over the leaves and snow that she sensed she was in grave danger of being burned at the stake for her crime.

She would have to leave at once before the villagers could pick up her trail.

"So, she wrapped her few belongings in a blanket, slung it over her shoulder, and set off into the wilderness well ahead of her pursuers. But soon enough, they gave chase, and it became clear to Old Berchta, as week after week passed that she'd underestimated their commitment to arresting her, as for months, they gave chase with the most dogged persistence.

"Crossing the frozen highlands she began to grow weary. Her blood ran thin. Her old body was starting to slow down. It will happen to you too, one day. You will see. When the journey became to much to bear, Berchta collapsed in a highland pass and cried out in a desperate prayer to any and all who might hear her that she would give anything, anything at all in exchange for the chance to escape the humiliating end that awaited her at the hands of her pursuers. Well, if you make an evil prayer like that out in the wilderness, then you'd better be ready for whatever comes calling, because Old Berchta soon found herself blinking in disbelief at the horned forms of the Fates. They'd heard her prayer. And they'd come to make a trade for her eyes."

"Her eyes? Why'd they want her eyes for? Didn't they have no eyes of their own?"

"Oh, the Fates had eyes, to be sure. But it was a set of glass eyes upon a black velvet pillow, magical eyes that they wished to trade for hers. They burned upon the pillow with all the color and brightness of fire, fused as they were from the red sands of Hades. With those eyes, the Fates promised her, she would see the world as a demon does, see in the dark just like a cat; see the sins of others, and into the very souls of men. The Fates tantalized her with the treasures, tilting them to make them sparkle in the moonlight. And then, they offered her a spoon."

"A spoon? You mean to take out her own eyes? Did she do it?"

"Berchta?" Luludja snorted. "Of course she did."

"Oye! But with a spoon? A dull old spoon? Wouldn't that hurt?"

"Once she'd pushed her new eyes into the empty sockets, she marveled at the sight of the world all around her as a devil sees it!"

"What did it look like?"

"Shut up."

"Did she have--"

"Shut up. The Fates handed her a book, a silver medallion and a purse of boiled manhide. *The Book of Wurm*, they told her, could only be read with a devil's eyes. To all mortals, its pages would appear blank. All she'd need do was ask the book to reveal the whereabouts of anyone, anyplace, or anything she wished, and it would show her the way. The silver medallion of Icarus, they explained, would harness the winds and give Berchta the power of flight. With these tools, she could find her way to a sip--if eternal life was still what she desired--from the legendary Fountain of Youth, the very wellspring of immortality. Well, of course that excited her! And she found strength to rise again and set off with her new eyes, *The Book of Wurm*, and the magic purse, which was in fact a bottomless and weightless Sack of Shadows, with infinite space to store whatever she wished to ease her burden. Inside, she was pleased to find that the Fates had already been good enough to stock it with a mountain of food and drink that would never spoil, as well as a dozen children."

"Now, wait a minute. She got magic eyes, a magic book, a magic medallion for flying around like a bloody bird, and even a magic purse filled with food and things and all the Fates got out of the deal, was a couple of bloody eyeballs?"

"Not so quickly." Luludja cleared her throat. "There is nothing given for free in this world, or the next. The Fates had larger plans for her than she might've ever known. One of the Fates, the Incubusz, had designs to bring her into his harem of human brides. And how could Old Berchta refuse, what with the angry mob of villagers in such close pursuit? Of course she accepted, and a ring of lead he slipped upon her gnarled finger, and I'm afraid that you are too young to hear what came next, but on that frozen highland pass, let us to say that their dark union was well consummated."

"What's consummated?"

Luludja cleared her throat. "When it was over, Old Berchta used her new devil's eyes to move like a cat through the night, distancing herself from her pursuers until at last, the *Book of Wurm* led her to a cave. Back, back into the bowels of that cavern she crawled, until she penetrated the deepest and darkest chamber in perhaps all of the earth, and there she was shocked to find that she was not alone. There, in the darkness, colorless as a cave fish, squatted a man squinting in the dull glow of her devil's eyes, sensitive as he was from untold centuries estranged from the light of the sun. He introduced himself as Lazarus of Bethany."

"You mean the fellow who got raised from the dead?"

"Berchta was confused as to why the book had led her to this old hermit, when she'd asked it to lead her to the Fountain of Youth. But upon reopening the ancient volume, *The Book of Wurm* displayed a fantastic image! It was that of a headless Lazarus of Bethany, gilded and dazzling in Hindu repose, and from the stump of his neck, spouted a golden fountain of eternal life!"

"Lazarus himself ... he was the Fountain of Youth ... the magic was in his blood!"

"Mmm, but as Old Berchta withdrew her butchering blades and set upon him, torchlight filled the chamber with blinding light, setting Berchta's hellish eyes aglow, and making Lazarus scream in pain, for not a ray of light had he seen since moment of his reanimation. The mob had found them. Berchta was cornered. There was no escape."

"What happened?"

"Well, the mob attacked poor Lazarus, presuming him to be the murderer they'd long been tracking. Berchta, they dismissed as his haggard old whore. So she was made to watch as the angry villagers destroyed her lifelong obsession, beheading poor Lazarus right before her devil's eyes. Once every precious drop of his immortal blood had soaked into the soil, the mob turned on Berchta. The leader of the group, father of the last boy she'd killed on the woodcutter's trail, strode up to the old witch and ran his sword right through her heart. In another world, another realm, you might've heard the screams of the Fates, for their plans for Old Berchta had been spoiled."

"The mob killed her?"

"So it would seem. Her assassin put the sole of his boot upon her face and pushed her back off his sword, wiped the blade across her tunic. The mob taunted her as Old Berchta retched blood, dragging herself across the cave floor like a crushed cockroach in the direction of Lazarus's sad remains. In another world, another realm, you might've heard the Fates cheering her on, pleading that she receive but a drop of that blood on her tongue. She outstretched her claws for the soil saturated with his essence, but before she could touch it, the mob pulled her away by her ankles and stuffed her screaming inside her own sack, which was then tied shut, forevermore."

"But what about the deal she'd made with the Fates, to cheat death?"

"Say what you will about mischievous tricksters and the like, but they always keep their dark bargains. Although the deal rarely amounts to a mortal's hopes, a Fate always keeps his word. She'd been led to the Fountain of Youth, as promiscd."

"Now wait a moment." Krengel sat up in his bed. "What good did any that business do for anyone? Lazarus was murdered, Old Berchta destroyed, and the Fates lost their bride and whatever hopes they might've had for her, had she made it to the blood of Lazarus as they'd hoped. She exchanged her eyes for a sip from the wellspring of immortality, and married the Incubusz. She'd gone through all that trouble for a sip. And all for what? No one gained!"

"Well, I suppose that if you weren't so greedy and stupid, always looking for whatever is lacking, then it might've been clear to you that I was not yet finished with my story."

Krengel sniffed. He rubbed his nose across the back of his hand, and then sat quietly until Luludja continued.

"The magic purse in which the mob bagged her, the same given her by the Fates, had upon it a curse that protected its infinite inner space and all of its contents from the passage of time, hence the mountain of food inside that would never spoil, and all the living things trapped inside that would never age. Nothing inside the Sack of Shadows ever aged, nor could it ever die. You could say that it was a parcel of Purgatory, and so long as Old Berchta remained inside, she would remain immortal. But if she ever dared set foot outside the sack, even for an instant, she would fall over dead from a skewered heart, and no doubt, some devil would be waiting to snatch up her soul. So, the Fates did in fact keep their promise. She received her eternal life, though not in the way that she or the Fates had hoped. You could say that her winnings amounted to an eternity spent waiting at Hell's gates."

"What about the magic blood of Lazarus? The cure for eternal life? What about the magic book and the Icaraus Medallion? Are they all still there inside that cave? Where is the cave, I wonder?" Krengel stood and reached for the fringed scabbard that always dangled from his bedpost. He withdrew the wooden sword and slashed at the darkness, jumping up and down on his bed. "I should like to find that cave myself some day, drink it up and live forever and ever!"

"Sit down!" Luludja barked. "You, so fat you barely fit in your braies! I'm afraid you wouldn't last but an instant, if you dared step a hair's breadth outside the borders of Christendom. You and your kind are only so bold within the walls of your guarded estates. But much beyond Lambsheim's towers, you're just a newborn sheep in a world of wolves."

Krengel sat with an indignant grunt. He scowled and rubbed his thumb along the wooden blade, glowering hotly at the servant woman through the corner of his eye.

"No one knows whatever became of those items that Old Berchta dropped during her struggle. Some say the mob scavenged every trinket. Others say they dared not touch any of it. They quit that cave at once, for they sensed within it a terrible evil. And still others say that many years later, the tomb of Lazarus was rediscovered by a traveling man of the cloth, who collected buried poor Lazarus's bones and blessed the site before taking with him the book, the medallion, and the sack. No one knows what became of them, for sure. Like so many great legends from the Age of Miracles and Magic, the choice is yours, what to believe, and what to dismiss as folly."

"What do you believe, Miss Luludja? What do you think became of the treasures, and the Sack of Shadows with Old Berchta trapped inside it?"

"Shhh." Luludja tapped a finger against her lips and shook her head slowly from side to side. "The story is finished. Best you never speak of Old Berchta again, because some dangers are uncomfortably close, little Klaas."

"How do you know so much, anyhow?" Krengel pointed the tip of his wooden sword at Luludja's throat. "You're nothing but a servant." Krengel could see the shine of Luludja's teeth by the light of the small candle that flickered upon his nightstand. Or was that her eyes? With one finger, she pushed his sword away.

"As so many naughty children just like you have learned through the ages, wherever light does not shine, there is always Old Berchta, watching you, not an arm's reach away."

"But you said she couldn't ever leave the Sack of Shadows, or she'll fall right over dead from her sword wound."

"She needn't leave her sack to reach you, Klaas." Luludja rocked in her chair and smiled, disappearing and reappearing in the candlelight. "She lives in the darkness between moments, and darkness is darkness from one world to the next. From between moments, her devil's eyes can always see you once the candles are blown." Luludja reached for the candle on the nightstand, raised it to her lips, and blew out the tiny flame. In an instant, her face disappeared. "Yes, she is looking at you right now, in fact. And when the time is right, she will reach through the darkness, take a fistful of your hair, and drag you screaming out of your world and into hers!"

Krengel lilted over the platter of venison, paralyzed by the painful memory of Luludja lunging across his bed and grabbing a fistful of his curls. She'd hissed into his ear that she refused to be bullied by a spoiled Lambsheim brat at the end of her long day of toil, at the only hour that remained of every day kept apart from her daughter. She then assured him that bedtime stories were officially finished, and if he dared report her, then she would see to it that something very real would come and visit him in the night.

Some dangers are uncomfortably close, little Klaas.

Of course, he'd believed her.

What a story to tell a five-year-old boy, whose own Mother had never once visited his bedside at dusk, never once kissed him goodnight. What a thing to inflict upon a child abandoned to the darkness at birth, to condemn him to years of night terrors. And for what? For simply speaking up, pointing out the fact that she'd been deceiving him, cheating him out of minutes of the only time he could ever hope to snuggle close to a motherly figure at the end of each day?

When Luludja left his bedroom chamber, the vibrations began. Tremors, nearly audible, pulsed rhythmically through every inch of his body, as the presence of his Forever Friend began to ooze forth from somewhere deep in his core, like the blackest heartwood sap from the innermost rings of a malformed tree. It was coming. Summoned by the feelings of anxiety, inadequacy. The counterpart. The evil twin. The anti-Klass. And this time, it was targeting little Lala.

Krengel released the hem of his tunic. It floated back to his knees. Four years, he'd spared her. Four years since that night her mother inflicted so much undeserved pain. Lala had done him no wrong but to love his enemy, her mother, and to receive her love back, in turn. She was innocent. She'd deserved no mistreatment, but the Krampusz would not relent. He was nothing if not persistent. There was no sanctuary from his daily barrage of lewd suggestions, inventive ways of humiliating her, new means of ushering little Lala into the same world of nightmares into which the girl's mother had so forcefully thrust him. Lala was not a victim, his Forever Friend assured him; she was but a perfect device that offered some leverage with which Luludja's injustice could finally be righted.

Krengel stared down through pooled urine at his own reflection on the venison platter. Despite the bathers' efforts, black circles of ash still hollowed his eyes. The pain in his head no longer throbbed, dulled by two goblets of metheglin, but a great goose egg of a lump remained. He wagged his head back and forth, examining his distorted countenance from various angles. The brutish face in the platter, disfigured by piss and sin, looked positively inhuman. And then another face appeared, red-hooded and bearded, leering right behind his own.

A massive arm hooked around Krengel's neck before he could scream, dragging him backwards off the counter. His heels plowed ruts through spilt pottage, smearing piss and pudding over the planks with thrashing kicks. There was an explosion of rabbit pottage. A goblet bounced across the floor. Krengel gasped for a breath as he was pulled off the table and into the air, feet flailing, as he swung by his neck in the crook of a locked elbow.

"You shouldn't have touched her."

Sour breath, heady with ale, steamed the blade of an eager dagger jammed up beneath his chin. He could feel the point of it tenting the inside of his throat. The stranger lugged him toward a row of open livestock barrels, topless, and shimmering. Krengel arched his back and clawed at an arm so unyielding, it might've been carved out of oak.

"You thought there would be no consequences if you attacked one of our children in the woods?" the stranger hissed into his ear. "You think you have the right to abuse us because you were born more fortunate than we?"

Krengel's tongue protruded through grimacing teeth. He began to feel dizzy, faint. Tremendous blood pressure was building up inside his head. It felt as though his skull was about to explode and paint the kitchen walls with something of minnow pie. His legs kicked weakly, like a frog impaled on a fish hook.

"We are the walls and the trees. Our ears hear the unkind words that you speak. Our thousand eyes witness every trespass you commit against our kind. Are you starting to understand now? We outnumber you. We surround you. We know when you are sleeping, and we know when you're awake. We know when you've been bad, and ohhh, you've been so very, very naughty, little Klaas."

The stranger seized him by the nape of his neck and bent him over the rim of a livestock barrel. Krengel gawped down into the bulging eyes of his reflection upon the surface of the brine, purple-tongued and flushed as a roasted piglet. Over his shoulder, hovered the face of the bearded stranger, the harbinger of death. One of his father's finest coats was draped over the assassin's shoulders, boasting brilliant crimson in honor of the Habsburg flag, exquisitely trimmed in snowy ermine. Stolen, no doubt, right off the racks of his father's exorbitant wardrobe. The beard, pale and wiry as a denuded thistle in the dead of winter, split in a terrible rictus-grin of rotten and missing teeth. If there were any eyes at all beneath that hood, they were lost in the swath of darkness.

Krengel gaped down, through the reflections to the bottom of the barrel, where knots of eels writhed as if eagerly anticipating the arrival of new company. Perhaps it was the lack of blood flow to his head, but the whole process of being murdered hardly seemed real, almost dreamlike in a way. Was this a joke? Would he really be joining those eels soon?

The assassin pushed hard, forcing Krengel's head lower into the barrel. Concentric rings expanded from the tip of Krengel's nose as it lit upon the water. Its coldness seemed to snap him back into reality. The fight for life surged back into him. He growled and wrenched back against the steely hands of his killer, but his efforts were so futile. The man who had hold of him was clearly a product of the lower class, forged into a work of iron from years and years of backbreaking toil. Krengel was accustomed to supple skin and polished nails, but the fingers of this brute were like great calloused sausages round his throat. The power in his hands was unfathomable.

Another forceful shove from behind and his snout dipped beneath the surface. Krengel choked, twisting his head to the side and spitting brine. His ear went under, muting half the ambient sounds, joined by half his face. He cried out for the first time since the attack began, then completely under. Back up again, sucking breaths through the side of his mouth, clinging to the barrel's rim, he tried to make a plea, to bargain with his murderer. Only a mewling burble escaped his lips before his head was forced under, and he could not bring it back up again.

A rhythmic chugging accompanied the threshing of eels, the ripple of bubbles from his nostrils, ringing in his ears. His veins burned. The tempo increased to a static vibration that pulsed through Krengel's drowning body from head to toe. Eel fins slapped his face and cheeks. He could hear the knocking, the banging, and the insistent drumming of his Forever Friend on the other side of the door. Wanting in. Raging at the gates for another chance to pull Krengel through from one world into another, to enable his escape from yet another of life's terrible moments. The demon's bellow resounded through every channel of Krenegl's brain with all the timbre of a war horn, vast and portentous, calling all soldiers to battle in a great war for Sundaloon.

Chapter Fourteen

The crabs advanced in garish legions across the battlefield. Each weighing no more than a biscuit, they gained ground between waves, resolute in what seemed an impossible resistance against the might of Mother Earth, herself. Armed only with crimson pinchers to ward off the diving seabirds, to shield them against pulverizing waves, they appraised the birds and thundering breakers through glistening eyestalks with what seemed some calculating aspect of intelligence. They coolly assessed the kinetic tonnage of the next ship-crushing blow, the speed of each plunging shorebird, and to each threat, they reacted, but they did not run. They never ran. Even as the curling wave loomed over them until it blocked out the light of the sun, gathering sand, substrate, and all things in its path with an elemental roar of wind inhaled through streaming seagrass like an oath of leagues deep and fathoms vast, amassing all the ocean's energy to deliver focused upon them like the down-stroke of a stupendous battle axe.

In the face of the oncoming breaker, a night heron spiraled down over the foam and lit shivering upon a rise. It surveyed the receding surf through hysterical yellow eyes, spotted something of interest, and loped drunkenly through the jungle of cockles and crags. Slowing, tiptoeing through the shadow of the plummeting wave, the bird struck out like a viper to snatch a crab from the foam, turning, goose-stepping, rising at once on heaving wings through the deafening roar, climbing, climbing, only to stall for unclear reasons at the wave's crest, twiggy legs kicking, spearhead shaking side to side as if it could not believe some bit of bad news it had just received, when the breaker snatched the shorebird out of the sky.

It disappeared, and then reappeared, a tumbling mass in the seething amalgam. Dark and disheveled, feathers sparse and vacillating, its carcass was cast upon the beach like a gruesome message to others of its kind. One night heron destroyed. One crab still attached released a death-grip across the bridge of the heron's beak. It was a pinch sufficient to rupture both of its predator's golden eyes. Unaffected by the glory of its victory against incalculable odds, the toy soldier crawled from the mouth of the heron and marched off to rejoin its legion, as another wave came thundering in.

All crabs flattened before the breaker, adjusting the angle of armored platelets, withdrawing eyestalks, gripping pumice rock with cherry-red claws. They bore down. They held fast. They clung to rocks and held through the scouring sandblast of seawater and stone, tumbling aggregate and shells, enduring all Mother Earth could muster, while waiting patiently, holding tightly, holding formation, holding their breath, until at last, the forward momentum depleted and the waters receded in a slithering carpet of foam. The toy soldiers rose bubbling from sandy foxholes and marched on.

"Look, ye. Look all about ye, Fat Brother, and see how it's done. Watch a pecker gnat stand up and whup the dog."

The crabs, and for that matter, all life on Sundaloon possessed the ability to endure, to withstand unending punishment. For what choice does a toy soldier have but to endure, when the might of his opponent is immeasurably greater? What defense can one so small adopt in the face of a looming enemy but one of endurance, until the last possible moment when a subtle shift of one's body might minimize the brunt of impact? When you're small, you must at least possess the fortitude to take a hit, because quite often you will have to do so. Anticipate the oncoming force and adjust yourself by whatever means to survive the blast, to welcome the pain that will inevitably follow. And when it is finished, you will rise. You will rise and follow. You will wait until the time is right and retaliate with a well-placed shot to the eyes, to the groin, to the chink in the juggernaut's armor.

"Feller's got you is big as all daylights, Fat Brother. Aim to butt heads with this one, might as well be trying to push a rope. Just let him have his go with ye. Let him drown ye. Let him reckon he's got ye killed."

Krengel would stay here on Sundaloon for a moment longer. Just waiting. Apart from death. Apart from the pain he knew would be waiting for him, back on the flipside of things. He would wait it out, because a murderous servant would not likely linger long at the scene of his crime, not in the house of his sleeping master. He's apt to flee the scene, yes, perhaps a bit prematurely, wild-eyed with guilt and fear, as he quits the terrible sight of a drowned child in a livestock barrel, heart hammering, tramping back up the stone staircase and out into the starlit forest. Whoever he was, he will not likely ever return to Lambsheim again.

"They's going to be others where he come from, huh. You bet ye. Once they see you ain't been killed for what ye done. Hell's got no scorn like a gypsy's revenge, Fat Brother. They's going to keep raising sand and you can better well bank on it. 'Til they get you killed, leastways."

The Krampusz had a point. Even if he managed to survive the assassination attempt in the kitchen, the servants could soon send another. There were so many of them all around the Habsburg-Krengel estate, working in the fields, the bakeries. Hundreds of potential assassins. They would follow him. They would find him alone in the woods. They would slip into his bedchamber once he'd fallen asleep.

"Ain't nowhere's in Lamsheim is safe for ye. Not no more."

But where will I go?

"With the Elves. A choir's passing through town, on the morrow. Choir of orphans, run by a blind feller. They are going past your gates midmorning. Best ye be there at the gates, in waiting, and don't ye dare let no one stop ye from going. Anyone tries, scream so loud they's apt to hear you in the New World. Don't ye dare muck this one up, Fat Brother. This here's the spot where it all begins."

Although he could not see the Krampusz, nor physically feel his touch, Krengel perceived the warmth of his Forever Friend's presence as something of an arm around his shoulders. But it wasn't much consolation. He'd never felt so small, so ghostly thin. The ocean had never looked so vast, so ominous. Miss Luludja had been right about him, four years ago. He was only brave within the walls of his guarded estate.

"Don't ye worry none, Fat Brother. Ain't nothing terrible's going to befall ye."

Chapter Fifteen

Simple lanterns constructed of bottles filled with luminescent mold swayed from pikes and saddle tethers that flagged each numbaec in the caravan. Tinkling fitments also adorned the hulking beasts, perhaps as a secondary means of locating them in the blackness should their lamps ever dim. They lumbered in total silence, but for the occasional popping hiss from an anatomical point of origin that was difficult to determine, and the tinkling of fitments that adorned the hulking beasts for the purpose of locating the animals in the blackness, should their lamps ever dim. Their march produced an enchanting music of jingling chimes that became a gentle constant, not unlike the ebb of river bottom sand. The beasts' mouths did not appear to be designed for any sort of vocalization, stuffed as they were with an assortment of delicate spoons, spades, and segmented fingers that fiddled anxiously between the upturned points of massive horns that flanked either side of their broad, flattened heads. Like a great collar, a thoracic shield swept back over the creatures' necks and shoulders to double their formidable frontal defenses. So far as Krengel could discern, this offered the numbaecs protection against head-on clashes with others of their kind. Thus far, he'd witnessed no violent tendencies in the beasts. They seemed quite docile. But many were badly scarred and chipped all about their armored carapaces.

"Do they fight? The numbaecs?" Krengel looked over Hiley's shoulder, watching her work the light reigns affixed to her numbaec's delicate mandible spades. Their mouthparts were evidently highly sensitive organs, because her animal responded to her most subtle slights-of-hand. It was interesting to observe such a hulking monster controlled by a girl holding little more than a pair of strings.

"Nah," Hiley replied, "unless a boar gets between an ol' sow and her grubs. Then, she'll just get to pushing him 'til she flips him on over. That's about as mean as they'll ever get."

"They all look so scarred, as if from fighting in great battles."

"They get those mostly from whistling sagra. We'll run into them sometimes up here, but mostly, you got to watch out for them down on the veldt."

"What are sagra?"

"They're like a … well; they ain't like anything else, really. They let out a smell, upwind of you, a sort of chemical that knocks you stupid. Numbaecs, anyhow. Gets them drunker than a keg of moonshine. Once they start to stagger around, whistling sagra move in." Hiley hooked the air with her index finger and made a glottal sound. "Stick them with their big ol' fang, folds up on the underside of their hood, like this. Guess it's kind of tough to explain a sagra 'til you seen one for yourself. Big strong arms and paws. Long skinny head. Big ol' yeller eyes. Bushy tail. Stink. Gawd, but they stink. Trouble is, once you smell them it's too late. Means they already done gassed your herd."

"But it doesn't affect people?"

"Not humans."

"Why not humans?"

"Cause humans ain't from here, Mr. Silly Pants."

"What difference does that make?"

"Makes all the difference in the dadgummed world. You're a god down here, Klaas Krengel. Didn't you know that?"

"I beg your pardon?"

"A living god. How's it feel? You're between moments in time. You won't never get sick, won't never grow old, and you sure as heck won't never die. In the eyes of the natives, you're a living god amongst them. Some will treat you like a god, too. But others, they'll treat you like you're the devil."

"Natives?"

"Just like anywheres. You got your naturals living here and your immigrants. We're the immigrants. Soon enough, you will meet the natives. But first, you've got to meet the Ike Man. Welcome to city of Iptintec, Klaas Krengel, capital of the Midlands."

Hiley snapped the thin reigns, and as their numbaec lurched around a bend in the mountain road, Krengel gasped at the brilliance of Iptintec, radiating from a bleak promontory that jutted over the Molithe Valley. Below, a river stained as if by the blackest well of ink, mirrored skyward a flawless rendition of the glowing city. Set aglow by tethered blimps of sodium gas, the strange skyline was a cloistered and swooning collection that appeared conjured from the earth, perhaps by the will of some Druidian sorcerer, writhing like fungi in the blackness, bow-stemmed, top-heavy and impossible, reeling in drunken defiance against all likelihood of intelligent design, against every physical law and platitude.

Sprays of the ubiquitous blue bioluminescence splashed the walls of the understory, waning yellow at elevations nearer the crackling yellow phosphorescence of the sodium blimps, which were set at varying heights to prevent collision, evidently, and looming like a clutch of moons lilting gently on their tethers. Higher, glimpses of the segmented underbellies of mauna gobas could be discerned passing in and out of visibility, circling the city, trailing their fountains of iridescent fibers through the lamplight like the nets of fishing vessels. Beautiful and deadly, the enormous creatures swooped near enough the skyline to capture the swarms of glittering life gathered there, yet maintained a respectful distance from the blimps, which perhaps served some secondary purpose as a deterrent to these leviathans that danced upon waves of light.

"Are there people here, like us?" Krengal asked.

"You betcha there's people. This is home, Sugar. All the humans live here."

"It looks like Atlantis!" Krengel exclaimed, gripping Hiley tightly around her waist. "At least, how I'd imagine Atlantis to be, teeming with friendly whales and all."

"Guess them damn mauna gobas do look kinder pretty from a distance, don't they?"

"They're beautiful."

Important creatures, though once reviled and shot down for sport, Hiley explained, the mauna gobas were hunted nearly to extinction before human immigrants to the Quick were made to understand that their regular flight patterns were the only measure of passing time, dependable as a rising and setting sun. Even the bioluminescent polyps and mold, timed their activity around the patterns of these clockwork predators, resulting in definite periods of brightness and lightlessness that were similar enough to the earthly cycle of day and night, as to help preserve the sanity of the human immigrants.

"They can only float around for so long before they all got to head back to the river and digest what all they've eaten, recharge their lift gases. Ye ever see one all deflated you wouldn't hardly know what it was."

"Why did you save me, back there on the mountaintop?" Krengel asked. His chin bounced lightly against Hiley's shoulder. "If what you said is true that humans are gods down here, and we'll never die, then what harm could've possibly come to me from that mauna goba?"

"I never said you was indestructible, Sugar."

"But now you're being contradictory."

"No, I ain't. You're a god, like I said, in the eyes of the Naturals, anyway, 'cause you won't never grow old, get sick, or die." Hiley turned, putting them nose to nose. "But that ain't to say someone can't walk right up and lop off your head."

"So, I can be killed, but I won't naturally die."

"You still ain't getting it. You won't never die, and you can't be killed, but you can darned sure be permanently disabled." Hiley clicked her tongue and lifted a reign by the tip of her index finger, drawing her numbaec close to the mountain wall.

Nearing the open gates, a cacophony of instruments filled the air in a jangling of a million canorous voices. The discordance of competing chimes was a ruckus sufficient to guide wayward travelers many leagues through the blackness and toward the city from across the Molithe Valley, beyond even the Midland

Mountains to those vast and deadly plains to which Hiley referred as the Paux Veldt.

Krengel's hands rose reflexively to cover his ears as they passed between the towers and into the deafening crash of noise. He gritted his teeth and winced, squinting up at the withered husks of people thrust up on pikes on either side of the road, twisted by the mummifying vacuum in which they eternally rotted, highlighted by the glowing mold that set their tenantless sockets afire in lilting skulls of curious shape. Krengel's eyes widened and his hands unclasped from his ears. The remains were not human. They were something else.

Despite all he'd been told about this realm, his rational mind had on some level clung to the fallacy that everything in the Quick had originated from the other side. The numbaecs, the mauna gobas, they were all creatures he thought had arisen from a stock of common beetles and things. Perhaps they were once things crawling on the floor of the cave of Lazarus. Or, perhaps, they began as tiny forms offloating life in the air, too small to be seen by the naked eye. It was possible that life such as this could be attracted to the scent of so much garbage wafting from the cinched opening of the Sack of Shadows and once trapped here, became gradually distorted to a size and shape more befitting the new and timeless niche. But those things impaled; they were not of earth, and they never had been. Krengel gaped crosswise into one of the elongated alien faces with batty ears, festooned with shriveled barbells about its parched mouth.

The jangling chimes all subsided at once into one unharmonious tone, as if the whole explosion of sound had been one to mark their entrance, or perhaps to mark the hour, like the bells of Bari. Only the trundling tonnage of numbaecs upon the grit of Iptintec's streets could be heard, as their caravan passed into the shadows of the arched and swooning structures that looked to have been frozen in motion, as they'd writhed up naturally from somewhere far below, like giant lava tubes from the sea bottom. High above the massive whorls, mauna gobas drifted through the ethereal glow of sodium blimps.

"All this is built on sodium," Hiley said, explaining that the city of Iptintec was designed and built by an ancient and extirpated race that had once flourished in the Quick. "Regular table salt's how it starts out, mined yonder in the foothills over the Veldt. Bring it in by numbaec and barge to the trams, where it's augured up to the electrolysis plant and gets distilled into pure sodium. That gets weaponized, traded as currency, and converted to light up yonder by them transformers. All from salt. You can sprinkle it on a steak, use it to light up your kitchen, or blow the roof clean off your house."

Krengel sat quietly, his arms around Hiley's waist. He understood precious little of Hiley's cheery dissertation, but he was boggled by the hidden possibilities unearthed by Iptintec's alchemists from a pinch of ordinary table salt. "What happened to them? The ones who built this place?"

"The Naturals? They're still here, relivin' their version of the Stonc Age. Those are the tribes I was telling you about. The Pancha, Wyanoc, Yibrasaw, Iridede … trouble is, when you got but one resource, sodium, makes you pretty easily whupped if someone sets their mind to whuppin' you. And that's pretty much what happened to the ancient Imbajaw when the witch landed here, by turning the Naturals against one another."

"The witch!" Krengel leaned back away from Hiley and groaned, smearing his hands down his face.

"What?"

"Honestly, a bloody witch? A bloody witch in a sack?"

"Would this place be any less weird if there wasn't one? Don't know what to tell you, Sugar. She's a fact of life down here, and a pretty big one."

"You don't understand. I know this story! By God, but do I ever know it! It's haunted me my whole life and you're telling me that it's real? It's really real? The legend of Old Berchta? I never believed it." He shook his head furiously from side to side. "I did, but I didn't. I couldn't! Badly as it scared me, I just couldn't!"

"Better get to believing it."

"But if she was imprisoned here after the assassination of Lazarus, then she couldn't have been down here for more than fifteen-hundred years. But you speak of her as being the destroyer of some bloody ancient world down here. How is that even possible?"

"I haven't the foggiest idea what you're talking about, Lazarus and all, but I'll tell ye, someone might could go missing into the Quick for a year, flipside time, but that year might amount to a million years down here. Time's relative. You're between moments. Lord knows how long I been down here, prob'ly a hundred years or better, and shit, I ain't hardly aged, far as I can tell."

"A hundred years? That's impossible. I'm from an earlier time than you, and I haven't been down here but a few weeks. It doesn't make sense!"

"Makes sense down here. Quick is the Quick. Time passed down here ain't got no relationship whatsoever to the time's passed upstairs, because time upstairs ain't hardly even passing. Not much, anyhow."

"But you said yourself that some of the other children down here were kids you knew from back home, kids who fell through later. Clearly, time is still passing by on the flipside."

"Look, the hour that you left home is an hour you left back at home. Folks might could be falling through from the past, present, or future, but your hour will still be waiting for you if you ever leave here, just the way you came. Down here, you're on Quick Time, where a minute means forever, and there ain't no one's been down here longer than the witch."

"The bloody witch in the sack." Krengel threw up his hands. "Not in all these years has the Krampusz ever once mentioned a word about a witch!"

"Well, he wouldn't have, or you'd likely not have been so quick to go along with all his schemes, if you'd knowed this place was where you was headed."

"If I'd known back then what I know now, you could bloody well be sure I wouldn't have heeded a word of his raving!"

Krengel thought of all the pieces that had so carefully been dropped into place, from coercing his attack on the girl in the woods, to his unwilling stewardship in Bari, losing every last thing he'd ever known and loved along the way, only to end with being trapped forever in a sack on the desert island of Sundaloon. Sundaloon … funny, how badly he now longed to be there, after having so intensely deplored that island in the months after crash-landing into its briar thickets. It's harsh and barren landscapes deprived of pleasures, devoid of people, were now remembered after a short time in the Sack of Shadows as a tropical paradise teeming with life and sunshine. In much the same way, his feelings toward Lambsheim had waxed toward fondness after departing with the choir, and how terribly he'd missed the same choir of orphans he'd come to abhor once he'd been shuttled to Bari, which seemed not so sterile a place at all after being transported to Sundaloon. Albeit in retrospective, he was aroused to notice that he'd learned to appreciate the value of people and places that had once seemed valueless. It was the ever-increasing levels of depravation to which he'd been exposed that had gradually exacted some sort of a change in him, one that helped him to appreciate what he had, versus obsessing over that which he lacked. Perhaps there was something yet to find appreciable in this place, the worst place of all. Because, God forbid, he be cast into a worse hole than this one in order to reveal its merits by contrast.

Hiley swiveled in the saddle. "Look, I know you're upset, but there's two sorts of people you'll meet down here, Sugar. You'll meet the kind who's bent on missing home and escaping this place--and believe you me, steer clear of them sorts, or they'll drag you right on down with them--and then, you've got another sort who's sat down and thought it all through, and decided that come what may, the Quick really ain't such bad a place to call home."

"… are you mad?"

"Maybe so. But here, you're forever young, without no worries over food or water or scraping by to make some kind of a living. Won't never starve. Won't never have to work no sorry job to pay the rent. And won't never get old and sick and waste away. Death can't never trouble you no more, down here. You been given the gift of eternal life! Use it. Make some real forever-friends. Fall in love with your true soul mate, without the ol' clock ticking. My philosophy is pretty simple: you either let the darkness make you crazy, or you string it up with lights!"

Krengel pondered Hiley's angle. If he lived down here a thousand years, he'd theoretically return to the same stitch in time from which he'd departed, still just as young in age, yet wizened beyond words for all he'd learned and experienced during his extended holiday. He wasn't on life's borrowed time anymore. This was extra time. Time for introspection. Personal development. Training … but for what?

Krengel drew in a heavy breath, purely out of habit, since he no longer had any physical need to breathe. It was a strange existence, dreamlike. Like being underwater, or in a new womb, awaiting rebirth. He emptied his dead lungs, relinquishing the useless bit of air back to the vacuum from which it had been borrowed. He felt like a living ghost.

"I won't ever eat down here?" he said. "Not ever again?" Krengel thought of minnow pies with a flakey lard crust, warm apple strudel, and steaming bowls of cinnamon pottage. How could he not despair the loss of his last remaining pleasure, his last and dearest love of all, like the others, stripped meanly away. It made him want to scream.

"You can eat if you want to. If you like the feel of a brick swinging in your gut." Hiley snorted. "We've all done it, in the beginning. Hard not to want to try and do something that feels so natural, at first. But, you'll live to regret it, if you do it."

"Why?"

"Food you eat just don't go nowhere. Just sits there, festering in your belly. Damned unpleasant. Especially if you eat something natural, something from here. It'll spoil. It'll rot and ferment right there inside your belly, and swell you like a poisoned pup with the worst gas you've ever smelled, until you finally decide to go ahead and bring it on back up." Hiley wriggled an index finger before her open mouth. "But it don't seem like you'll ever get it all out. Takes days and days of drinking water and flushing it out, over and over again, 'til your breath starts smelling right again. Trust me; you'll learn not to do it after going through all that business a time or two."

"But the Naturals can eat. The numbaecs. The whistling sagras. And the witch."

"Yeah, but the witch ain't a Natural. She's from the flipside, just like us."

"But you said she devours children."

"Oh, she does."

"But if she eats, then wouldn't she have to …"

Hiley nodded and wriggled her index finger. "The Naturals can't speak our language, and we can't even try to speak theirs, but we've taught more than a few of them to write. The stories they've written about that place … land, ho … say she sits all alone at the end of a great long table. Servant on her right keeps a glass rod on a velvet pillow. One on the left holds a silver basin."

"But why …"

"'Cause she's evil incarnate. A kinder evil like you ain't never seen."

Stable hands with catch-poles appeared without greeting or affect, as Hiley's caravan neared the gates of the municipal stables. The hands approached with profound disinterest, looping nooses lacadasically around the numbaecs' mandibles and leading them by their poles into a great corral. At its center, a terrible showdown could be discerned through the billowing dust, between an unruly numbaec and a seemingly suicidal wrangler. Equipped only with a whistle and a catchpole, the lad invited the ludicrous mismatch with every jab of his loop in the enraged monster's face. The beast tossed its head and reared, returning to the ground with a thunderous impact and eruption of dust, met only by another poke and a cheep from the herder's whistle. This time, the looped end dropped over a mandible and the wrangler pulled taut, directing the titan's forward momentum round and round him in a circle, in a trot reminiscent of a horse near breaking.

The corral was fenced by a low mud wall that seemed unfit to contain the might of creatures of such stupendous size. The wall looked to be constructed by the same primitive methods and materials as all the buildings in Iptintec, smoothed to a slick and rounded finish as if by a thousand patting hands.

At the back end, uncovered stalls ill-lit by the usual sodium lights segregated the various life stages of the numbaec. Clutches of elliptical eggs neighbored low pens of hatchlings, blanched, and rippling grubs with button eyes and translucent skin that clambered and rolled over one another in their effort to have a turn at what seemed an undersized feed trough brimming with a curdled yellow paste. Heaped pupae in another, solemn and nutty brown, shifted the pile with their larval twitching like a litter of dreaming dogs. All movement halted as a great shadow spilled across the corral, when a mauna goba passed beneath a tethered sodium blimp, and gradually resumed once the sky devil had floated on.

Hiley dismounted. She shouldered her sodium musket and approached the stable hand who led her beast by its mandible. She took hold of the pole. "I got this. Why don't you go and tell Ike Man that we got him. Santy Klaas."

Krengel slid off the back of the numbaec. He met the inquisitive stare of the herder with a defensive surliness that he could neither justify nor explain. The stable hand smeared the back of his hand beneath his nose, nodded, turned, and sauntered off in the direction of the wrangler at the center of the corral.

"I wish you'd stop calling me that." Krengel hotly recalled his last night in Rome, the taunts from the leering Inquisitor, the taking of the Gottlieb sisters, the death of Friar Otto. The very sound of that cruel nickname ringing in his ears immediately recalled every detail of the terrifying and humiliating ordeal.

"I'm sorry, Sugar," Hiley said, "didn't know it bothered you. That's the name the Ike Man gave me when he paid me to find you and haul you in." Hiley hitched her chin at the distant wrangler, who was now conferring with the stable hand. Both boys were looking over in their direction.

"That's him?" Krengel asked, with a twinge of irritation cracking his voice.

"Yup. That's Ike Man."

Krengel's head whipped back around in the direction of the approaching figure, filthy and ragged, cheeks streaked with phosphorescent blue mold. "But I presumed him to be the king."

"The king?" Hiley snorted. "Ain't no kings or queens in Iptintec. Folks around here wouldn't have it. Guess we got our dignitaries, but ain't no leader to speak of. Round here, you're on your own."

"He paid you?"

"Course he paid me. Dozen sodium slugs, for starters. Wouldn't risk my danged neck out there for nothing."

The wrangler strode up to them, barefoot and threadbare in his sackcloth tunic. He glowered at Krengel through matted bangs, and then spat into the dust at their feet. "So, where did you find him?" His face split into a lopsided loutish grin. "Clinging to the bottom of the staircase, no doubt, crying like a motherless child?"

Krengel sucked in a gasp of recognition. He covered his mouth, lowered his hands, and then covered his mouth again. "Ludolph?" he whispered, stepping forward, a wide smile of disbelief spreading across his face. "Ludolph Eichmann? Of course! Ike Man!"

"Actually, no," Hiley replied. "He'd made it on his own all the way to the summit."

"Then the trip took half as long as you'd estimated," Ludolph said, his eyes flicking from Hiley to Krengel, and back again. A half-dozen stable hands drifted in and settled to either side of Ludolph Eichmann.

"Price is the same."

"Does he have it on him?" Ludolph narrowed his eyes.

Hiley shrugged. "Check and see for yourself."

"You mean you brought him all this way without even bothering to check and see if he had it?"

"Payment was a dozen slugs to find him and bring him in. Dozen more upon delivery."

"I don't give a damn about this brat!" Ludolph jabbed a finger at Krengel like a catch-pole in the face of a numbaec. Motes of spittle flew from his lips and sparkled in the sodium light. "I want the myrrh!" He seized Krengel by two fistfuls of ragged tunic. "Have you got it on you or not?"

"Y-yes," Krengel said, nodding in disbelief.

"Good!" Ludolph shoved loose of him, sending Krengel back a couple of steps. Ludolph nodded to one of the stable hands, the biggest fellow, with a web of scars around his throat. "Give the lady her fireworks."

The boy unfastened a rope belt around his waist to remove a bulging purse. He loosened the thong and spread the folds, then handed the bag over to Hiley. She pawed around inside, seemed satisfied, and nodded back at Ludolph. "Pleasure doing business with you." She cinched the bag tightly, looped the thong around her belt, turned, and walked away.

Krenegl watched her go with some measure of panic. Something about the situation didn't feel so very right. He'd at first felt so pleased to find Ludolph, a familiar face, if not a friendly one, bound through life experience. But it seemed to him that their old hatred of one another had inexplicably worsened, in what must have been more than a year of separation.

Ludolph extended his filthy hand, beckoning with fluttering fingers. He flipped his bangs with a toss of his head. "Give it to me."

Krengel's gaze swept the hardened faces of the other stable hands, who for whatever reason, appeared loyal to this bully who'd somehow been first to invade this realm and establish himself. He was clearly at a disadvantage and outnumbered. Just like before. Just like always. Krengel locked eyes with Ludolph as his slipped his hand down the front of his braes. He retrieved the tarnished flask that had for so many months been sloshing around down there, and he dropped it in the dirt at Ludolph's feet.

Ludolph allowed that sordid grin of bestial complacence to creep across his face. "You all know who he is, don't you?" Ludolph pointed at Krengel, turning round to his cohorts and shouting loud enough so everyone in the corral might hear him. "The only one who could've delivered us the holy myrrh; he is the reason that all of you are trapped here. This lad! Santa Klaas! Hailing from an earlier time than the rest of you, but conveniently. Oh, but I know this fellow so very, very well." Ludolph circled him, grinning maniacally. Something terrible gleamed in his eyes. Dozens of people emerged from the stables and stalls. They began to wander up and gawp at the scene.

"Here stands the fraud who ruined our lives. Fraud, I say! Not because he's the first to have befriended the monster that damned you to this living Hell -- and make no mistake, I have seen it, brothers and sisters! I've seen the place where the monster's foul name was etched into stone behind the very house where they were shat upon the earth, side by side." Ludolph wagged his head up and down. "Krengel and the Krampusz. Twin seeds of evil sowed by the same stud, one through the loins of a demeaned household servant, and the other from the blood of the witch, herself, delivered to the other side in the sting of a captured bee." Ludolph spun on a heel and whipped one finger up into the air. "But only one of these half-brothers is a true Habsburg heir. The other, I'm afraid, is a fraud. A lovechild. A common bastard, posing as an aristocrat." Ludolph snorted and spun toward Krengel, leaning in to bring the two of them nose to nose. "Would you care to know which one you are, Santa Klaas? The terrible truth of how Lady Adeline couldn't bear the sight of her malformed offspring, so she claimed instead, the child of her husband's poor slave, and thrust her own little monster, the true heir to the Habsburg fortune, upon the bosom of her husband's whore? Which one do you suppose you are, Santa Klaas? I know."

Krengel's eyes felt oily, his ears hot. "Just another of a thousand lies about my birth."

"Oh, but there you would be wrong, because I met her. Your true dam. I enjoyed a little chat with her in the moonlit garden nook right beside the grave of your half-brother. And she was kind enough to tell me the truth, right before she shoved me through a hole in the sky." Ludolph drew back his lips and pressed his forehead against Krengel's. "You're the son of an old servant named Luludja. Penniless. Worthless. Of a lower class, even than I."

Krengel shook his head back and forth, his lips parting, contorting, but producing no sound. Because he knew it was true. Deep down, some part of him knew it all along that he shared neither flesh nor blood with that alabaster doll behind the red door. He'd always wondered why her creation was not something more beautiful. Perfect. Something more like her. His crown of Moorish curls, his common and portly features, they reflected no part of Lady Adeline Habsburg-Krengel. It had all been a terrible lie. And it all made perfect sense where it hadn't before.

He was a product of Krengel infidelity, defined by Habsburg pride, unloved and unwanted by every hand in his upbringing. And how could he blame any one of them? What love would be expected of Count Krengel for his servant's bastard child, the living evidence of his adulterous misgivings? What love had Lady

Adeline for the bastard son of her husband's whore, the living proof of his infidelity and all the attention he'd denied her? The only reason she adopted him was to shame her husband's concubine, to put her in her place by reminding her of her lack of entitlement to anything in this world, to force instead upon the poor woman a monstrously deformed to spare her self the indignity of coddling her frightful creation. Even Luludja, his true mother, could hardly be expected to feel anything more than resent when faced daily with the product of Count Krengel's forcible affections.

And the Krampusz, his loathsome half-brother. No demon at all. Just a lad born woefully disfigured. Truly, if there were one who walked the earth more wretched than Krengel, it was the Krampusz, buried alive in that gruesome nook by an unwilling foster mother after she'd caved in his face with a stone. Exiled. Despised by any and by all unfortunate to have encountered him. Cursed forever to wander the nameless threads of time and space, collecting people and things as he rabbit-holed from one world to the next, hoarding enough junk practically to fill a nether realm in his effort to compensate for the love forever denied him. In that respect, Krengel could certainly sympathize, and he found in that moment that it was even perhaps possible to pity such a wretched creature.

"You know what the worst part is, Santa Klaas? The worst part of all."

Krengel could only glower, unable to defend himself against whatever accusations were coming. He could only glower back like a fox in a snare, awaiting the final blow of the trapper's club.

"The worst part is that it was all for nothing." Ludolph lowered his voice to a whisper. "The Hound of God truly believed he was on the trail of the Habsburg fortune, and Friar Otto went to his grave protecting it. The Gottlieb sisters were taken for it. And all the rest of us lost everything we ever knew and loved, scattered to all the ends of the earth, and for what? What, Santa Klaas? All that suffering, misery, and death? All to protect you and your nonexistent fortune, you penniless son of a whore."

"Stop it, Eichmann." Hiley suddenly stepped between Ludolph and Krengel. "You got what you wanted. This kid ain't had no more control over what's happened here than anyone else."

"How would you know?" Ludolph shouted in her face. "Aye? I shared the last months of my natural life in the company of this simpering brat, and I didn't see you there." He stabbed an accusatory finger in Krengel's face. "No, I didn't see you there when this boy's greed led to the ruin of so many promising lives. This boy is the antichrist!"

"Ain't that just a little much?"

"But it was all an accident!" Krengel wailed.

"I hold you personally responsible for every minute of misery suffered by every one of us since the moment you crossed our path, and for the deaths of Friar Ottomar and poor Pascal."

"Pascal?"

"Shattered like a bird fallen from its nest on the rocks of your devil's island." Ludolph scooped up the flask of myrrh from the ground and popped the cork. He waved the bung beneath his nose and sniffed it cautiously. One of the stable hands leaned forward. Ludolph extended his arm and offered the lad a whiff. The boy sniffed it and raised his eyebrows, blinking his eyes.

"Why?" Krengel asked, tears streaming down his dirty cheeks. "Why do you even want the myrrh? It's the only thing I have left."

"Not any more." Ludolph recorked the flask and smiled. He tossed the flask lightly into the air and caught it again. He gripped it tightly, as though relishing the feel of the vessel in the palm of his hand. He clasped it with both hands and held it against his breast. "This is the whole reason I'm here, little Santa Klaas. The whole reason your Forever Friend banished me to this place."

"But I risked my life to get it."

"Good for you." Ludolph grinned. "But I'm afraid you're nothing but a delivery boy. Funny, isn't it? Something so harmless as an aromatic oil, could be so deadly--if you happen to be a witch. One drop of this holy myrrh on the tip of an arrow … just get me within a thousand paces of that succubus and I'll blow the gates of this Hell wide open."

Chapter Sixteen

"You want to see a monkey? Come on, Klaas. Let's go and see a monkey."

Krengel couldn't for the life of him recall the man's name. His mother's effeminate manservant, he had an oversized and dazzling smile, Krengel remembered, an orange tunic pinstriped with gilded threads, and breath that always smelled of licorice. Lithe hands and polished fingernails that always fidgeted, had once produced an amazing shadow of a wriggly-nosed rabbit on a garden wall, and sometimes fashioned chain necklaces from dandelion stems. He was a fine and whimsical companion, theatrical, childlike, equipped with a seemingly endless supply of wry tricks. It was on one memorable morning that this nameless handler from a bygone age would usher a toddling Klaas Krengel toward a rendezvous with destiny.

"Have you ever seen a monkey, Klaas? Do you know what one looks like?"

Krengel had never seen any animal from beyond Lambsheim's white towers, aside from those portrayed in his picture books, of course. Monkeys were people-like, but sillier. Krengel knew that much of them. His flamboyant handler puffed out his cheeks and pulled out his ears, delighting Krengel with a bow-legged dance, knuckles swaying side to side in the air. Somersaulting end over end through the verdant carpet of grass, he beat his chest and hooted crazily in the midmorning sunshine. Krengel was delighted. He clapped his fat hands until his nanny sauntered back, panting to catch his breath, and led the small child around back of the estate in the direction of the servants' quarters.

Soon enough, they stood before a splintered door. His nameless chaperone was behind him, goading him into opening it. Krengel remembered the popping sound of the leather hinges as he'd pushed against the door until the pine slats gave way to the lightless interior of the shack.

"Where's Miss Luludja's monkey, Klaas? Do you see him? Where is he? Wherever could that funny monkey be?"

Miss Luludja was not home. He remembered thinking it queer she'd leave her monkey unattended in such a place while she went about her daily duties. He shuffled inward a few steps upon the packed earth floor, surveying the simple furnishings by the light of a fire pit still dimly aglow with the morning's embers. White motes of ash hung in the air, all around him. The fire popped. And out of nowhere, the thing came at him.

It emitted a scream that permeated his very soul, as a melee of teeth and claws upset a chair into a kettle that vomited a steaming river of gruel all over the creature, and over the tops of Krengel's feet. It all happened so quickly. And it was his own scream joining that of the scalded monster he remembered best of all, their unrehearsed harmony of shared agonies raised one and for all in the gloom like a cry in the night for a mother they both knew would never come. But his handler appeared, swiping at the globs of molten oats on Krengel's feet. With haste, they quit that frightful place and left the squalling goblin in its lake of porridge. But not before it delivered Krengel a parting glance that burned more deeply into his forming mind, than gruel could ever scar his fair skin. There, blue eyes blazed back at him through the blackness like twin portals to a midsummer's sky. Filled with an unfathomable despair, those blue eyes were the poignant detail Krengel would most clearly recall when he was informed, some time later that Miss Luludja's monkey had died.

"What'cha looking at? Found my comic collection, did ye?"

Krengel sat cross-legged on the floor of Hiley's dormer. He hadn't much felt like speaking for the last several hours, so he'd withdrawn, immersed in picture books, surrounded by dozens and dozens of the thin and glossy pamphlets known as comics. Page after page displayed rows of colorful tiles that depicted scenes involving a pantheon of pagan gods, and masked warriors dressed in lewd tights with colorful boots and capes. Their violent engagements with their sworn enemies were portrayed in the most dramatic and spectacular fashion imaginable, so vastly different from the stylized hieroglyphics often stamped around the borders of the dreary books of his own age.

"Who is he?" Krengel picked up a pamphlet that featured a warrior not flamboyant like the rest, dressed all in black, his face hidden behind a horned cowl, crouching on a rooftop like a dark assassin, an angel of death leering over a damned city. "Is he a wicked man?"

"No, he's actually a good guy. He just dresses like that to look all tough and scare the bad guys. He was afraid of bats when he was a kid, see. More afraid of bats than anything else in the whole world. When he grew up and thought to go out and fight evil, he reckoned he'd take the form of that one thing that scared him most, and use terror as a weapon against the bad guys. That's how's come he's dressed up like a bat."

"Did it work?"

"Hell yeah it worked." Hiley tittered a little.

"Is he really a knight?"

"Oh, well that's just one of the names they call him."

"Have you ever met him?"

"Well, no. He ain't real. None of them are. They're super heroes."

"Super ..."

"Super heroes. They're fake. Imaginary. Ye know, for entertainment."

Krengel frowned at the books scattered all around him.

"Don't they got no entertainment where you're from?"

"Choir and the arts, I suppose. Theater."

"Bore-ring." Hiley sat cross-legged next to him. She snatched up a comic that featured a man in blue, with a flapping cape unfurling from his shoulders that was just as red as the flag of the Habsburg Netherlands. "See, it's fun to read these stories because these guys can do all sorts of cool things that regular folks can only dream about. Like, this feller can fly." Hiley pointed at the man on the cover. "Lots of them can fly, actually. This one can, and she can, too. Some turn invisible--poof--disappear and reappear wherever they want, or they have super seeing or super hearing and can hear someone scream from like a hundred miles away, and zip right over to save them in a flash. All sorts of nifty powers like that."

Krengel's eyes brightened. "I know of someone with the same nifty powers of which you speak!"

"Do ye? Hell's bells, about time you and I had something to talk about. What comic's he in?"

"No, he's not from any comic. I mean, I actually know of someone, a real person, who can really do those sorts of things. All of those things! God bless! All of them that you mentioned!"

Hiley furrowed her brow.

"Saint Nicholas!"

"Santa Claus?"

"Stop it!" Krengel pounded the floor with a fist. His sudden outburst made Hiley jump in surprise. "I'm hardly a saint! It was a bad joke to begin with, made by a wicked man in very poor taste, I might add, and I'm sick to death of being called that!"

"Whoa-whoa-whoa, settle down there, Tiger. I was just asking, is all."

"Asking what?"

"If your Saint Nicholas and Santa Claus weren't different names for the same guy. They're the same guy where I come from."

"What in heaven do you mean? I'm Santa Klaas."

"You're a fat man from the North Pole with a sleigh and flying reindeer? Not where I come from, ye ain't."

"Flying deer? Have you gone mad?"

"You mean to tell me that outside of your own nickname, ye ain't never once heard of no one else called Santy Claus?"

"I've positively no idea what you're talking about."

"Figures." Hiley tossed her comic and rose to her feet. "There for just a second, I thought we might actually have a real conversation."

"Saint Nicholas of Myra." Krengel rose, cleared his throat and clapped his hands together. He skipped after her. "There was only one, and he couldn't possibly be confused with any other. He lived in the third century, and he was the very first super hero. Look here, with his super powers, he was able to raise the hacked bodies of three dead boys from a meat tub to testify against their murderer, the village butcher, before they could be eaten!"

"Now, that's just creepy."

"But wait, there's more. Lots more! I know everything about Saint Nicholas. I once served as a steward to his basilica in Bari, right up until the last Festival of the Translation of the Holy Relics."

"Now you're speakin' Chinese again."

Krengel's eyes fell to the comic book still in his hand and tapped the pad of his index finger on image of the rooftop knight, crouched atop a gargoyle. "Look, he was just like him, in life. He wore a dark cloak like him, moved from rooftop to rooftop by night, just like him, and he dropped sacks of gold down the chimneys of whores."

"I don't think that's hardly even the same --"

"But wait! He stood up to evildoers."

"Guess that's a little better."

"He confronted evil wherever he encountered it. He sought to bring balance to an imbalanced world. He was the Christkindel."

"Chris Kringle?"

"Christkindel. The Gift Bearer ... oh, and he could fly, just like that one!"

"He could fly?"

"Oh, but of course he could! How else might've he harnessed the winds to lift poor little Basileus out of slavery in a faraway land?"

Hiley shrugged. "Whatever works."

"With his super-hearing, he heard the boy's whispered prayers from half a world away and he whooshed him off into the sky and safely home again. You've really never heard of these feats? Why, they're immortalized in glass and tile all over Bari! He appeared on the decks of imperiled ships at sea whenever sailors cried out his name. He moved objects with the power of the Holy

Spirit. He walked on water. He raised the dead!" Krengel smiled fanatically. "Now what do you think?"

"I think those all sound like a bunch of Bible-banging miracles to me, but not super powers."

"Whatever's the difference?"

"One's religion. The other's entertainment."

"Well, if you must be that way, then I submit that all of yours are fake, and at least my Saint Nicholas of Myra was real."

"Guess that's a matter of faith." Hiley took up a comic and thumbed through the pages. "You can believe whatever you want to believe, but that don't make it any more real than my comics."

"His acts are depicted in works of stone."

Hiley sighed, but did not reply. She stretched out upon the floor and thumbed through her comic.

"So you've traded your faith in miracles for entertainment? What joy can that possibly bring into your life? Why would you do such a thing?"

"To each their own." Hiley swept away the comics, rose from the floor, and stepped out onto the balcony. She placed her hands upon the rail and stared out over the lights of Iptintec. The vast shadow of a mauna goba passed over her, losing her in the darkness for a moment. Hiley never even flinched.

Krengel rose from where he'd reactively cowered and searched the black skies above like a squirrel at the base of its tree, before slipping out across the veranda after her. "Whatever happened to magic, Miss Hiley?"

"Ain't no such thing as magic. Not where I come from."

"That seems to me such a terrible shame." Krengel placed his hands on the rail beside hers. He gestured toward the flickering sodium blimps with a hitch of his chin. "How can you fail to believe in magic while standing here in the glow of those great floating lanterns? Magic, right there before your eyes!"

"Not magic. They're lights. Chemical lights. Just like neon or phosphorus, you pass an electric current through certain gases, and bam, you got light. It ain't magic so long as it can be explained, and everything can eventually be explained."

"But what about the magic of possibility?" Krengel's eyes twinkled in the sodium light. "Instead of explaining how something is possible, try explaining why it's possible."

Hiley wrinkled her nose.

"Look, take away all that exists, all that you know, and reduce the whole universe to a great state of nothingness, as it was in the beginning. Now then, from this state of nothingness, which is more likely the universe as we know it, or nothing at all? Existence or nonexistence? Something or nothing? Ask yourself, which is the more likely state, the more natural one?"

Hiley just shook her head.

"Nothingness is clearly the more natural, given the nothingness from which it all began. Ask not how, but why? Why should there be the possibility for anything else? Why should nothing ever give way to something? It's impossible, against all odds, completely illogical … yet against all odds, here we stand. You and I. Living proof of magic, of miracles; explainable perhaps, right down to our tiniest particles, yet still wholly unjustifiable in the greater sense for daring to exist where existence is impossible."

"You're still awful new around here, Klaas Krengel. You'll see. Gets harder and harder to think straight in this place. Longer you're trapped here, longer it gnaws at ye. Memories of the other side start to fade. What ye left behind starts to seem more dreamlike than this here place once did, and that's when it starts to get scary. You got no time to argue for miracles and magic, where ye feel like ye might be nothing but a figment of your own imagination, and ye got to keep reminding yourself every other minute that this place is real. A physical realm that existed long before we got here and it'll still exist long after we're gone. But it ain't even safe to think that way." Hiley shook her head, her bottom lip beginning to tremble. "Because thinking that way gets ye wanting to escape. And there ain't no escape. Not from this place."

"Then you don't believe that Ludolph Eichmann will succeed?"

Hiley snorted. "Hell no. Ye think he's the first? Ye think Ludolph Eichmann's the first jump up and decide to lead some kinder charge?"

"Perhaps there's another way, then. A way around the problem, rather than through it. What of the story Ludolph told, how the witch created the Krampusz with a drop of her own blood dabbed on the sting of a captured bee? That bee had to have found its own way in, and a way out."

"Bunch of hooey." Hiley shooed the air with her hand. "All them stories … ain't like anybody even knows what she's about, imagining a green lady with a pickle nose and a pointy hat, down there stirring a bubbling cauldron … just stories! Stories invented by folks who ain't never confronted her. No need to build her up to be anything greater than the child-eating predator that we know for sure she is."

"But the bee … and the Krampusz?" Krengel cocked his head. "How was he coming and going from this place for so many years?"

"I don't know if I believe none of it, no more," Hiley whispered.

"Believe what?"

She bent at the waist and rested her forehead upon the rail. "Maybe I just dreamt it all. Every bit of it"

"You must believe in something, Miss Hiley."

"I believe in insanity." Hiley turned her head and hitched an eyebrow. "Thought maybe when I'd met him, I'd just lost my mind, and funny thing was, I was okay with that."

"Met whom?"

"All's I needed was him, my Forever Friend, from the first moment he crashed into my life, even if he was just a sign, like a symptom that something just snapped in my head when Pap died. Part of me still kinder thinks that, that maybe I ain't really even here at all. Maybe I just keeled over in the bog and this here's all just been a great and terrible dream."

"But how do you explain me?"

"Maybe you and everyone else in here's just a figment of my own imagination, just like me, just like all of it. One big crazy dream."

Krengel felt something. An ant crawled over the back of his right hand. It traversed the rail in between, and then crawled over the back of his left. So filled with purpose, this tiny creature. So bent on the direction in which it was headed. And where could it possibly be going?

Krengel moved his left hand to block the ant. It hesitated, studying the new wall of flesh, antennae shifting, calculating height and width, redirecting. The ant lurched forward again, bore hard left, and circumvented the obstacle by way of the railing's underside, walking upside-down, effortlessly, seamlessly, as it passed beneath Krengel's hand, then returned topside, marching determinedly toward Hiley.

It occurred to Krengel that the ant was not natural to this place. Just like Krengel and all the other children of Iptintec, it was a creature from the flipside. Ants, flies, and other meaner forms of life, perhaps rats and mice, might've found the Sack of Shadows lying on the floor of Lazarus's cave, as it had remained undisturbed for untold years after he and the witch had been dealt with. It would've been attractive to vermin, the sack, with the mountains of garbage therein, the tons of food that never spoiled, and eventually they would find their way in.

Krengel snatched up the ant and closed his fingers tightly around it. He could feel the thing scuttling anxious circles around his palm, searching for a way out of the trap within a trap. But there was no way out.

It was not so very unreasonable that a witch could trap a bee in this place. But what unnatural element had she in her blood that could infect such a creature's sting to create a monster on the flipside, once the terrible payload had been delivered? If the story of Old Berchta once told to him was true, the witch was made a bride to one of the Fates. Perhaps by way of the consummation of their unholy union, there was some lasting affect on her constitution. Perhaps the witch was no longer a human being at all. Perhaps as a bride to the Incubusz, she had been transformed into something else. Something evil.

Krengel felt a tickle on the back of his hand. He rotated his wrist to find the ant circumnavigating the outside of his fist. Somehow, as if by magic, the tiny prisoner had found a way out of the trap. Krengel raised his hand and extended it toward Hiley. "Does this look like a figment of your imagination?"

She stared down at the little link to the world they'd left behind, a living vestige. It was undeniable. Real. In her face. She blew the ant off his hand and over the railing. It cartwheeled down into the abyss.

"We are here," Krengel said, "and by might or by magic, we will escape this place."

"Ye really need to quit believing that kinder thing, or you'll wind-up just as crazy as Ludolph Eichmann."

"The Krampusz told me quite sincerely that I'd been sent here to rescue you, lead you out of this place, and even after all you've told me that's still just what I intend to do."

"Klaas, what's the last thing he had you do, right before he dropped you through that rabbit hole?"

"What do you mean?"

"What was it that he had you fetch?"

"I don't have any idea what you're --"

"You fetched the holy myrrh, Sugar. The witch poison. That there's your how's come and what for. I'm afraid you wasn't never nothing but a delivery boy. He knew he couldn't have told ye the truth, or you'd never have done your chore. But he knew if ye thought ye was going to be some kinder big hero, you'd do him right."

"Don't be upset. I'm telling ye this for your own good. Ye need to accept a few things. Your Forever Friend knew what you were good at, what part you'd best play in his big plan. Call him what you like, but he does know a thing or two about using people. You was a thief, and now your job's done. Every one of us down here in Iptintec thought we was special, Klaas. Believe me. Come to find out you ain't the only one with a Forever Friend, to find out he's tricked you, stolen your childhood, and robbed ye of your whole life ... well, kind of comes as a kick in the pants. I remember how I felt when the whole weight of it hit me. Bad enough he had us all under his spell the way he done, but come to find out you wasn't even special at all to him, just one of a million other kids ... yeah, that kinder burns."

"At least he trusted you enough to tell you about your part in the plan."

"Wanna know the truth, Klaas? I'll be honest Injun because I think ye really need to hear it said." Hiley took him by the shoulders and looked him dead in the eyes. "Only reason the Krampusz latched onto ye, was because he knew you was the one friend he had available at just the right place, at just the right stitch in time, to go and steal the holy myrrh. That's all. That's the whole reason he bagged ye, roped ye into his plan."

"Killing the witch, then. That's the whole plan."

"Yup."

"I presume, so the Krampusz can have the Sack of Shadows all to himself, to come and go whenever and wherever he pleases."

Hiley shrugged. "Reckon that's prob'ly the truth."

"And what about you? If I'm the thief, then what exactly is your part in this rather complicated and silly assassination?"

"Playing mam to you." Hiley tousled Krengel's hair. "Said you kinder needed one. Deserved one. Said you'd never had a real mama before."

"I don't need a mama." Krengel wrenched his head away from her hand.

"Well, our Forever Friend seemed to think ye did. Sent me straight out to fetch ye and take ye under my wing, teach you the ways around here. Same as I once did for him, the day he come fallin' out the Alabama sky."

Chapter Seventeen

The Chukchi herders dully regarded the sleigh as it grated to a halt on the frozen floor of the ice cave. Like prehistoric men thawed from frozen tombs in the glacier wall, they closed in with spears and torches and advanced upon the team of panting animals. Expressionless faces, dotted and striped with black ink, peered through darkly slotted eyes set within the fur-rimmed portholes of their deerskin parkas. They set to work without speaking, expelling plumes of breath as they unharnessed the reindeer team. Clearly more concerned with the condition of the animals than that of the three passengers, they closely inspected each reindeer and led them one by one back into strange whalebone stalls that were stocked with heaps fresh hay. The clicking heels of the beasts resonated through the glassy caverns like the chatter of whales beneath a floe of ice.

Black Pete stepped from the sleigh. He brushed the snow from his parka and removed a wooden mask to reveal a face immeasurably more frightful than the grimacing countenance carved into its former covering. He strode to the mouth of the cave. Silver bells jingled along his boot seams. There was no trace of worry in his mind over the girls, their safety, or any chance of their escape. From this place, there was no escape. They'd survived the journey. That would suffice, given they wouldn't be alive in another hour.

He drew his fur parka more tightly around his shoulders. Strings of yellowed teeth rasped the edges of the silver medallion upon his chest, as if giving a little nip to test the metal's worth. No steamy plumes arose from his colorless lips, for there was no breath within him. All that filled his body cavity were things that writhed and churned against the frigidity of this bleak land. They did not like it here, those things that lived inside him, and he could not blame them. They would only tolerate this place for so long before they began to gnaw. They would gnaw at his insides like a cask of acid, pining for their release until he harnessed the reindeer and set course for the starlit streets of some faraway land. In those places, they could be released to spread their message, to satiate their bloodlust. He pulled the folds of the parka around his breast, protecting the restless swarms, therein.

His buttermilk eyes surveyed the glacier valley, where the perpetual reconstruction effort continued. Through the haze of steam and smoking manure fires, Chukchi tribesmen lumbered about like frost giants, hauling and melting cartloads of snow. Skins filled with colorful dyes were emptied into the melt just before the steaming water was poured from cauldrons into great leather forms, where massive blocks of colored ice were born. It was an impressive operation, requiring the daily efforts of an entire Chukchi tribe. One by one, he'd captured and brought them here, all descendants of the same walrus hunters unfortunate enough to have invoked his eternal wrath by killing the man he used to be.

Black Pete scanned the ragged domes of their little village. Wisps of steam rose from their vents. Nothing seemed out of place. Everyone was busy in this prison valley, where no one entered and no one left. For there was no way to overcome the sheer ice walls of this crevice except behind a team of flying reindeer, and the Chukchi, who'd long come to regard Black Pete as the god of their small world, were no closer to discovering his secret of flight than their ancestors had been five hundred years ago.

Black Pete's hand rose to his breast and closed around the silver medallion. With the pad of his thumb, he stroked the engraved image of Icarus. He knew that the Chukchi were all too aware of his presence, and that he was standing there watching over them, and it pleased him that they dared not look up from their labors. He supposed that their ancestors must have felt equally powerful when they were clubbing his brains out into the snow. But now, trapped for countless generations between the walls of ice, whatever fleeting moment of power these people had once enjoyed at his expense, was long forgotten, though their debt was far from being paid. Those who were born, lived, and died in this place were entirely dependant upon their master, their god, for their most basic rations. They were less than slaves were, he supposed. They were his pets.

Black Pete turned his head toward the crack of a whip. From the fire pits, twin teams of harnessed, dragged a ruby-colored block toward the citadel. By way of a precarious whalebone scaffold, massive fulcrums and counterweights of ice, an emerald-colored block was already being hoisted into place on a tower wall, just beneath a striped onion dome.

They'd developed their own unique culture over the years. The shifting rivers of ice beneath the glacier valley was a rather dynamic substrate on which to lay a foundation, but the location of his fortress was an otherwise perfect one. Perfectly hidden in plain sight, the great crevice that concealed his citadel gaped like a wound in the frozen heart of this land of eternal ice. Packs of ravenous wolves, prowling ice bears, and armed bands of Chukchi deermen added formidable layers of defense that extended for days upon days in every direction. Most important of all, the sun never shone.

This far north, the sun took an orbital path, eternally circling the glacier valley on the frozen horizon, as though Black Pete's citadel was the center of the universe, and never passed over it. This of course made the climate all the more severe. Another layer of defense, all to protect his children. Those who'd received him. And now, just like him, they could no longer tolerate the light of the sun. He was the first of their kind.

How many centuries had passed, and still, he could taste that dirty blood in his mouth, a lasting vestige of the life he'd left behind when the Fates had offered him a new one inside a corked silver vial. A new life in one cold swallow of what tasted like coagulated metal, stratified into musty layers of grit and sediment that retained the flavor of the cave floor from which it had been gleaned. In his last act of life, he'd uncorked that vial with trembling hands and he'd swallowed the precious blood of Lazarus of Bethany.

And he'd risen.

Father Pabichka Napien, no more, the Fates called him their Sacred Vessel, the Living Arc of a covenant between their Guilds, for vested within him, would reside the living means to their merged agendas. The fearsome one had then seized him by the jaw, lifting his bare feet from the snow to draw their faces together. Black Pete's new face was reflected a hundred times over in the Fate's bulging mosaic eyes. He could only stare back into his duplicated visage of horror, as a wrinkled trunk extended from its cowl, dabbing, probing his lips with its whiskered pedestal as he spat against it, and gritting his teeth. The Fate then squeezed until he was sure his jawbone was just about to shatter, and finally, he opened his mouth.

In great surges, they came, and in great swallows, he received them, while strange instructions were buzzed into his ear. He had been chosen. He was chosen to be the Steward of the Sacred Artifacts, the Vector of Wurm, the Lure of Fiend, and the Arc of the Dark Covenant, the Harbinger of Pestilence and the Father of the Revenant. Naked legs flailing in the blistering wind, he swallowed mouthful after mouthful of fleas until the shifting skin of his belly protruded like that of a wealthy glutton. When the Lord of the Flies was spent, Black Pete was dropped upon the ice. The Book of Wurm and Icarus Medallion were cast upon his bare chest. He would use these gifts to spread their message of Black Death, and to raise an army of the ones down there, the ones he kept hidden beneath the ice.

Black Pete closed his sallow eyes. He could hear them. Rustling. Far below. Down in the frozen grotto beneath the crystal citadel. Waiting patiently. Waiting for their hour to come. Waiting for the vessel that he'd promised them. The perfect vehicle that could transport them untouched by the light of the sun and deliver them, en mass, upon an unsuspecting world. He could hear their slackened folds of leathery skin, rustling. Stabled reindeer grunted anxiously and tossed their antlered heads. They didn't like them, the ones down there, especially on feeding days, when he brought them a meal of fresh blood.

Black Pete turned to the sleigh where his two captives still cowered. Hopeful as he'd been, the girls had been of no good use to him. At one time, they'd been in such close company with the one he tirelessly pursued. The boy had huddled between them in the back of a jostling wagon. He'd seen it all in the pages of the Book, and he'd risked it all to pursue them across the boggy fens, through Lambsheim, and then to Ischgl over the highland pass, releasing his legion of messengers at every civilized place, until no man, woman, or child, remained alive. And at last, he'd caught up to them, to these girls to whom Klaas Krengel had once been so attached, and found that the boy was no longer with them.

He reached into the folds of his parka and pulled out the Book of Wurm. The silver medallion around his neck bumped amiably against the worn leather volume. Three of the greatest artifacts from the Age of Miracles and Magic he possessed: the Book of Wurm, the Icarus Medallion, and the Blood of Lazarus that flowed in his veins. But he lacked the fourth and final treasure that would at last complete him, and would at last enable the dark mission for which he'd been created. But first, he needed the boy. The boy would lead him to it, the Sack of Shadows.

The children below began to beat their leather wings, raising their undead metabolism in anticipation of what they sensed was about to come. They could smell the two girls. Their teeth rattled. Because they understood, in their own way that the scent of any new blood in this frozen land was a treat for them.

Black Pete's fingers tightened their grip on the Book of Wurm as the minions inside him began to churn, boiling up his throat in one seething mass, as if they could somehow sense that his mouth was going to open, and that he was about to speak. But when his lips parted and the frigid air rushed in, the angry rope of fleas retreated back into his gullet. For years, they gagged and choked him with their terrible antics, but he'd come to anticipate the volatile behavior of his horde of deadly mites, and even to admire them.

"Show him," Black Pete whispered, relaxing his grip on the Book's spine, allowing the volume to fall open in his hands. "Show Klaas Krengel to me."

His murky eyes rolled downward in their sockets. The black pages before him showed nothing. No imagery. No pictures that he'd learned over the course of many centuries to decipher. No answers to his question in the form of illustrations scratched by claws from the other side. The things on the other side had their limitations. They could not directly interfere in the world of men. But they could hint as to what a man should do. They could tempt and manipulate. They could empower their key players with gifts, and they could most certainly punish the insubordinate. But when asked the whereabouts of Klaas Krengel, with all their mysterious power and guile, the Fates could show him only darkness.

"There is no place on earth where a boy could hide from you!"

The twin swatches of blackness faded away to two pages of blank parchment.

He'd been so close on the boy's heels. But it was the changing seasons that ultimately deterred him, soon after he'd passed through the village of Ischgl. The boy had been assimilated into a vast caravan of Spaniards, which made it difficult even for his minions to search the hundreds of rolling wagons, but winter's chill had put an abrupt end to the chase, close as they were to their goal, for if the fleas were not housed safely within him in cold temperatures, his precious minions would perish. Spring and summer were the ideal killing seasons for the Black Death.

From Rome, the Book showed him how the boy had been taken to the seaport of Bari. And it was from that place that Klaas Krengel had disappeared. He'd simply dropped right off the map. He hadn't died. Black Pete was fairly certain of that. If the boy had met with an untimely end at the hands of some fiend, then the Book would've shown him Krengel's festering corpse and the place where it had been laid to rest. And if he'd asked, it would've shown the identity of his killer, the killer's place of residence, the whereabouts of every living member of the assassin's family. No, there was no question that the Book of Wurm could not answer. Yet the question of Krengel's location remained an enigma. Always blackness. Whatever had happened to Klaas Krengel in Bari was something stranger than death. He suspected the boy had been abducted, and taken to someplace … unnatural.

The sound of scratching claws tipped Black Pete's head to one side. What was this? A new message was being sent to him from the other side. A clue. Something being scrawled in the usual flurry of knitting claws. Gradually, it took form on the parchment, a scratched image of something. Something strange. Black Pete cocked his head from one side to the other, trying to make better sense of the bizarre illustration.

"What are you trying to tell me?" he whispered.

Hash marks flitted into place amongst the pattern of hexagonal plates, deep relief between the scales that bejeweled its trunk-like legs, as thousands of scratches manifested the likeness something somewhere between ordinary and surreal. The thing taking shape before his eyes was the image of a boy, Klaas Krengel, neatly seated upon the great domed back of a giant tortoise. But there was no such animal in existence. Or was there?

Black Pete's eyes widened. His lips stretched reflexively into some perversion of an expression that he might once have known and understood as a smile. It was a remembered expression of something called joy, which people experienced whenever good fortune smiled upon them, whenever things finally went their way. It had taken them half a year, but the dark ones on the other side were pretty clever, if nothing else, and perhaps they'd devised a roundabout way of answering that niggling question: Where is Klaas Krengel?

The tortoise was as large as a sheep, with twice the amplitude. Its knobby head, surmounting a great serpentine neck, peered quizzically back at him from the parchment. This fantastic creature was apparently a denizen of the land where Klaas Krengel had disappeared, someplace yet undiscovered, a blind spot in the Book of Wurm's eye. And although the ones on the other side had repeatedly failed to give him a clue on the whereabouts of Klaas Krengel, they were evidently eager to divulge information on this particular tortoise.

Fleas spilled from the corner of Black Pete's grinning mouth. They sprung crazily from his lips and parchment pages to die wriggling upon the ice and snow. A gray tongue protruded and swept the eager minions back inside their hollow. The lips closed briefly, as he swallowed the wad down.

"And where," Black Pete tapped his fingertip on the image of the fanciful creature, "can I find this King of the Turtles?"

Chapter Eighteen

From Iptintec's capital spire, sprayed a fan of radial lines like spokes from a wheel hub, spanning taut to every building across the city like the framework of an enormous tent. These vast and glimmering cables harped mournfully in the unnatural breezes that came with every vacillation of the Sack of Shadows. But when the city alarm was sounded, this sinuous network was the very mechanism devised to produce an altogether different sound, like a thousand wagonloads of shattered glass, all being dumped at once from some great cliff to the rocks below. The crier need only wrench his helm to and fro to hoist and lower the entire web through a series of cogs and worm gears, lifting and crashing massive canopies of silver chimes, trumpeting air through bellows by way of pumping hydraulic pistons, drumming mallets upon titanic diaphragms in the core shaft of every building in the city.

Like the schedule of bells in Bari, the unique pitch and timbre, Iptintec's every municipal instrument was calibrated to herald a specific event throughout the streets and plazas of the Midland capital. Each effect could be isolated with a thrown lever and sounded apart from the rest, or harmonized with the toll of one or more others. But on those emergencies, when order was given to the city helmsman to sound the high alert, he would throw every lever in his command and heave to the wheel with all his might. The resulting cacophony was so tremendous that it assaulted the body on every level, from the eardrums through the nervous system, to the very marrow of the bones, for the strange and swooning aspects of all the buildings of Iptintec, were designed less by their sightless architects for any aesthetic purpose, than they were built to serve as the pipes of a terrible organ.

Krengel screamed in distress as he fell to the floor of Hiley's dormer, palms pressed against his ears, writhing like a Dervish in her mess of scattered comics. The blast of sound droning up through her building's core was so intense, he was sure that every vertebra in his spine had unfastened, his limbs pulverized, reducing him to a bewildered and boneless puddle of jelly on Hiley's floor, by the time the alarm finally subsided. Before he'd a chance to utter his first word of inquiry, one of her Starlings came skidding through her doorway, antennae rattling atop his helmet, strings of sodium lights disrupted and flickering around his arms and legs.

"Y'all hear that?" he asked.

"Well, how do, Alva," Hiley replied.

"How do, Miss Hiley." He gave a nod to Krengel, sprawled on the floor. "Pancha raid, down at Tencotha."

"Eichmann's dozen?"

"Yes'm. I'd surely reckon."

"Can't say we didn't warn them, when we seen how he was getting them all riled up down there at the stables."

"Yes'm. We surely did." Alva cocked his decorated head at the comics strewn over the floor, causing his antennae to knock together over his helmet like a pair of clapping hands. "What ye reading, Klaas? Some comics, are ye?"

Krengel looked to Hiley in disbelief.

"Say, got ye some new ones there, don't ye? Don't mind if I borrow me a couple?"

"Am I hearing this right?" Krengel scrambled to his feet. "Something has happened to Ludolph Eichmann's party?" Krengel looked back and forth from Hiley to Alva, but neither seemed eager to return eye contact. "Hey! Have you all gone mad?"

"Ain't nothing can be done for them, Klaas," Hiley said, gently.

"Well, we surely must do something!"

"They're gone, Klaas."

"How do you know that? What do you even mean, gone? What is gone?"

After a moment's silence, Hiley spoke. "Listen, I know what you must be feeling. But, this place? This ain't our world. Never will be. It belongs to the Naturals. We took Iptintec years ago, and we've managed to hold it, but it's known and accepted around here that if ye get ancy and strike off on your own outside the city walls, well … you're on your own."

"So you're not going to do anything about it?"

"Me?"

"No, your sweet Uncle Clem! Of course you! Alva? Anyone!"

"Klaas, I been here long enough to remember what it was like before we had Iptintec, when we crawled through tunnels in the garbage like vermin, waving light sticks back and forth to send a message across the divide. You remember them days, Alva? Back when we lived in fear every minute that something awful was going to snatch you up. And I remember what it took to capture Iptintec. How many we lost. A lot's changed around here, and I guess for the better, but one thing's never changed and never will." Hiley leaned in close and poked Krengel in the chest. "If ye get so brave ye decide to strike off on your own, then you'll get taked by the Pancha. And once ye get taked by the Pancha, then you're off to meet the witch, quick as that." She leaned back, put her hands on her hips. "That ever happens, ye ain't coming back. Least, not in one piece, ye ain't. Them kids are gone."

"We tried to tell them, Klaas," Alva said.

"We warned them over and over, but that boy Ludolph was dead-set. Couldn't tell that boy nothing!"

"Been others like that."

"Yep, there sure have," Hiley said. "Ain't like we're a herd of cattle down here, Klaas, calving more and more of us each spring. We got to be careful. We're a dying breed."

"We just worms on a hook, down here," Alva said.

"That's right. Worms on a hook. Getting picked off one at a time. Get ye to wriggling all around and pop! Something will see ye and snap ye right up. And I ain't never seen nobody get to wriggling as bad as old Ludolph."

"Couldn't stand it."

"Couldn't stand it! Had to get out of here right now-now-now."

"Well, what else would you expect of him?" Krengel shouted. "He's lived his whole life like a bug beneath a boot heel, never knowing an hour of peace or freedom! You wouldn't know a thing about what he's been through. You couldn't. Neither of you. And besides, he had the holy myrrh, the secret weapon against the witch! Does that mean nothing to you?"

"Klaas, I never honestly expected it was bound to turn out any different. There's been plenty of folks before him--"

"I don't care how many have tried and failed before him. This time was different. He had the myrrh. The secret weapon."

"But ye got to be able to use it for it to do ye any good. Got to get within range of her. And that's impossible. She lives at the bottom of a river, Klaas. In the ruins of an old Imbajaw foundry. Ye got to take the old conveyer system down to the river bottom and be taken inside to see her, and ye know what? Ain't no one has ever seen her and come back in one piece."

"Then how can you know so much about her? Her glass rod and silver basin and all, if no one has ever seen her?"

"The Naturals. Some of them are permitted. All we know of what goes on down there on the river bottom is through the stories passed on by them. There is no way into her fortress, Klaas. Not without being taken."

"But the myrrh."

Hiley shook her head. "Just forget about it, Klaas."

"She's right." Alva nodded his head, waggling his antennae.

"But do you have any idea how much trouble I've been through to deliver it? Aye? My entire life. My entire life was manipulated into finding it!"

"We all just pawns, Klaas," Alva said, reassuringly. "Don't matter what ye do with life. It all pays the same."

"No." Krengel spun toward the doorway, nearly slipping on all the comics. "I'll be damned if I'm going to stand idly by and allow my whole life to amount to nothing!"

"Klaas, wait a minute." Hiley made a move to halt him but he threw off her arm. "What the heck do ye think you're going to do, Klaas?"

"Hide here in your pile of comic books for all eternity if you like, wrap yourself up in a warm cozy blanket of entertainment, and try to pretend all the while that there's not a whole world out there that you've left behind. Have you ever heard of honor? Either of you?" Krengel glared at Hiley and Alva. "What has happened to you? I suppose that much like the forgotten Age of Miracles and Magic, the concept of honor has been lost in time as well."

Iptintec's stables slumbered in the darkness that veiled the vast corral. The center ring resembled an empty theater with no booking for a show. Near the stalls, the voices of boys echoed like the chatter of stage hands from where they sat, three in a row, along the far wall. The flow of their conversation waned erratic and dissipated, as Krengel marched steadily toward them through the gloom across the center of the corral, swinging lantern in hand like a wayward wizard bent on some curious errand that defied intuition. They were silent when Krengel stopped beneath their lamppost in a halo of sleepy light. The shadowy figures looked like cutouts, loitering extras in the wings of a dream.

"Have you heard what happened to Ludolph Eichmann?" Krengel asked.

One of the boys was whittling a stick. Pale wood chips bounced rhythmically off the shoulder of the slouching form seated next to him, who seemed not to mind. The third lad chewed lackadaisically on a bulging wad in his cheek. He leaned forward and spat a dark rope of juice into the dirt, then resumed chewing. The whittler lowered his stick and swiveled his head to deliver a long and faceless stare. The slouching middleman, littered with his neighbor's chaff, might've been carved out of stone.

Krengel glanced in the direction of a dull ruckus emanating from the nearest stall, where rippling numbaec larvae suckled the planks that contained them with their vacillating lamprey mouths.

About the size and shape of a seal, the grubs wriggled over one another's bodies like a clutch of oversized maggots. Every board on their stall had been rubbed furry with their incessant and voracious habits.

"What do ye want, kid?"

Krengel turned back to the three gargoyles perched on the wall. He wasn't sure which of them had just spoken. He guessed it was the one who'd most recently spat. "I need to borrow a mount, or rent one. But I don't have any money. I say, are they free to borrow, or ..."

The middleman glanced at the chewer, shifting uneasily on his rump. The chewer spat again, sat up tall, and straightened himself. He wiped his chin with the back of his hand, and then stared at Krengel down the bridge of his nose. "Want I should saddle up one of them grubs for ye? Looks to be about all ye could handle."

Krengel cleared his throat. He swapped hands on his lantern. "Can you at least point me in the direction of Tencotha?"

"Heck for?"

"Didn't any of you hear what just happened to Ludolph Eichmann?"

"Eichmann hated your guts, boy." The chewer leaned forward and spat again. "Best ye leave it alone. He gone."

"Is that what you intend to do? Just leave it alone?"

Middleman's head spun quickly back to the chewer. All eyes were on him, now. He appeared to be the designated spokesperson. Just visible in the lamplight was his bulging cheek and about half a grin. "Boy, you might just want to go ahead and skin out of here, while you're still able."

The level of apathy in Iptintec was indefatigable. Such wry and veiled personas. Hadn't anyone in this godforsaken place committed any act at some point in their past that cried out for redemption? Had no one the urge to strive for some modicum of validation of their lukewarm lives? And how they judged! As if Krengel were the only sinner in Iptintec!

Before he realized what he'd done, he'd hurled his lantern with such force into the chewer's smug face that the boy was blown clean backward over the wall in an explosion of luminescent mold and shattered glass. The middleman straightened right up and the whittler dropped his stick. Krengel waited for the chewer to rise and come after him, as he would have expected of any opponent he'd ever fought, but the boy stayed down, just moaning on the far side of the wall. And that was lucky for him, because had he risen, Krengel would have beaten him within an inch of his life. Maybe even to death. Not since the days of challenging Ludolph and Cardinal Moretti, had he enjoyed the heat of a hard scrap. It felt good, all the dark energy pumping through his veins. It had been too long, and he craved some more. "Which way to Tencotha!" Krengel shouted at the other two.

"West gates." The whittler pointed a quick finger in the direction of the Molithe River Valley. "Take the tram down, riverside. Tencotha's just a few clicks upriver."

"Bunch of posturing pigeons. No honor or faith in anything. You people disgust me!" Krengel paced, eyeing them like a caged beast. "Weak of spirit. Flaccid cowards from a soulless age! Tell me all that you know of it!"

The whittler shrugged and glanced quickly at the boy next to him. "Just a place of rendezvous, between the Pancha and the witch. Used to be the upper docks of the old foundry before she dammed up the river. Can't miss it, all the uprights, cables, and diving bells."

Although he'd hardly understood what much of any of that meant, Krengel at least understood the directions on how to get there. Now lightless, Krengel turned from the two remaining sitters on the wall and struck off back across the corral in the direction he'd come.

"Wait!" one of them shouted, behind him. "You're really going down there?"

"Well, of course I am."

The two boys looked at each other, and then back at him. "Better at least come and get you a weapon."

The stalls on either side were rank with numbaec excrement, a mostly liquid substance that smelled something of spoiled mushrooms. Every stall was occupied, displaying ranks upon ranks of the humpbacked beetles, some with carapaces so high they bumped the strings of amber bulbs, causing shadows to leap and cower along the walls. Most of the beast's heads were lowered into a common trough, where a constant flow of water trickled. From every direction, Krengel could hear the gentle paddling of numbaec mouthparts against the walls of their aqueduct. That and the shifting of their great ponderous limbs were the only sounds throughout the vast stables.

Krengel had always lived in close proximity to livestock, and never had he encountered a creature so docile, so mute. Many stood absolutely motionless, doing absolutely nothing, not the least indication of thought's passage through their alien minds. Yet, they appeared as though they could spring into action at the least provocation, in much the same manner as a lit fly remains utterly statuesque, until the instant of its explosive return to livelihood. In that respect, the numbaecs made Krengel uncomfortable. They seemed reliable enough, but so detached of that unspoken connection between a horse and a rider, a dog and its master, surely founded at some basic level of mammalian familiarity. Instead, there was something about the presence of a giant insect that left so much to be desired, with their dull and expressionless upturned bowls for eyes, alien smell, and of course, their utter quietude. Krengel feared that he could never fully trust one.

He so suddenly and intensely missed the lively bucolic atmosphere of an ordinary stable filled with whinnying horses, buzzing flies, and lazy shoals of dust floating through the sunshine. Never before had he any real affection for livestock, but now it made him smile to imagine an afternoon picking stalls, pitching sheaves of golden hay, running a curry brush over an animal's shivering flanks. Normal, everyday chores in another world, a warm and brighter place he might've imagined in a dream.

His smile faded. So, this was how it all began. This was how he would be transformed into one of them. Escape from this place seemed suddenly critical. Because once homesickness piqued and hope waned, a creeping uncertainty would prevail, a thinning of the human spirit that was satisfied by apathy, one that craved entertainment to replace the erosion of faith in miracles and magic that maybe hurt just a little too much to remember. Faith became a door that refused to open. Hope was a cry in the night for a mother who'd never come.

The hands led him back to a sort of store room that they called the bunkhouse. This was evidently where they lived. Bedrolls guarded segregated piles. The garbage and litter was ubiquitous and repulsive. Krengel's eyes were drawn to a comic book on the floor.

"Did you know he was most afraid of bats, so he decided to dress as one?" Krengel pointed at the image of the bat-fellow. "However, he's not really real. He's fake."

"Yeah ..." The whittler made a strange sound and cleared his throat. "Over here, this here's Ludolph's locker."

The hand stepped over garbage in his pointed leather boots. His grimy pantaloons were faded blue, like a swift autumn sky, and his sleeveless shirt was perhaps once white, but had yellowed with age and filth. He appeared comfortable here in the stables, the bunkhouse. Almost at home. He grabbed a handle and pulled open a sort of cabinet door on the wall.

"He liked to keep all kinds of weapons around." The kid smiled, reaching in. "Looks like he done took his good sodium musket, but there's still all his bows, arrows, and things. You're welcome to whatever stuff of his ye think ye might could maybe use." The hand then stepped awkwardly aside, hands jammed to the knuckles in his pockets, and looked expectantly up at Krengel.

"Thank you," Krengel replied, stepping up to the locker and peering inside.

Amongst the bramble of longbows and quivers of arrows, the first item really to draw Krengel's attention, was a ragged tunic of sackcloth, splashed with red paint. Folded upon it was a pointed hat of rolled, red paper. He reached into the locker and removed the battered garments, the same outfit that Ludolph and the others had been forced to wear during their humiliation at *Miso de Gallo*. Perhaps the most heart-wrenching aspect was the realization that this mock clergyman's costume was Ludolph's only set of clothing.

They all came back in an agonizing rush, their little faces, and the ones whose lives had been utterly crushed as a result of his self-centered ambitions. And the ones who'd died. Krengel closed his eyes against the hot tears of shame, knotting his brow as if to brace his mind against the impact of the worst memory of all. The forced rehearsal came back in piercing flashes, stabbing his soul with broken memories of a Roman stable, where they were all forced to witness Friar Otto's torture, confession, and undignified execution.

Krengel took up the stack of folded garments from the floor of the locker and pressed their rough fibers against his face. So much had happened since the dawn of that terrible day, where his benefactor, his friend and the best person he'd ever known, was strangled to death in the manure with the leather coils of a donkey's bridle. What sin had that saintly man ever commited to deserve an end so terrible? Krengel sniffed, wiped his eyes, and looked up from the stack of clothing. There, on the locker floor, he noticed a simple leather pouch.

Krengel laid the garments down gently. He removed the leather satchel from the locker floor. It had been hidden beneath the clothing. This purse, he did not recognize. He brushed off the lint and dust. Probably an article Ludolph recovered from the mountains of garbage in the Quick, or pilfered from just about anywhere between here and Rome. Krengel unfastened the wooden peg sewn on for a button and lifted the flap. Inside was a wadded, silk handkerchief and load of ashen sand that could've come from nowhere but Sundaloon. Projecting up from the sand were lavender shards of shattered glass.

Krengel pushed the handkerchief aside and withdrew one of the shards. He held it up before his eyes. There was no denying its place of origin. He yanked out the handkerchief and shook the sand from the flag of purest white. Upon one corner was embroidered in the finest crimson silk, an ornate letter "K." A baker's meager wedding gift to his cold porcelain bride.

Ludolph had spoken the truth. He'd been back to Lambsheim. Somehow, he'd escaped his benefactor and found his way back to the Krengel estate, with a mind to loot, no doubt, but if he'd been truthful about that visit he'd paid, odds were he'd no reason to lie about his conversation with Miss Luludja. If there had been any remaining doubt that the servant was truly his mother, it had now been washed away. The Krampusz really was rightful heir to the Habsburg-Krengel estate.

Krengel scrunched the silken kerchief in his fist, and let the glass shard fall from his fingertips. It bounced musically against the packed earth of the locker room floor.

But was the Krampusz aware of his unclaimed inheritance? Had his monstrous half-brother, in all his years of rambling, gained some understanding of his entitlement to a fortune so vast that it nearly defied reckoning? Perhaps not. He was nothing but a hermit, a loner, a beach-combing hoarder whose only friends were crabs scuttling around him. But if he did know, what then?

The Krampusz had never given the least indication of awareness, with respect to this matter, but Krengel's eyes were the portals through which the Krampusz had forever peered. He must have seen the ruined corpse of Lady Adeline Habsburg-Krengel, her fingers scattered amongst the shards of stained glass. He must know something. But what, and how much? And what would be the next logical move for a player occupying such an interesting position? Why was the Krampusz still fooling around on a beach with his sad sack of human pets, when he could instead have launched his triumphant return to Lambsheim and laid claim to his sprawling estate? It made no sense that he would know of his entitlement and care nothing. Unless, he too was somehow trapped.

Krengel knotted his brow. He dropped the satchel back into the locker with a tinkle of glass. A gout of Sundaloon sand spewed from beneath the flap. As he stared down at it, he felt a darkening begin to well within his brow, his chest. His fingers tightened around the wad of silk kerchief.

"See anything ye like?"

Krengel didn't respond. He snatched the finest looking bow off the peg, and then a rattling quiver of arrows, all fletched and served with strange, synthetic materials. All were brightly painted and daubed about the nocks with phosphorescent mold. Krengel slung the quiver hotly over his shoulder and turned for the locker room door.

"Careful with them arrows."

Krengel stopped and glanced questioningly at the stable boy.

The kid walked up and took the quiver. With his fingertips, he pinched an arrow by the nock and withdrew the long shaft from the quiver. Krengel was surprised to see that at its leading end, was no barbed point at all. There was just a blunt cylinder of clay, affixed to the shaft with catgut serving and resin.

"What is it?"

"Sodium grenade. Miniature one." The kid twisted the arrow shaft back and forth, rotating its clubbed head in the wan light. "Ludolph spent a lot of time bothering the lab rats down there at the electrolysis plant. Most of them Naturals. Must've done them boys some favors, I guess, because generally they ain't too sociable. Least, not in the normal way."

"How does it work?"

"Well," the kid replied, rubbing his nose with the back of his hand, "each round's got two wax-lined chambers, see. One in front's a slug of pure sodium. One in back's plain water. Smash the round and the water sets off the sodium."

"Ka-boom?"

The kid smiled. "Bet your ass, ka-boom." He gingerly slid the arrow back into the quiver. "Don't ye trip and fall when you're toting these around. Blow ye clean in half."

Krengel nodded uncertainly.

"Got a bunch of other stuff in here." The kid leaned against the frame of Ludolph's locker. "Plenty of sodium slugs and flash-bombs, looks like. All the usual stuff. Feel free to snort around and take all ye like, just be careful. One of them things goes off here in the stable, and you're liable to start a stampede. Numbaecs hate them damned things."

"Thank you," Krengel said.

"Don't mention it," the kid replied. He shoved off the frame of Ludolph's locker and strode off toward the door.

"Hey," Krengel called out to the boy, who hesitated in the doorway and turned, "I'm sorry for -- the things I said."

"No worries," the kid said. "From different worlds, you and I." He reached to doff an imaginary brimmed hat, and then swaggered off through the door.

Chapter Nineteen

"All rise, for His Most Reverent Grand Friar-Inquisitor, Brother Ignacio de la Rabida."

Their common chain had rattled the ringbolts of their manacles as the row of orphans clambered hastily to their feet. No one took him for a joke. In the last twelve hours, they'd bore witness to the Hound of God's impatience, and the lengths to which he would go to exact compliance from those in his clutches. The gruesome evidence dangled from the rafters, just above them. Trying not to look up, the orphans shivered in the swaying shadow of their new decoration.

Flanked on either side by his hooded entourage, the Grand Inquisitor floated toward the stable's center. Like some angel of death, misery incarnate, he exuded a palpable pall that flattened spirits and cooled the blood, for agony was all that this man delivered. Hovering wordlessly before them, head bowed as if in commune with some higher power, he pressed the pads of his fingertips ever so lightly together and raised them to his thin and colorless lips. Like dark manna, a ruby droplet fell from somewhere high above, where strained rope fibers creaked. It spattered dully in the mud, The Hound of God allowed a wry smile. No one moved. And no one spoke.

"Bring him down," the Grand Inquisitor said.

One of the wraiths in black habits plodded through the mud to the back wall, where he released the knot with a twitch of his wrist that dropped what was left of Friar Otto from the pigeon roost. Birds flushed with a tumult of flapping wings. It was a wonder the poor man had a scream of pain left in him, but scream he did when his body followed the barrel of manure bound to his ankles to the stable floor.

"Remove the device."

The minions fussed around sad heap, where strange joints bent limbs in new directions. Broken, defeated, he looked like a crushed spider dying in the mud. It was nothing short of a miracle that he'd survived through the night without asphyxiating after the weighted barrel was hung from his broken legs.

Fidgeting fingers loosened a nut threaded onto a bolt on the back of his head, which gradually relieved tension on the leather straps around his jaws, withdrawing the iron phallus from his throat. The great bulb was extracted with a swinging rope of slobber that bridged the device and the mouth from which it had emerged. Friar Otto moaned thinly.

The Grand Inquisitor strode over and leered down at his prisoner. He smiled and cocked his head with an air of whimsy, as if bemused by the silly predicament that this fellow had somehow gotten himself into. "Can you hear me, Friar Ottomar?"

The friar licked his lips and winced at the sound of the Inquisitor's voice. He swallowed, cleared his throat, choked, and then swallowed again. It appeared as though he wished to speak, but was not yet able. A blind eye flickered open and blinked colorlessly at his tormentor, then closed again.

"I say, which of these children is Klaas Krengel?"

Breathing heavily, the broken heap seemed to be drawing on the last reserves of its strength, shifting what shattered limbs would still obey, rotating the head upon the neck. Blood bubbled from the stumps at the ends of the shattered arms, where every last digit had been hacked off to ensure that never again, would he bless a forehead or place a Eucharist upon a tongue. The mass gurgled, facedown in the mud. The head rotated, openmouthed, and masked completely with manure, and it groaned some unintelligible oath.

"I'm afraid I didn't get that."

"I said I cannot identify one whom I've never seen." Otto said, startling even the Hound of God with his surprising resilience. "My hands have long served as my eyes. And now you've rendered me twice blinded."

"You still have ears."

"I will never!" Friar Otto raised his head from the muck to seemingly impossible attention, scattering rats back into the furthest reaches of the gloom.

The Hound marched over to squat beside the crushed friar and took hold of one of his ears. "But Ottomar, you've already confesed to heresy!" the Hound shouted. "What good sense does it make to further prolong your agonies, when I've already promised you no harm will come to the child?"

"You're a liar and a dog, just like the wolf you serve."

"I'm a servant of God, Friar Ottomar."

"You're the Hound of Satan!"

The Inquisitor shoved his head away and rose to his feet. "I've no patience left for this game. Perhaps your assistance in this matter will not be needed, after all. Something has just occurred to me." Hooking his finger around his lips, he squelched through the mud down the row of shackled children, brow furrowed as if in deep thought. When he reached the end of the line, he turned on one heel to stand directly before Krengel.

"Such a talented choir." He smiled down at Krengel. "I've long had an ear for sweet music. Perhaps too critical an ear, some might say; too sensitive to the slightest errors in tempo and intonation, but I am, after all, a naturally critical person, so it stands to reason...

"You wouldn't know it to look at me now, but there was a time in my life when I was not so very different from all of you. I too was once in a choir. Can you even imagine?" He turned to the nearest of his hooded entourage, behind him, who smiled dimly back at him with a toothless grin. "I was quite talented, actually. Had the voice of an angel. But my voice one day changed, as will yours, and I was called to serve God in another capacity. Oh, but I do still love the sound of a perfect hymn!"

The Hound clapped his hands together and squelched back up the row. "The most renowned choir ever to be birthed in all of Germania. My-my-my. I would expect from any one of you perfect pitch, a Cappella, as well as a keen ability to follow commands, yes? I am certain that all of you would all be familiar with the hymn, Pange Lingua, by Aquinas, of course." The Hound turned on a heel and spun to face Albert Amsel. "Girls, be seated. This rehearsal is just for the boys. You! Sing for me the first verse of the last two stanzas."

Albert's chest rose and fell. A sheen of terror brightened his eyes. He tried to clear his throat, but produced instead, a strangled little cry. The Inquisitor seized him by the jaw.

"Are you Klaas Krengel? Heir to the House of Habsburg? For only he amongst you would fail to sing for me Pange Lingua, line for line!"

Albert closed his eyes. He opened his misshapen mouth, and from his throat gushed a chilling crescendo. The Inquisitor released his grip on the boy's face and stepped back as the child sang.

"Tantum ergo Sacramentum." His voice was the best, among them. Clear and lovely as a mountain spring. Born with a badly cleft pallet, he was not expected ever to speak clearly, but it was in fact the malformed features of his mouth that enabled those heart-stopping acoustics. At least that's what the other orphans believed. "Veneremur cernui."

"Perfection," whispered the Inquisitor. "Absolute perfection." He pulled up the sleeve of his habit and showed Albert the hairless pimpled flesh of his forearm. "You gave me the goose bumps." He sidestepped over to Albert's younger brother, Emil. "His act will be quite a tough one to follow. I wouldn't want to be in your shoes, right now. Go."

"Et antiquum documentum."

"Poco accelerado!" the Inquisitor erupted with sudden fury.

Emil's eyes darted to and fro, as he remembered the meaning of the command, then nodded, and repeated his verse with a bit faster tempo.

"Next!" The Inquisitor pointed fiercely at Benedikt, the youngest of the Amsel brothers.

"Novo cedat ritui."

"Next!"

"Praestet fides supplementum."

"Con brio!" The Inquisitor plunged into his purse and withdrew his sopping sponge as Rolf widened his mouth and sung again with more spirit. "Con brio! Con brio!" He mashed the sponge to his face and inhaled so forcefully that it looked as though his whole throat might collapse. His eyes were crazed when the sponge fell, bloody medicine running from one nostril. "Go!" he screamed at Theodore Weissmuller.

"Sensuum defectui."

Medicine sloshed from the purse down the front of the Hound's habit as he slid through the mud past the Gottlieb sisters, making it appear as though he'd pissed himself. Wolfram Faust was already singing before the Inquisitor had arrived.

"Genitori, Genitoque. Laus et jubilatio."

"Go!" he shrieked at Ludolph Eichmann, sucking another massive draw from the sponge. Blood was now streaming down his throat and over the back of his hand.

"Salus, honor, virtus quoque."

"Legato!" The Inquisitor slapped Ludolph across the face, splattering Krengel's cheek with blood and medicine.

Ludolph began again, repeating the verse a little more softly. "Salus, honor, virtus quoque."

"Legato!" The Inquisitor struck him again. First on one side of his face and then the other. Ludolph sang, his cheeks painted scarlet with blood. The Inquisitor threw back his hood to reveal an entirely hairless head, laughing maniacally in a snuffling staccato. "Legato! Legato!"

"Enough!" The booming voice of Friar Otto stunned the room into silence.

The Inquisitor turned away from Ludolph, who breathed hotly through his nose, blood and tears dripping from his chin, and stormed over to the ruined heap of flesh in the manure. "What have you now to say, Ottomar? What good news would it please thine lips impart?"

"He's dead."

"What?"

"Dead. Dead in the woods because I killed him in the mountain pass, south of Ischgl."

"Klaas Krengel? You really expect me to believe that you murdered him?"

"Believe whatever you like, but I spared the child his suffering."

"Explain."

"Because of the evil within him. Klaas Krengel was possessed by the devil." Friar Otto reared up and sucked a breath, blinking eyes like pearl onions in a mud pie. "I slit his throat in a cave whilst he slept. Then I forced every child in the choir to swear an oath before their lord God almighty that they would never in their lives speak a word of what I'd done." Otto's neck then weakened. His face returned to the wallow in the ordure.

The Inquisitor looked to the row of children, one end to the other. "Is this true? Is this entirely true, what he said?"

The children cast uneasy glances at one another. Albert and Wolfram were first to nod their heads. Emil and Benedikt imitated their brother. Rolf sucked his fingertips, glancing left, then right. Nele looked to Mitzi, who nodded last. Nele looked slowly and fearfully back to the Inquisitor.

The Inquisitor sighed. He walked down the line past bloodied Ludolph and Krengel to remove a fitment hanging from a peg on the stable wall. He tossed the marriage of leather and steel into the mud near Friar Otto's head. "I believe the time has come to fit this stubborn ass with a proper bridle." He nodded to his toothless henchman. "You are a liar, Friar Otto. A liar, blasphemer, and a heretic, no longer of any real service to neither God nor man."

The orphans watched in horror as the executioner waddled over. He sat full upon Friar Otto's back, situating himself like a rider in a saddle. With a half-witted smile, he pulled Otto's face up from the mud, looped the bridle reins twice around his throat, and then wrenched back with all of his might.

###

Sister.

Krengel dipped his index finger into the spittle. He stirred the warm foam into mud. Staring into the tile of mirrored glass that was mounted in the back of Ludolph's locker; he brought his fingertips to his face, and smeared dark hollows around each of his eyes. The blue eyes floating in the pools of ink blinked back from his distorted reflection.

The girl in the woods had been his sister.

He spat again and stirred another spot of mud into the locker room floor. Black ash would've been preferable, but not a single flame flickered anywhere in the Sack of Shadows. No need for it. No use for fire when you couldn't eat. Not when the temperature was always the same, acceptably lackluster. Not where even the smallest flicker would endanger the lives of a dwindling population of humans by attracting unwanted attention, by inviting devastation with a wildfire raging through mountains of trash.

He dragged his muddy fingers from the corners of his mouth down either side of his chin.

He wondered why no one had ever succumbed to that impulse, setting a fire, setting the whole godforsaken place ablaze, burning down the Sack of Shadows, all around them. What would happen, he wondered, if the sack burned to ash and all realms at once collided? Would all threads of time and space unravel and curl in the inferno like a nest of hot wires, precipitating a universal cataclysm? The end of days?

He widened his eyes, opening and closing his mouth.

Perhaps nothing at all would happen.

He wiped his fingertips off on his pile of old rags that he'd worn all the way from Bari. Now, he donned Ludolph's sackcloth tunic from *Miso de Gallo*, still slopped with red paint and streaked with the snowy droppings of flapping chickens. He placed the tall steepled hat upon his head and examined its effect on his reflection. Pinching hold of the brim, he pulled it down over his brow just to the tops of his eyes. That looked better, in a more frightening way. Gruesome, like a deranged puppet come to life.

Had Lady Adeline not stolen him from his birth mother, he'd have grown up with a sister. He imagined a very different childhood, growing up inside that cramped little shack, where their mother might've lovingly brushed both their heads by the light of their crackling hearth. Not cramped. It would have been cozy. Not sprawling and ghastly, like the Habsburg-Krengel estate. How much happier he might've been as the child of a servant, son to an adoring mother and protective brother to a sister. But no, he'd been robbed. And that life had instead been wasted on a so-called monkey, otherwise known as the Krampusz.

Krengel lifted the silk handkerchief by its corners and shook it square. He then folded it over into a triangle and raised it just beneath his nose. The tapered point hung to his chest. It concealed the lower-half of his face like a long snowy beard, surmounted by cavernous blue eyes. The effect was perfect. He looked just like him. Or, at least, an artistic rendition of that murderous phantom. Krengel turned his head side to side and studied his reflection from every angle. In the same manner as the bat-fellow, he'd adopted a look resembling that of his greatest fear. All the terror once inflicted by that midnight assassin was now Krengel's to own, to project like a weapon upon his enemies, to disarm and disorient them in the gloom.

He emptied the sand and glass from the leather satchel. No room for sentiment on a mission of vengeance. He gathered up sodium slugs and flash-bombs by the handful and arranged them carefully inside the purse. In order to survive whatever awaited him at Tencotha, it was imperative he look past those insurmountable obstacles even to greater challenges that lied beyond the Sack of Shadows. The witch, she was not a barred gate. She was merely a flimsy barricade through which he would smash to engage a new path in life that was becoming increasingly clearer. Without a doubt, there existed sins for which there was no good penance to absolve one's self of the burden of guilt. But that was not to say that a lifelong quest could not be fueled by the need for absolution, as well as revenge.

There before him in Ludolph's tile of mirrored glass was the manifestation of a gypsy assassin, the vindictive ghost of a dozen humiliated Elves. The costume and war paint suggested something of the duality of his self-appointed mission, a rather extreme task of rewarding the good, and punishing the wicked. For he had no more choice in the matter of rescuing the survivors of his former choir, than he did in the matter of avenging the deaths of those slain.

"This shall forever be my path, until my wrongs have been righted."

The path was clear. There was no other choice but to confront the Wolf wherever he found a lair. Today, a witch would die. And before her blood had even begun to seep into the earth, he would be hounding the trail of the next persecutor of children, the next devil who dared abuse those less powerful than he. Save the children. Lead them like an army of toy soldiers into battle, for they only needed be trained to withstand the might of their oppressors until just the right moment to strike. They outnumbered their persecutors, if they confronted them one at a time. Their collective eyes and ears could become the walls and the trees, who would know then that the wicked ones were sleeping, and when they were awake. Perhaps in dark parody to the habits of the Spanish Inquisition, they would keep a ledger filled with the names of every offender, and a record of their each and every sin. Turn the terror they inflict right back against them.

Chapter Twenty

Krengel peered down onto Tencotha from the overlook, just as the Westgate guard had advised. Evidence of the battle was apparent. Lifeless bodies lay scattered about the ill-lit yard of what looked to be a sort of wheelhouse, situated at the foot of a watchtower. And the carcasses, he noticed, were not human.

Round shadows like negative spotlights swept over the dead, as an endless train of great glass orbs surfaced from the Molithe River on a system of cables pulled taut around a massive pulley up at the wheelhouse, where they made their turn at the end of the line and headed back down toward the water again. Most of the globes were lit from within by the usual blue lanterns, setting the string of bulbs ethereally aglow, as they plunged one after another back into the inky abyss on an endless promenade to the river bottom.

A staircase was affixed to the tower's hip that looked something of a gallows. Here, Krengel intuited, the inhuman workers must have bustled up and down those switch-backing stairs, to the dock platform where the cargo of those bulbous vessels could be loaded and unloaded. Perhaps the Naturals had been engaged in that ordinary duty when Ludolph and his band of fighters had attacked.

Krengel squinted his eyes and stared at one of the bulbs as it came around. Something different about this one. The inside of the glass was darkly streaked, smeared with handprints, sanguine hieroglyphics writ by flailing hands. A gory testament by some doomed captive dragged down into the river to meet the witch.

It occurred to Krengel at that moment that he might ought be better served to abandon this suicidal course of action. No human being had ever returned from down there. None had ever seen it and survived. He stared into the roiling water where the blood smeared bulb disappeared. Only the Pancha were permitted to venture down and back. Only they knew the truth. And the stories they brought back to the surface, were so horrific, they defied the imagination.

A devourer of children. A fountainhead of nightmares.

Evil incarnate. A kinder evil like you ain't never seen.

Glass rod on a velvet pillow to one side. A silver basin on the other. So she can still consume the flesh of children. Endless consumption without filling.

With his resolve teetering on the brink, Krengel spotted something down in the yard. It was small, square, and metallic. It winked rhythmically in the gloom as its polished surface reflected the procession of glowing bulbs.

Krengel slipped over the ridge and slid on his rump down the slope to the edge of the battlefield. He waited in the shadows, scanning the ridgelines all around him. The squealing wheelhouse pulley, the surge and plunge of the globes in and out of the river was an altogether noisy affair, and more than a little unnerving as it deprived the senses of being heightened. Crawling forward on his hands and knees, Krengel edged his way closer to the object of his attraction. It flashed weakly at him, like a tiny cry for help. As he planted his arm forward, he felt something warm and yielding against his palm. He gasped, and retracted his hand as if the thing before him was a coiled serpent.

The head was oblong. No eyes to speak of, but there were great, fringed, batlike ears. From the wide, thick-lipped mouth, sprouted long and whip-like barbells nearly the length of the creature's body. It was dead. A massive hole was blown through its chest. Probably inflicted by a sodium musket.

He reached out and dared to touch the creature. It was silky smooth, like the muzzle of a horse. Or perhaps it was the horse-like shape of its head, its rubbery lips that made him think of a horse. It was like a cross between a horse, a bat, and a catfish. Three-fingered and three-toed. Thin and sinewy, overall, a camel-grey in color with darker splotches along the spine.

"But no eyes at all," Krengel whispered, stroking the thing from muzzle to crown. Truthfully, he wouldn't have known the best spot for a pair of eyes to be located, so unusual was the shape of its skull. He knocked gently on the hollowed bridge of its … no nose. Just the flailing pair of barbells. "Lucky for you," he said, for the odor of the thing was somewhat sour, doglike.

"Klaas!"

Krengel jolted upright at the sound of his name. "Hiley?"

"They've taken the dam! They're going to blow it!" She came sliding down the slope behind him with her musket slung over one shoulder. "Oh, my gosh." She stopped and covered her mouth with one hand.

Krengel at first assumed that it was the sight of the dead Natural that had given her pause. But she was not looking at the dead body. She was staring at him. It was his costume.

"What do you want?" Krengel jerked down the snowy handkerchief that served as his bearded mask.

"They took the dam. Ludolph's stand here wasn't nothing but a distraction. Main force swung south along the reservoir and took the dam. They're gonna blow it to Kingdom Come! Drain the whole reservoir. Witch will be flopping like a fish on the bank. Ain't never seen so many sodium kegs. Come on back to Iptintec." She slapped Krengel on the shoulder. "We're fixing to have us a siege."

Krengel gawped around the bloody scene at Tencotha. He rose from beside his fallen Pancha warrior and strode over to the object he'd spotted. It was his flask. He picked it up, shook it. It was still tightly corked and full. "Where is Ludolph?"

"Klaas." Hiley slipped up behind him. "It ain't safe here."

"Where is Ludolph?" Krengel turned to face her.

She shook her head. "We're going to do something about all of this, ye know."

"Where is he, Hiley?"

"They took him." She dropped her gaze toward the riverbank. "They took him down."

"Then I'm going down after him." Krengel marched off toward the wheelhouse. "Are you going to show me how to work this fangled contraption, or will I have to figure it all out, myself?"

"Klaas, they're going to blow the dam. Ain't no reason to go down there. We're bringing the ol' witch topside."

In the background, the city of Iptintec raised its alarm once more in all its grotesque cacophony. Even as far away as Tencotha, the noise was practically deafening. It could still be felt at one's core.

"Ludolph is down there!" Krengel shouted over the blast. "Do you even know what it means to be part of a siege? It could take months, Hiley! Ludolph has hours at the most!"

"Why do you care so much about someone who clearly hated you?"

"He doesn't hate me. He just resents me, because he's already suffered so much on my account. We all have! Even you!"

"What are you talking about? I got myself into this big mess all on my own. Me with my Forever Friend."

"Don't even call him that anymore! He's not your friend! He's never been a friend to any of us. He's only used us as his means to an end. This is all about money, Hiley! He's stuck on that bloody island with no means of returning to the time period of our birth, where he stands to inherit a sizable fortune. The witch is the only thing standing in his way. That's what all of this is all about. See? The Krampusz is nothing but a devil! He's the spawn of a Succubusz, the bride of the Incubusz, seeded into the living world through the poisoned sting of a bee. All along he has been doing precisely what you'd expect of a devil: manipulating everyone around him, ruining lives, and corrupting the innocent, all out of greed."

"Then how's come ye think it's your fault the rest of us got into this fix? Ye don't owe us nothing."

"Because I was the first." Krengel knotted his fists and began to tremble. "I was the first victim to be corrupted. Had I been stronger and resisted him, he'd have spent his days in exile on Sundaloon the way God intended, but it was my own greed that spoiled God's plan, and destroyed countless innocent lives as a result."

"Klaas … I think you're taking all this a little too hard."

"No!" Krengel held up the flask of holy myrrh. "This was my mission. Mine. Stealing a flask of God's Tears right from the tomb of Saint Nicholas, a man canonized for his miraculous heroism and his acts of profound generosity. I stole his relics at the command of a devil! This was a mission suited for the worst sort of scum, the most soulless of unscrupulous thieves, and I was chosen." Krengel nodded his head. "And I succeeded."

"You were manipulated."

"No. You were manipulated, Hiley. I was perfect for the job."

"Klaas, get down!" Hiley shrieked. Unshouldering her musket, she dropped to her belly, pulling Krengel with her to the ground. There came the staccato pop of rifle fire from some point high and to the right. Geysers of dirt leapt from the ground, all around them. Hiley swung the hefty barrel of her weapon over Krengel's body and let loose a thunderous report. With surprising speed, she jacked a second slug into the chamber, snapping a cap behind it with the pad of her thumb. Krengel plugged his ears as the weapon discharged a second time. From the bluffs overlooking Tencotha, he saw a spotted body fall roll limply down the slope onto the edge of the yard.

"We have to go!" Hiley grabbed his arm and pulled him to his feet. "Now!"

"No." Krengel jerked loose her and slipped the flask of myrrh into his leather satchel. "I told you, I'm going down there. I'm going to save my friend." He pulled an arrow from the quiver and nocked it onto the bowstring. Rather front-heavy with the explosive tip, he guessed it was going to require quite an arch to hit a target much beyond a stone's throw.

"Fine. Go on and kill yourself, if ye think it'll make ye feel better." Hiley took a couple steps backwards to deliver him a parting glare before she turned and jogged back up the escarpment. She clambered up over the bluff, using the butt of her musket for support. She rose to her feet, shouldered her weapon, and disappeared.

At last, Iptintec's terrible alarm fell silent, yielding to the machinations of the lifeless wheelhouse yard. And then came Hiley's scream.

###

The Naturals used a language that sounded like rubber friction, like a thumbnail dragged over the teeth of a comb. Surrounded by the creatures all vocalizing at once was not unlike the ambiance of a twilit marsh of croaking frogs. But as they dragged Krengel and Hiley out into the middle of the yard and began to strip them of their weapons and other effects, it seemed as though they were not so much communicating thoughts as they were constantly perceiving their surroundings, like chittering bats.

Alien hands swept purposefully over their bodies, touching, feeling, almost as if they were calculating, appraising the worth of their new captives by some strange system of value. They seemed particularly interested in Krengel, paying special attention to his portly waistline. Rattling and croaking, they tapped his round belly with their slimy barbells, measuring his amplitude with noticeable excitement. A barbell stroked against his leather pouch and a three-fingered hand struck out for it. Krengel grabbed it by the strap and played a game of tug-of-war with the would-be robber.

"Let go of it. It's mine!" Krengel pulled the strap to his chest and barrel-rolled in the opposite direction, bringing a flurry of beating staffs upon his body. He curled into a ball to minimize the exposed surface area of his flesh, clinging stubbornly to his last possession. At last, the strap snapped. He heard the Pancha warrior fall backward onto his spotted rump, the clatter of sodium slugs and the tinny bounce of a flask upon the ground.

Krengel flipped over and dove through the jungle of sweeping barbells, three-toed feet and grappling hands. The flask was his. Or, at least, its contents. He'd be damned if the Tears of God would be the spoils of these heathens. He snatched it from the chaos and clasped it tightly to his chest, rolling over on top of it to protect it from the ravenous hoard. All the clicking and chittering in his ears made him half-mad, if he wasn't already. They knew he had hold of something, in their own strange way, and they were trying to roll him over to get at it. It wasn't long before they'd succeeded in doing so, with so many involved, and try as he might to keep hold of his last precious thing, they were soon yanking it from his grasp.

"You won't get it." Krengel growled, biting onto the cork stopper. "Not this!" He popped the cork free. Squinting his eyes, he yawned his mouth like a baby bird to receive a cool and fragrant stream of perhaps the world's most powerful relic. He had to admit, he'd tasted better things. Certainly not spiced hippocras. But it brought him some satisfaction to drain the flask to its very last drop, before at last, relinquishing the spent vessel to the heathen army.

Flipping him onto his belly, his handlers crooked his knees and elbows behind his back to bind him, wrists to ankles. Once pinioned, the horde lifted him from the ground like a trussed hog and carried him toward the wheelhouse. No mystery where he was headed.

Up six flights of stairs to the dock, he swung facedown over a forest of tramping, three-toed feet. Somewhere behind him, amidst the mob's rattling chorus, he could hear Hiley's screams as she cursed them. Cursed him. Cursed her Forever Friend.

A glass bulb was conveyed up the cable and into position. A lever was thrown, derailing the large globe from the drive cable and dumping it over onto its sedentary sister. Two of the Naturals squatted beneath the swaying orb and took hold of opposite sides of a steel helm that loosened the valve over a manhole. The covering swung free on its rusted hinges. Positioning Krengel directly beneath the gaping porthole, they hooked some fitment to his bindings, and winched him easily up inside the bulb from an internal block and tackle. Swinging and spinning round and round from an upper eyelet, Krengel watched in horror through the bleary glass as the manhole was slammed shut beneath him, and the valve retightened. One of the Naturals slapped the side of his bulb twice. Somewhere, a lever was thrown that reengaged his vessel to the drive cable. And then, he was floating away.

Spinning helplessly, he watched a more and more distant Hiley kicking against her handlers, as she was being loaded into a bulb of her own. He watched this intermittent show as he came round and round again, until his vessel heaved suddenly and violently as it slammed against the surface of the Molithe River, clanging his head into the glass wall. The internal lantern pitched and pinwheeled from the eyelet, as a surge of murky bubbles rushed around him. Good God almighty, he was going down.

Dragged down, down, deeper into the darkest place of all, in a world without light, every turn of the cog pulled him further from a surface world he'd so recently departed, strange as that world had been, and ever deeper into another one devoid of familiarity. The darker it became outside his glass bubble, the more accutely he yearned for light, as someone drowning yearns for a last breath of air. Now he longed for the glow of Iptintec's sodium blimps, the solitude of the numbaec stables, the strewn comics on the floor of Hiley's dormer ... could it be so? Like Hiley, he'd on some level come to develop a fondness for life in the Quick.

Perhaps there had been some wisdom after all in her philosophy, to accept that which fate dealt you and make the best of it. He had, after all, been given the gift of eternal life, had he chosen to accept it at cost. He could've made himself some real forever-friends, found a soul mate, and lived together forever in Iptintec without ever having to suffer the indignity of watching the ones you love most, grow old and waste away. Nothing was ever free in this world, nor in any other, he supposed.

You either let the darkness make you crazy, or string it up with lights!

Deeper and deeper he plunged, until the glass began to sing and the seams around the portholes began to fizz. Dark water pooled in the bottom of the bulb. Cold droplets rained down upon his back from what appeared to be a second manhole, up above him. The bulb tore through black mats of snotty material, still spinning, once bumping hard against something huge that floundered greasily against the glass.

Coming around from a spin, Krengel noticed an orange glow that appeared to be emanating from the bottom of the river. Faint at first, the light gathered intensity as he was dragged ever closer to the source. The cables whined as he was pulled through encrusted crossbeams that leveled off his direction of travel to one parallel to the river bottom. Water sloshed sharply in the bottom of the bulb. A steady stream pizzled from above. The outside pressure of so much water felt tremendous, as though at any instant his bulb might give, crushing he and his vessel both into a chum of organs and shattered glass. He shelved these inconsolable worries, watching instead, the muddy river bottom scrolling beneath his glass carriage like a pocked and lifeless moonscape.

Ahead, the flumes of orange light leapt blearily into the gloom from great cones of mud like ancient pyramids. But quick as they were appeared, the fires were snuffed by the frigid gloom into which they were born. As he drew nearer, the phantasmagorical play of magma in the void was bright enough to make him wince. Floating through a volcanic gauntlet with all the power to disintegrate him with one hellish belch, he could not bring himself to close his eyes and spare himself the sight of it, for something even worse lay just ahead. Dead in his path, it was so vast in size and so ominous in shape that it seemed somehow to slow the passage of time to a crawl. Even the harping cables on which he rode were stilled into respectful silence, as they neared the man-made structure looming up from the river bottom.

Flattened and clenching the muddy substrate with a jungle of hooked columns, twin portholes seemed to stare out into the void like the eyes of a gigantic crab. Open magma vents pulsed demonically against the underside of the fortress, which happened to be the direction in which the cables appeared to be strung. As Krengel was drawn beneath, he perceived a gradual ascent. The volcanic fury below grew more distant and less threatening, as the drive cable rose along an inclined channel in the fortress underbelly that sloped upward toward its center. There, Krengel discerned the shape of a circular opening.

His bulb lurched as it clanked through a set of steel uprights that redirected the cables vertically. Up into the gaping maw, he felt helpless as a polyp in the tentacles of a mauna goba. It was indeed much the same feeling of terror he'd experienced back on the plateau, where Hiley and her Starlings had appeared in the nick of time to save him from being devoured alive. But no one was going to save him this time. His bulb, half-filled with murky water, surged dripping from the surface of the subterranean pool, and into a lair of inexorable blackness. He had arrived. And this time, he was on his own.

A lever was thrown that derailed him from the drive cable and left him hanging in the blackness like a cut of meat dangling upon a hook. Minutes seemed like hours as he waited, until at last he spotted the dark villous forms slithering about the floor beneath him, grabbing hold of the wheel valve on the bulb's lower manhole and loosening its threads. His ears felt as though they might pop, as hissing air and streams of bubbles around the seam gave way to a total release of pressure that dropped the porthole on its hinges like a sprung jaw, regurgitating a massive gutful of water down into the gloom with a horrendous splash. Krengel was left swinging, pinioned from the inner pully, gaping down into the blackness of inner space.

He could hear them. Hundreds of them. Their rattling language reverberated off unseen cavernous walls. Whipping barbells brushed his flesh as the rope from which he was bound descended in jerks. Before he landed in a pool on a smooth floor, cold as a tomb, their three-toed hands were all over him, feeling him, measuring him, appraising him once again in their inconceivable way. There was some disagreement and two of them lashed out against one another over his hogtied body. There appeared dissention in the ranks as his handlers divided over what best be done with him. Their prattling cries resounded in the blackness as they took sides over the two fighters now wrestling in the water. Pushing, slipping, their rattles escalated into glottal bellows. It was an awful sound, not unlike a pair of sparring sealions on Sundaloon. With a deafening concussion and a salt-white flash, one suddenly took the life of the other. Krengel grimaced in the acrid smoke as a spray of warm droplets rained down upon him. The loser of the skirmish crumpled wetly to the grotto floor. The victor barked, clacking the butt of his musket against the floor. Two Pancha then seized Krengel beneath his arms and lifted him with renewed purpose from the floor.

Moving forward, barbells sweeping and tapping, occasionally brushing Krengel's shoulders, his invisible captors lugged him deeper into the bowels of their subterranean stronghold. Never in his life had he experienced such absolute impermeable blackness. It was disorienting. Sickening. Were it not for the grips of the Naturals firmly upon him, he might've spun off the face of the earth and into space. Their clicks and chatters bounced off distant walls and what seemed an impossibly high ceiling, where unimaginable life forms slapped their invisible wings. Despite being deprived of sight, Krengel sensed by the exorbitant resonance of every sound that this room was far and away the largest he'd ever occupied. What unseen wonders and gruesome works of art must decorate the walls and ceilings of such a cavern, he wondered. What scenes must be captured in its arcade frescoes to befit the temple of their goddess, the flesh-eating witch?

The reverberation of their tramping footsteps and clicks gradually assumed an air of closeness, as his handlers approached what certainly was a wall, or a solid object of considerable size. Strange, how he could perceive such a thing without sight, but he knew it was there, even as they hefted him up onto an immense table, situating him upon a clattering tray of cold metal.

Here began the most peculiar preparations. Handfuls of cool and rustling sheaves that smelt of fresh vegetation were tossed around his trussed body. Once he was completely encircled, toiling hands rubbed him down, head to toe, with a warm and sticky salve that reeked of fruity vinegar. The Naturals purred and clicked in the blackness, antennae tapping, sweeping, and sampling the flavors of his skin with every flick. Their hands dipped and rubbed until he was completely covered in the stuff, his hair gelled into a peak. Orbiting grinders cracked strange seeds above him, pulverizing their contents into a gentle shower of astringent grit that burned his nose and stuck fast to his marinated skin. How it irritated the lining of his nostrils, causing his nose to run, but Krengel dared not sneeze.

A Natural then approached with a basin emanating blue light. Three-fingered hands plunged into the container, and returned with luminous scoops of sliced polyps, which were scattered fussily around him amidst the leafy garnish, setting his body aglow on the serving platter like a showcased dish, the main course of a terrible feast. Once the polyps had been arranged to the chef's satisfaction, a great domed lid was slammed down over him, and latched shut from the outside.

Partly entranced by all the activity on his behalf, Krengel hadn't yet had time to fear his predicament fully, until he heard Hiley's screams, muffled by the platter covering. It was his sudden awareness of her terror that ignited his own, as he felt his platter being lifted and carried forward, possibly toward a waiting oven to roast him alive. Tears spilled down his cheeks, both from fright and from the burning grains of seasoning in his eyes. He quite vividly imagined what a roasting would entail in a place he could not die. Hour after agonizing hour of smelling his own fat liquefy and stream from his pores, while his flesh and organs were gradually transformed from a familiar vessel of life into a cannibal's savory dish. And then, the blades would find him, carving him up alive, boning cooked flesh and shuttling him piece by piece into some horrible masticating mouth, all while he watched the whole process of being devoured by the glow of sliced polyps.

The sound of his breathing was close and tinny as he sucked humid shots of air through his nostrils. Panic began to whistle up through his core. He'd never been claustrophobic, but then, he'd never been trussed and sealed beneath a metal dome before. Hiley's shrieks grew more distant as his servers carried him away from the food preparation area, and onward to the next step in this unthinkable process. The guilt he suddenly suffered over his years of gluttony took him by complete surprise. In that moment, he actually pitied every living creature that he'd ever eaten. Being devoured by another organism was such a terrible thing. He truly understood that now. He mourned the undignified end of every last animal that had been trussed, broken and carved, roasted, ground or sliced to bits within that dreadful Krengel kitchen, where he'd strutted through leavings and pissed upon their remains like a spoiled child-king. Tears rolled down his cheek onto his pillow of leafy garnish. Never again could he view the habits of eating in much the same way. If somehow he survived this predicament, he vowed to God never again to devour the flesh of another animal.

They slammed down his platter with a jolt that jostled the garnish and set halved polyps to wobbling to and fro. The purrs and prattles of the Naturals faded softly away, as did the splash of their feet through unseen puddles. At last, he was left in the company of an ominous silence. Only the sound of his breathing inside the dome. The occasional plop of a water droplet, somewhere in the depths of the grotto. For the time being, it seemed there would be no oven roasting. All things considered, he supposed that was good fortune.

By the fading glow of sliced polyps, Krengel stared into his own distorted reflection on the polished walls of his tiny prison, where his made-up eyes gaped hollowly back at him. His skin was glistening with marinade, his hair hanging in sticky locks. Of all the things his captors had stripped of him, they'd somehow overlooked the silken mask that still covered the lower half of his face. The light of the dying polyps still waned. Ironic that the last face he might ever look upon, would be that of his own worst nightmare, reflected. He wondered, had Ludolph suffered this same end, staring into his own terrified face as a final indignity before being eaten alive? Had Chad? Would he soon be joining a collection of former people in the garbage mountains as living leftovers? One day, eons from now, would another lost child find and stroke his severed hand in their lap?

Krengel balled his hand into a fist. He closed his eyes. A thin whimper slithered up his throat to escape his burning nostrils. When he reopened his eyes, the polyps had burned completely out. Blackness filled his cramped cell like the inside of a coffin. The residual image of his midnight assassin continued to hover before his eyes as a blanched and greenish negative until eventually, even that too dissipated.

This is what it meant to have nothing.

Only now, at that moment, did Krengel truly understand absolute divorce from everything, including hope. How selfish he'd always been. Such a piglet. Such a swine. To think he'd cried foul over his circumstances at any point in his life prior to this one. Even the terrible descent to the bottom of the Molithe River had been awesome in its stunning visions of natural wonder and volcanic might. Such a wasteful fool, wishing away his life, minute by minute, while forever lamenting life's inequities. At last, he understood that no price could be put upon that gift, which he'd forever taken for granted.

There was a sound.

Krengel's ears pricked. He stopped his unnecessary breathing, shutting down all receptors for distraction from the source of what he'd just heard. A rustling. So close that it must have been inches from his head. There! There it was again. The tap of the tiniest footsteps he'd ever heard. Picking its way through the leafy umbrage that encircled him. Not unlike the trundling gait of a microscopic numbaec, the little visitor drew nearer his face. Antennae flicking, the unseen creature clambered inquisitively from the garnish onto the point of Krengel's nose. It was an ant. A smile broadened Krengel's face. An earthly ant had somehow found him at the bottom of a river, in the uttermost depths of a netherworld, and it had come to comfort him in his final moments -- at least, as a wholly corporate and sentient being.

As the insect crept up the bridge of his nose, to perch purposefully right between his eyes like some bejeweled scarab of mystical portents, Krengel wondered if this could possibly be the same ant he'd gently handled at the rail of Hiley's veranda. Were such unlikely circumstances even possible? If so, then this was not just any visiting ant. This was an old friend. A friend of the most loyal kind.

Krengel quieted his thoughts. He detected another sound, somewhere just outside his serving platter. The thunder of distant breakers against pumice rocks. The tumultuous yelping of seagulls. Wind through the seagrass. Rippling water.

The domed lid of his sanctuary was torn suddenly free and rocketed upward to untold heights, as chilly grotto air rushed against his exposed body. The stolen lid clattered as it struck a distant wall and rolled dizzily through the blackness. There again, the sluicing of water, set into fluid motion like lapping waves upon a beach like the wake of a passing ship. Krengel dared not even twitch. The blackness swam with his ideas, imagined phantoms and revenants. None could be worse than what his own mind conceived. This is what he told himself, as he knew that whatever ripped away and threw his covering was standing there. Right there.

Another rippling slosh of liquid, but nowhere near the floor where logically, it should have been. No. The sounds of water were coming not from down below, but from somewhere high up above. Had the world turned upside-down? Krengel bent his neck from a cowering angle, upward, and to an awestruck gawp. It was right there. Everywhere. Like a titanic skin of wine of such enormity as to contain the vintage of an entire region. And high above, surmounting the invisible leviathan, blazed a hot pair of eyes, burning down upon him with red hate.

Awestruck at the foot of this mountain of evil, Krengel found himself awash in pale blue light. Some poor polyp, or part of one, swallowed deep within this mass, flickered miserably to life in its semi-digested state. It was this poor devoured polyp that set its entire trappings aglow by the flickering light of its own despair, exposing the stupendous dimensions of its transparent devourer. The crystalline blob brimmed with a stew of sloshing filth, sausage skins and other nameless indigestibles, skull fragments, whole feathered seabirds and shattered bones. At the height of a castle turret, useless vestigial limbs dangled feebly like tripish and useless teats. Higher still, that hairless head of normal proportions split wide in a gaping mouth filled with rows of triangular teeth.

Whatever Old Berchta had been on the flipside meant nothing to the new form she'd assumed in the Quick. Hers was a form befitting her life of perpetual consumption, termite queen of the lightless void that she had terrorized for untold millennia. Not a trace remained of whatever humanity she had forsaken back on that frozen pass, when she'd consummated her unholy union to the Incubusz. Krengel trembled in the crimson spotlight cast down upon him from those inhuman eyes, for which she had traded her immortal soul. Long ropes of silvery mucous dangled from her jagged grin, as the ancient predator of children lowered herself upon him.

Useless clubbed feet descended, drumming lifelessly with scraping shins against the table's edge. Still, she sank, clawed and withered hands knuckling down to rest upon the platter, curled nails but an inch from the tip of Krengel's nose. He grimaced when a thread of her saliva coiled upon his cheek. Hovering over him, her eyes burned his skin like two peepholes through the walls of Hell. He could feel the otherworldly heat emanating from her glare, wilting the leafy garnish, sending his loyal ant scurrying down over his nostril and into the silken folds of his mask. This attracted the witch's attention.

Lowering herself still further until she was eye to eye, she edged a withered claw toward his face. Bristling with stiff hairs and reeking of rancid meat, the yellowed hooks pushed through the ring of garnish until they pinched hold of his mask. With surprising strength, she ripped it loose of his head with one vicious thrash. The knotted rag sailed off into the blackness.

The witch grinned, revealing gums black as a dog's and a tongue like marbled cheese behind those rows of needling teeth. The stinking claw returned, pushing up once again through the garnish until it slipped between his pursed lips, scratching at the enamel of his front teeth. Clear fluid passed between his lips to trickle down her gnarled finger. The witch cocked her bald head and flared her nostrils. Aroused, she leaned in closer to the new scent of perfume until the heat of her glare threatened to blister his skin.

That is when Krengel lunged. He threw himself straight at her, spewing an entire mouthful of holy myrrh directly into Old Berchta's face.

Hurtling skyward like an enormous grubworm thrust up from the earth, the witch emitted a scream more terrible than the alarm of Iptintec, spurting a geyser of inner fluids clear to the cathedral ceiling through the ragged hole dissolved into her face. Arching the whole of her spineless horror, the monster toppled backward and struck the floor with a thunderous slap that shook plaster from the ceiling in a disconcerting shower. Her enormity twitched and sloshed, flickering dimly by the pulse of jubilant polyps stewing inside her as she deflated, gushing the foul tonnage of her stomach contents across the grotto with rhythmic sucks and spurges from her neck's ragged stump.

The witch, she was dead.

Chapter Twenty-One

They blew the dam while Krengel was using the serving platter's sharp edge to slice away the cordage that bound his ankles and wrists. There followed the prattling ruckus of fleeing Naturals amidst resonating aftershocks that still rumbled through the river bottom. And then began the movement of vast volumes of water.

He rolled onto his belly and slid off the table's edge, cowering in the roar of rushing water, above and all around him. The witch's lair groaned in the changing pressure, as if the fortress itself mourned the beheading of its queen. Scattered bits of phosphorescent life once devoured now blipped intermittently across the grotto floor like fireflies on a summer's eve. Krengel edged through the mess, arms outstretched before him. He picked his way gingerly toward the hellish glow of the vanquished witch's eyes. They served as something of a beacon through the ruin of flaccid skin upon lakes of liberated fluid. It felt a bit like walking across the surface of an enormous collapsed tent.

The witch's eyes, they were not a pair of loose and independent marbles, as he might've imagined. Instead, they were inset into the orbits of a leather mask designed to wrap neatly around the temples and tie with a thong at the back of the wearer's head. As though the black circles of mud and ash he'd sometimes painted around his eyes to assume the guise of a frightful character had always foreshadowed this very moment, Krengel pulled the black mask over the bridge of his nose, covering both his natural eyes, and pulled the leather thongs tightly around his temples. The blackness of the witch's lair was gone, replaced with every brilliant hue of crimson, from the deepest sultry purple to a nearly white-hot shade of pink. He held his hand up before his eyes to open and close his fingers, to turn it round as if he'd never before seen such a thing, and he hadn't, not to this level of profound intimacy where his every nerve and vein pulsed so clearly within a living matrix of cells. This is what it was to see the world through a devil's eyes.

The room was indeed immense, ballooned to its greatest width in the center, and cinched around portals to other rooms at either end. All around him, there were bodies. In various states of decomposition, the carcasses of Naturals grimaced quietly in the manner that corpses do from the spots where the witch evidently crushed them during her fits of displeasure. Some were so flattened they looked to have once served as the mortar between great stone blocks. Dropped serving trays and smashed lids littered the floor. Wings and feathers of shredded seabirds that had no logical business being in this place. A mangled iguana, bitten in half but forever twitching. Along the far wall, a small severed hand dragged itself through sucked bones by two remaining fingers. The feeding room of the bloated queen, Krengel decided, was one best experienced in utter blackness.

Krengel picked his way through the mess to a dropped sodium musket. He retrieved it from the floor, checked it over and opened the chamber. It looked good. Inside, was a single capped slug behind an ugly ball of lead. One shot was better than nothing. He closed the chamber and spun at once in the direction of a wavering cry. This was not the glottal rattling of a Pancha warrior. This sound was human.

"Hiley?"

His voice echoed through every whorl of the immense fortress, resonating for what seemed an eternity. The Naturals were clearly gone. Their goddess was dead, and they'd abandoned the temple. Probably, they'd ridden the cables back to Tencotha, unless they were brilliant swimmers.

"Klaas?"

The reverberations of her responding cry joined his in a miserable discordance that dissipated in a torturous decrescendo. Klaas splashed through standing pools toward the portal through which it seemed her voice emanated. He ran first toward the nearest edge and followed the concave wall down into the narrows, where he slipped into a tunnel like a tiny parasite exploring the gut of a host turned to stone. There was light at the end of the passageway, perhaps only detectable by the ultrasensitive Devil's Eyes. And as he drew nearer, he could discern through solid walls distinct sources of wriggling luminescence. There were two of them. A third source, ovate in shape, was situated somewhat deeper into the fortress than the first two. This one glimmered like a halo of warm and inviting brilliance, like sunlight upon the sea.

At last, he reached the distant room. The light from the blazing portal was too bright to bear through the Devil's Eyes. He slid the mask atop his head and rubbed his eyes. It appeared to be another room assigned to food preparation, or perhaps for dining. Heaps of stripped clothing, purses, weapons and assorted effects surrounded a table of scalloped stone, where two serving trays had been set. Their lids were locked down into place, just as the lid of his own tray had so recently imprisoned him. Beyond, the purest white light he'd perhaps ever beheld emanated through an arched doorway. Krengel cocked his head in the brilliance and listened intently. Just for an instant, he swore that he had heard the crash of ocean surf and the keening of seagulls.

"Klaas!"

Krengel shook loose of his trance and shouldered his musket by its strap. He approached the table and unfastened the hasps on one serving tray, followed by the next. Gripping each by its oversized handle, he dramatically lifted both lids and smiled down at the dumbstruck faces of Ludolph Eichmann and Hiley, trussed in nests of garnish like a pair of Christmas geese.

"Where's the witch?" Ludolph asked, in a near whisper. "Have you seen her?"

"Aye." Krengel smiled. "I saw the witch. And no other child shall ever suffer the sight of Old Berchta, not ever again."

"She's ..."

"Dead." Krengel worked on the knots in Hiley's bonds.

"You?" Hiley asked, her eyes widening. "But how did ye ...?"

Krengel winked. "A bit of a miracle. And a bit of magic."

Their bonds at last freed from around their wrists, his friends sat on the edge of the preparation table and picked at the knots around their ankles. While they were occupied with this task, Krengel turned back toward the blazing portal, where the smashing hiss of ocean waves against rocks beckoned to his very soul.

His perspective was that of a hermit crab, peering out upon the world through the opening of his shell. There before him spread a sandy beach. Sunshine and freedom. But he turned away from the portal, for he could not permit himself to believe that this scene of white sand and sparkling water was truly tangible, available. It could be nothing less than the cruelest joke yet played upon his mind in the entanglement of nightmares in which he'd been ensnared since the moment he joined the traveling choir and passed through Lambsheim's ivory gates.

He swatted at some buzzing thing that flew too near his ear. He closed his eyes and inhaled a briny lungful of the warm ocean breeze. Sand blew through the portal to tickle the tops of his bare feet. Dear God, it could not be true.

Krengel knelt on the gritty floor and crawled to the hem between worlds, where sand met stone. There, he reached one trembling hand through the portal, gasping at the warmth of sunlight beaming down upon his pale skin, exposing in lurid detail every pore and shining hair on the back of his hand. Overcome with emotion, he sprawled on his belly and plunged his arms to the elbows in the hot sand, scooping a great sandy pillow against his face. Tears spilled from his eyes as he squeezed sand through his fingers. It was real.

Blue-black feet tramped down on the portal's flipside. Krengel recoiled out from the sunlight back into the safety of his shell. The creature knuckled by, dragging a pulverized iguana through the sand as it stilted lackadaisically down the beach to the edge of a tide pool, where it lowered its onion-shaped body to the sand. It had not seen him. At a distance of about a stone's throw, the Krampusz crossed his spindly legs and prepared what looked to be his lunch.

Krengel glanced back at Ludolph and Hiley, still picking at their knots around their ankles and chattering to one another. He turned back to the portal, glaring grimly at the exposed backside of his so-called Forever Friend.

The monster had probably never meant any real harm. Not really. He was just looking out for himself in a world set against him from birth. Unloved and unwanted, aimlessly wandering the earth in his miserable state of hermitude, he was despised by all who encountered him. Just trying to escape his latest set of foul circumstances and perhaps glean some modicum of real happiness, before life ground him down to a nub and forgot his scattered bones in the dunes of a desert island. Krengel did pity the wretched creature. But that did not change what he knew he had to do.

Krengel removed the musket from his shoulder. Resting the weapon on the pillow of scooped sand, he slowly extruded the barrel out of the Sack of Shadows and into the Sundaloon sunlight. He took a deep breath and slowly released it, lining his blue eye up with the rear sight. And then, he squeezed the trigger.

"Why, ye sheep-killing dog." The Krampusz rolled onto his side in the tide pool, floundering in a cloud of red and billowing blood. A wisp of smoke uncoiled from the gaping hole in the middle of his back.

Krengel seized his ankles and dragged him out of the water, lest he drown before imparting any last words of real importance. This was a repugnant duty. No less repugnant than the duty of stealing myrrh. But it was one needed done.

"How's come ye done me like this for, Fat Brother? I never done ye no harm?"

"Have you forgotten the arrow you put in my backside? I'm not your 'Fat Brother' and you know it. I'd like for once to hear the truth from you, as however you might know it."

"You am," the Krampusz said, spitting-up blood with a grunt, "my Fat Brother from another mother. And that's the truth of it."

"No. We share no blood at all. You were seeded into my father through the sting of a bee, and he delivered that seed into a womb. The product of witchcraft is all you are. But I'm ..."

"A fly in the ointment." The Krampusz smiled. "A beautiful mistake."

Krengel knelt close to the dying demon and shielded his eyes from the brilliance of the sun. "What do you mean?"

"Took Mam nigh two years to born me, and meanwhile, Daddy sired ye in his spare time with that ol' servant gal." The Krampusz coughed on a lungful of blood. "Ye wasn't never meant to be part of the plan, but ye was. You was the only natural thing to come out of it, Fat Brother, just as natural as bare feet. And I guess I'm for one glad of it, or I'd surely have suffered every inch of this path all alone."

Krengel sighed. He lifted the creature's head and scooped up a pillow of sand.

"Thank ye, kind sir." The Krampusz lifted a trembling hand to touch Krengel's cheek. "You've always been a mighty good friend."

"What are you?"

The Krampusz's blue eyes widened. He licked his lips with a purplish tongue and swallowed, but seemed unable to answer the question. He closed his eyes for a moment, and then reopened them. "This ain't a world of black and white, Fat Brother, simple as ye might like her to be, huh. No, Sir. This here's a world of vagaries within vagaries, where angels fall from grace and devils get redeemed, and all kinds in between walk right among us."

"The witch is dead," Krengel said, "I thought you might be interested in knowing that."

"Half-interested, I guess."

"But I thought that was your whole plan all along, to corrupt innocent children and turn them into assassins, to kill the witch, control the Sack and return to Lambsheim to seize your fortune." Krengel glared down into the mystified eyes of the dying creature. After a moment's thought, the Krampusz slowly shook his head.

"What do you mean, no? Why did you kidnap us?"

"I liked ye." The Krampusz gurgled and rolled his eyes. "Loved every one of ye. Keep ye safe, forever, where ye won't never die."

"But why would you have me steal the holy myrrh? The secret weapon to kill the witch? Aye? Why would you need witch poison unless you meant to have her killed?"

"Cause she was -- a real bad -- person."

"Then why didn't you kill her, yourself?"

The Krampusz shook his head. He smiled weakly, lowering his eyelids. "She was my Mam."

"You've made a real mess of things, you know. Boogered-up a whole lot of innocent lives. And I happen to know a thing or two about that." Krengel rose, grabbed the Krampusz by his ankles and began once more to drag him. The sand beneath him was saturated with blood. "You want absolution? I can help you redeem yourself. I've just the perfect job for you, in fact. But you'll need to hang on."

"I can't -- Fat Brother. Not much longer."

"Oh, yes you can, my Forever Friend." Krengel smiled down at the weird caricature of Count Richwald Krengel in the sand. He gave the Krampusz a wink and poked him on the end of his bulbous nose. "The amount of time it would take a sparrow to peck a diamond mountain into dust, that's just the very start of the new life you'll have, so long as you stay put inside my magic sack."

Chapter Twenty-Two

Krengel tugged on the Sack of Shadows until it had swallowed the Krampusz whole. He then cinched it closed with a leather thong and swung the bulging, yet oddly weightless bag over his shoulder by its knotted carrying strap. He turned then toward the sea with an unfathomable sigh, and for a moment, he was content just to stand there, to stand with nothing requiring his doing on an empty beach at the end of the earth with the weight of a whole hidden world upon his shoulders. He crinkled his eyes in the glare the sparkled off to the farthest reaches of a shining and sun-dappled sea. He had no idea how he would find his way back home, if ever. But for the moment, he didn't care.

This was precisely the moment for which he'd always lived, for which he'd being born, toward which he'd worked so long and so hard without the slightest reckoning of the ultimate reward: a single moment in time that would be forever preserved, and appreciated for its absolute perfection. Never again would he wish his life away in yearning from one moment to the next, pining for the next bit of graftification beyond that which he'd been blessed, for who knows what hardships the next moment might bring.

Leather folds rustled near his ear. The thong slowly unraveled as the sack flowered open to extrude a blue-black nose. "Fat Brother?" the Krampusz whispered into his ear.

"Yes, my Forever Friend?"

"Reckon ye ought'er get in here. Have a look at all's happened since ye left."

Beyond the Krampusz, from some place deeper within that other realm between moments, there arose a chanting distant as the echo of some forgotten childhood dream. Sounded like quite a large crowd gathered. Again and again, it was three syllables being repeated like the raucous champing of a legion of toy soldiers into battle, shouting their war cry in unison, loud and clear, far and wide, such that any enemy with ears would hear it and begin to tremble.

San-ta-klaas ... San-ta-klaas ... San-ta-klaas ... San-ta-klaas ...

Krengel swung the sack down from his shoulder and parted the flaps to peer inside. He shielded his eyes from the brilliant sunshine and wrinkled his nose like a child examining his collection of weird bugs in a dirty jar. He saw Hiley and Ludolph waving up at him. Feeling a bit like a hovering deity in the sky, Krengel giggled and waved back at his tiny friends. No longer dressed in their filthy rags, they had somehow bathed and preened, adorning perfectly tailored outfits trimmed to the upmost heights of Iptintine fashion.

"Come on down here, Santa Klaas," Ludolph shouted, holding up a new robe of shimmering crimson and snowy trim. "Come on down and have a look at what trouble you've caused this time!"

Krengel nodded. "I will. I'll be right down."

He clenched the folds of the bad back together, wincing at the very thought of returning to soon to the Quick, even if only for a short visit. He'd only just escaped that awful place, and the thought of ever returning to the Sack of Shawdows was one that filled him with unspeakable dread. Here, in the middle of his absolutely perfect moment ... could it not wait another day, or at least until tomorrow morning?

Krengel scowled out over the sea. Where before, a sky of the purest azure had raced unchained to the hem between worlds over sun-spangled leagues of open sea, was a horizon now, besmirched by one ugly black cloud. Krengel cocked his head and glared at the crazy thing. There was just one. But one raincloud was enough to upset his sublime moment, to tarnish the sheen of his seaside situation. The play of lightning within the cloud was strange and ominous. Krengel cranked his head around each shoulder and to all sides. Nothing but dazzling blue skies in every direction, but to the far north, where loomed the lone thunderhead.

"What queer sort of weather."

Stranger still, was the speed at which it seemed to be approaching. He could discern now its agitation and ill-nature. Billowing like a great wad of brimstone soot, it rumbled toward him over the sea. Erupting, boiling, metastasizing new and grotesque outgrowths like blackened cauliflower, its maleficent energy seemed to grow the closer it encroached upon the desert island.

Krengel noticed a bewitching breeze that slithered up through the seagrass tussocks that festooned the rolling dunes like wild hairstyles. As the wind picked up, flocks of mockingbirds rose, shattered and fell fragmented back into the briar thickets, while far and away rattled the branches of the daisy forest. Krengel rubbed the goose pimples that had broken out all over his bare arms. The temperature was plummeting by degrees.

He frowned, squinting deeper into the core of the elemental mass. Because for an instant, just one instant, he swore he'd glimpsed something at its center. Something even darker than the clouds that enveloped it. Krengel rubbed his eyes and blinked and thing was gone. If there had ever been anything there at all, it had been swallowed back into the roiling folds.

He nearly leapt out of his skin when the black-skinned arm of the Krampusz struck out from the Sack of Shadows to seize hold of his wrist. The creature's sapphire eyes burned like low flames in the darkness. "Join us, Fat Brother."

The spittle of rain struck him now, cold and sharp upon his cheeks like splinters of ice. The wind lowed through the dunes, stinging his legs with blown sand. Twin harpoons of lightning struck the sea, setting the waves aglow.

"Alright! I'm coming for goodness sake!" Krengel snapped free of the monster's grip. Begrudgingly, he quit the squall that had fastened itself so suddenly on Sundaloon. If there had ever been a time when squatting out in a violent storm would've seemed preferable to going indoors, then this was certainly it. With a groan of despair, Krengel stepped back down into the Sack of Shadows.

###
San-ta-klaas ... San-ta-klaas ... San-ta-klaas ... San-ta-klaas ...

Hiley and Ludolph helped him into his new robe. It felt like a warm embrace after the rain and bracing winds and it smelled of lemon and clove. Not since the days of his Lambsheim pampering has he worn anything half so lavish. Hiley eased the leather mask with the Devil's Eyes down from his forehead and over his face to a better spot around his neck, and then she pulled a pointed hat atop his head. Hewn of the same lurid, crimson fabric as the robe, the hat resembled the conical hats forced upon the Little Elves back at <u>Miso de Gallo</u>, but this hat was of such fine quality and material that it actually succeeded in mocking the mockery intended by the Spanish Inquisition, back on that fateful night in Rome.

"We found this while we was tidying up the place, about a week after ye left." Hiley held up the white silken handkerchief ripped from his face by the claws of the witch. "Thought maybe ye might want 'er back. Went ahead and washed it for ye."

"A week after I left?" Krengel hitched an eyebrow. "I've not been gone but ten minutes."

"Down here, guess it's felt more like half a lifetime."

"Why don't next time you think to leave the bloody sack open for the rest of us, next time you decide to go out there mucking about," Ludolph said, as he approached Krengel with an exquisite recurve bow in one hand, and an embroidered quiver and matching purse of the finest leather he'd ever beheld, in the other. "Because I might've liked to join you."

"I'm sorry," Krengel said, with a gasp, "were you all locked in here the whole time?"

"Just joshing you, mate." Ludolph grinned. "I've been doing a little mucking about myself. And like she said, we've had lots of tidying up to do, what with that big mess you left and all." Ludolph held out the articles that he was carrying. "Here. These belong to you."

"For me?"

"Aye. Take them. They're yours. I crafted each of them, myself."

Krengel took first the bow and admired the perfect balance of the graceful limbs, through the sturdy riser. Driftwood in color, with fantastic emerald highlights, the leading edge of each limb was decorated with glyphs that depicted scenes from the battle of Tencotha, and Krengel's victory over the witch.

"Carved in one piece from the wishbone of a numbaec. Nowhere on the flipside will you encounter another, nor its equal."

"I don't know what to say."

"Then don't need to say anything, right now. But on some other night, when the perry cider flows by the light of a crackling campfire, I demand that you recount every last detail of your fight, and how in heaven you managed to win."

"Agreed, then." Krengel took Ludolph's hand and pulled him in. The last time they embraced was on the floor of a stable, muddied and bloodied, when Ludolph had tried to drown him in wet manure. This was a very good change. With a slap on the back each, they released their grips.

"Well, are ye ready?" Hiley hoisted her eyebrows and bounced on her tiptoes.

"For what?"

"To be embarrassed in front of a whole shitload of people."

"Foller me, Fat Brother." The Krampusz knuckled by with that queerly pendulous gait, rising and falling like a stilted onion. He ducked as he entered the mouth of the tunnel that led back to the witch's feeding room, and disappeared inside.

San-ta-klaas ... San-ta-klaas ... San-ta-klaas ... San-ta-klaas ...

Panic sent a jolt through Krengel's every nerve at the very thought of returning to that room of death and dismemberment. His rate of breathing must have changed, or perhaps he made some involuntary sound or a move in the opposite direction, because Ludolph put his hand on Krengel's shoulder. He seemed to sense what was going through his head.

"It's alright, mate," he said, "everything's changed."

"Just listen to them." Hiley smiled and pointed in the direction of the tunnel, where the raised voices of hundreds, perhaps even thousands, of people all chanted his name. His nickname, anyway. Strange, how his ears seemed not to burn at the sound of that nickname any longer, perhaps cooled by the air of celebration.

Ushered by his two friends, Krengel's feet found the will to move. One step and then another, he at last borrowed the rhythm of the voices and tramped ahead until the long tunnel was at last behind them.

San-ta-klaas ... San-ta-klaas ... San-ta-klaas ... San-ta-klaas ...

"They love you here!" Hiley threw an arm around his neck and hugged his head. "We all do. I want ye to know you've made a believer out of me. I do believe in miracles and magic, and I most certainly believe in you. You're as real as it gets."

Krengel was dumbfounded, craning his neck to take in the stupendous dimensions of the room. Every column and radial arch bedazzled with strings of twinkling sodium lights, the entire room glittered as though wholly encrusted with gems and precious metals. The arcades originally left devoid of artwork by those sightless architects whose appreciable aesthetics were limited to sounds and smells, now popped with vivid frescoes depicting scenes from the glorious victories that led to reclaiming this lost structure. Krengel's eyes seized upon one arcade depicting the final confrontation between him and the witch. Hardly portrayed as a chubby boy, stripped and bound to a serving platter with a mouthful of myrrh, the artist instead, captured a scene not unlike the cover of one of those comic books. Midair, they clashed, a masked dynamo enveloped in the flapping folds of a crimson cape versus a bat-winged succubus, whose enraged head of flowing black hair he'd neatly severed with one slash of his eager blade.

"Ye like them paintings up yonder?" Hiley jostled Krengel's neck and beamed. "I had a hand in 'em."

"They're -- very nice."

Higher still, around a dozen of those great glass balls had been relocated from the cable system to the heights of the cathedral ceiling, where, set forever aglow by lanterns of phosphorescent mold, they rose and dipped in orbit of the central spire by the massive gears of their mechanized mobile. And directly below, upon the sacrificial alter at the room's center, where only minute's ago, Krengel had fought for his very life against the queen of this underworld, now loomed a fantastic sculpture carved from a pillar of salt.

Sparkling like new snow, the grand effigy of the masked Witch Slayer rose mightily from the pedistile in a tall peaked hat. A bow and quiver adorned one shoulder, while over his other; the impish face of the Krampusz leered from the folds of a great bulging sack.

San-ta-klaas ... San-ta-klaas ... San-ta-klaas ... San-ta-klaas ...

Ranks of Pancha warriors stepped forth from the cheering crowd of human children alongside their Natural enemies. Covered crates clutched to their breasts, the warriors assumed a semi-circular formation around the statue's base. At once, they removed the cloth coverings to release a rising flock of fluttering tearpins that pulsed excitedly with pinkish light as they whipped their golden tendrils to the ceiling. The great cheer that followed was so deafening and so enduring that Krengel feared it might never end, but at last it subsided and the mixed crowd parted as a hush fell over the auditorium.

Down the central aisle formed by the respectfully shifting masses, loped the Krampusz. Bobbing smoothly up and down, as he vaulted feet over knuckles, he swung his head to gawp at the murmuring crowds. Immediately behind him, two armed Pancha warriors escorted a hunched and shuffling figure whose exorbitant decorations suggested that he was, amongst their kind, a dignitary of some importance. His knobby hand clenched a painted staff that clinked with countless hooked teeth and claws of nameless beasts. His ponderous limp betrayed his great age. One barbell had been sheared off to a nub, while the other had grown so long and withered that it dragged behind him upon the floor. The Krampusz stopped at the base of the sculpture and waited patiently, until the wiseman and his handlers caught up with him. Once finally in place alongside the Krampusz and settled, the old Pancha took a step forward, smacked his lips, then inflated a great pouch of skin on his throat to emit a glottal purr that terminated in three sharp pops.

The Krampusz cleared his throat. "Chief here wants first to thank ye all kindly for coming. He's for one awful glad the ol' witch is dead and her reign of nightmares is all done. An age of darkness is finally broke by this here dawn of a new kinder Renaissance, huh." The blue-furred devil then sniffed and rubbed his forearm beneath his nose, deferring once again to the Pancha Chief.

The loose skin on the Chief's neck vacillated as his clicks and pops resounded through the cavernous auditorium. No one moved while he was speaking. In the background, someone coughed.

"For generations, his people was exiled to the Paux Veldt, where they done learned of a thousand new ways of dying. Learned to overcome suffering likes of which none's ever seen on account of that witch. And now, they's awful happy to get back home. Chief here reckons they owes the lot of ye a great deal of debt for all them lives ye lost at the battle for Iptintec, at Tencotha, and down there on the dam, I reckon."

The Pancha chief whacked the base of the statue with his staff.

"Oh, and then for all them lives was lost right here upon this table, where folks was served as some kinder awful supper."

The Chief's throat ballooned for a prattling bellow.

"Feller here just wants to thank ye, each and ever one of ye, who done fought tooth and nail and suffered hard in their stead. But most specially of all, Chief here aims to thank Ludolph Eichmann and my own Fat Brother, for showing the rest of ye fellers how to stand up and give the ol' witch and her minions what-for. He wants to thank ye, Ludolph, for all your bravery at Tencotha, knowing all the while yours was a battle meant lost so the war on the dam might be won. That was awful good of ye. And then he wants to thank you, Santy Klaas, for your big scrap with the ol' witch herself, right here in her dreadful lair. Proud of ye."

Uproarious applause set the terrified tearpins to whipping their tendrils round and round with the orbiting globes. Whistles streamed and wavered. A small sodium grenade popped. Once the crowd had finally settled, the Krampusz raised a hand and cleared his throat.

"And now, I got me an announcement of my own to make. Like I said, I'm awful proud of ye, Fat Brother. I'm lucky to have had ye and proud to know ye. I ain't mad at ye for shooting me in the back like ye done, 'cause I reckon I prob'ly deserved it. We ain't never had no hard feelings between us, and I don't aim to let there be none now. I owe the lot of ye a great big apology." The Krampusz looked around the auditorium and nodded his head, waggling his tuberous nose. He sniffed and wiped it with the back of his hand. "I ain't never meant a one of ye no harm, and it pains me that harm did come to some of ye on account of what I done. I love each and every darned one of ye. Reckoned if I didn't keep ye safe, ye'd hope to leave me one day and I couldn't bear to let a one of ye go. But after this here party, I aim to do just that. Any one of ye wants to quit this place, I'll be glad to show ye the way back to your proper homes. All's I hope is one day ye can find it in your heart to forgive a wretch like me."

The auditorium remained strangely quiet. Krengel gazed around through the awkward silence to find that everyone in the room was looking to him. He stepped forward. Drawing a chestful of air, he walked straight and tall across the room toward the Krampusz, whose head hung in the shadow of his looming effigy. Krengel put his arms around the furry monster and held him close. "I forgive you, Forever Friend."

"I'm forever in ye debt and in ye service, Fat Brother." Tears rolled wetly down the creature's misshapen cheek. He enveloped Krengel in a spindly embrace. "If ever ye needs a favor, just ye ask it and it's done."

"I do have one niggling question." Krengel placed his hands on the Krampusz's cheeks and looked into his identical pair of blue eyes, as if he were looking into his own.

"Ask it."

"How was it that the Sack of Shadows fell into your hands?"

A chilly breeze whipped suddenly through the crowd, jingling the strings of sodium lights and rocking the great glass globes. The crowd began to shift, facing, and turning uncertainly. A murmur grew at the same rate as the moaning wind came snaking through the tunnel, bringing with it flecks of moisture and the fishy scent of the Sundaloon Sea. The sluice of lapping waves.

"They buried me alive in it, when they thunk they'd killed me with a stone."

"Who did? Who buried you in it?"

"Your mam done it." The eyes of the Krampusz burned back at him like twin embers of the hottest blue flame. "Her and the Council of Flies."

"The what?"

At once, a godlike roar from the tunnel evoked shrieks of terror throughout the crowd. The gathered masses all surged away from the mouth, as a flume of foaming seawater came gushing forth, casting a wake with sand and floundering fish across the tiled auditorium floor. A red crab scuttled over the top of Krengel's foot, waving its claw threateningly up at him.

"Fat Brother, ye ain't left the sack a-lying on the beach, have ye?"

"I ..."

"Tide's come in. By God, ye gots to be careful for where ye leave a thing of such power! Never dare ye leave it just to be taken!"

"I didn't think ... I didn't kn--"

"Run, Fat Brother! Fore the tide takes us all! Rest of ye, foller me!" The Krampusz vaulted off and extended his spidery arms, capturing masses of children with them as if in a net and herding them gently away from the tunnel and toward the front of the fortress.

Another massive surge of sand and seawater erupted through the portal, delivering with it this time a mass of kelp and one confused giant tortoise, legs sprawled, sliding, and spinning across the tile. The dazed beast raised its neck and peered sleepily around at all of the hysteria.

"I'm going to help with the kids," Hiley shouted, in passing. Then, she wheeled and grabbed Krengel in a quick hug. "Good luck to ye. I'd better see you again, sometime!"

"You will," Krengel replied, "I promise."

"I'm coming with you, you know."

Krengel turned to find Ludolph standing poised, ready and waiting. A bow and quiver of his own were shouldered. A belted satchel of certain surprises slung accessibly at his right hip. "Let's go, then," Krengel said, "quickly, before the next wave hits!"

The boys had sprinted more than halfway up the tunnel before a frigid gust of briny air forewarned the blast that was soon to come. Just as the roiling white water thundered upon them like the head of a battering ram, they flattened together, digging their nails into the cracks between tiles like crabs against the tides and they held, they withstood nature's might until the blast was finished, then they rose and charged forward again.

The portal room to Sundaloon was an ill-kept zoo of floundering sealife and displaced creatures of a neighboring world. The portal itself was like a window in the bottom of a boat. Jagged reefs and ribbons of kelp scrolled dizzyingly by.

"By God, Klaas, we're at sea!"

"We couldn't have drifted too far. Let's go!"

The boys leapt together and cannonballed through the portal, and at once were tossed and tumbled by the might of a churning sea. Krengel grabbed the Sack of Shadows and clenched its folds tightly shut, swimming with all he had toward the surface. He emerged gasping and choking in a squall of briny blackness and stinging sand. They had been taken. And there was no way now of telling which direction was the shore. Krengel heard Ludolph choking in the darkness, somewhere at arm's length, but the storm was so terrible that even at such close proximity he could not be seen.

And then suddenly, Krengel remembered the goggles round his throat. He fought the leather mask up over the bridge of his nose, and then clenched the Sack of Shadows in his teeth. A shot of seawater sluiced down his throat and nearly drowned him, quick as that, were he not so quick to cough the salty fluid back up again.

"Klaas!"

He could hear Ludolph's screams, more distant now than before. They were drifting apart. At last, he was able to position the Devil's Eyes over his own, and a world of darkness was instantaneously bathed in sanguine light.

He swam furiously for Ludolph until he'd seized the hood of his friend's tunic. Drawing the boy close, they synchronized side-strokes as best they could until at last they felt the sifting solidity of sand beneath their feet. An indignant breaker rushed up from behind and shoved them facefirst onto the shore.

"I can't see anything, Klaas!"

"I know! Just follow me!"

The howling tempest raged with such ferocity that the boys could barely hear the voice of the other, even when shouted directly into the ear. But at least with the Devil's Eyes, they would not be deprived of sight. Krengel lugged his blinded and deafened companion up the beach, until they found some slight shelter in the lee of a pumice outcrop, where the worst of the storm blew over them.

Krengel gazed around the embattled hellscape of Sundaloon. The Devil's Eyes seemed to turn darkness in, against itself, resulting in photonegative vision that exposed the best in the worst lighting. He could see why such a tool would've been so treasured by a witch, or by anyone with an affinity for operating under the cover of darkness.

"Do you hear that?" Ludolph asked, cocking his head skyward. "Sounds like a numbaec caravan!"

Fearing at first that his companion was suffering some sort of madness wrought of transitioning too quickly between worlds, Krengel then detected the same sound heard by his friend. It emanated from somewhere on high, near the center of the storm's elemental mass. It did indeed resemble the music of those chimes affixed to the great beetles of Iptintic that lumbered tinkling through the Midland Mountain pass. It was the sound of sleighbells.

Krengel gaped up into the tempest. And there, he saw a thing that could never be, not in this world nor any other. Stark against the chaos as the moon upon its zenith, black as a dreamless sleep, a lone driver slashed his whip through sheets of rain. His beasts pawed thin air, anlters pumping, tonges lolling, where each was but one articulating segment of the terrible whole, that undulating form thrust up from the abyss like some enraged sky dragon of the Orient, wheeling through the elements in a nightmarish promenade.

"What is it, Klaas?"

"I don't know," Krengel whispered, "but I believe it's come here to kill me."

The End

www.ingramcontent.com/pod-product-compliance
Lightning Source LLC
Chambersburg PA
CBHW051453170626
46811CB00002B/465